MORE MYSTERIES FROM THE
BERKLEY PUBLISHING GROUP...

CHINA BAYLES MYSTERIES: She left the big city to run an herb shop in Pecan Springs, Texas. But murder can happen anywhere... "A wonderful character!"—*Mostly Murder*

by Susan Wittig Albert

THYME OF DEATH	WITCHES' BANE
HANGMAN'S ROOT	ROSEMARY REMEMBERED

KATE JASPER MYSTERIES: Even in sunny California, there are cold-blooded killers... "This series is a treasure!"
—Carolyn G. Hart

by Jaqueline Girdner

ADJUSTED TO DEATH	MURDER MOST MELLOW
THE LAST RESORT	FAT-FREE AND FATAL
TEA-TOTALLY DEAD	A STIFF CRITIQUE
MOST LIKELY TO DIE	

LIZ WAREHAM MYSTERIES: In the world of public relations, crime can be a real career-killer... "Readers will enjoy feisty Liz!"—*Publishers Weekly*

by Carol Brennan

HEADHUNT	FULL COMMISSION

Also by the author

IN THE DARK	CHILL OF SUMMER

BONNIE INDERMILL MYSTERIES: Temp work can be murder, but solving crime is a full-time job... "One of detective fiction's most appealing protagonists!"—*Publishers Weekly*

by Carole Berry

THE DEATH OF A DIFFICULT WOMAN	GOOD NIGHT, SWEET PRINCE
THE LETTER OF THE LAW	THE DEATH OF A DANCING FOOL
THE YEAR OF THE MONKEY	

MARGO SIMON MYSTERIES: She's a reporter for San Diego's public radio station. But her penchant for crime solving means she has to dig up the most private of secrets...

by Janice Steinberg

DEATH OF A POSTMODERNIST	DEATH CROSSES THE BORDER

CHILL OF SUMMER

CAROL BRENNAN

BERKLEY PRIME CRIME, NEW YORK

CHILL OF SUMMER

A Berkley Prime Crime Book / published by arrangement with
the author

PRINTING HISTORY
G. P. Putnam's Sons hardcover edition / May 1995
Berkley Prime Crime mass-market edition / May 1996

The Putnam Berkley World Wide Web site address is
http://www.berkley.com

ISBN: 0-425-15309-6

Berkley Prime Crime Books are published
by The Berkley Publishing Group,
200 Madison Avenue, New York, NY 10016.
The name BERKLEY PRIME CRIME and the BERKLEY PRIME CRIME
design are trademarks belonging to Berkley Publishing Corporation.

PRINTED IN THE UNITED STATES OF AMERICA

10 9 8 7 6 5 4 3 2 1

To Eamon.
Thanks for sticking around.
It would be sheer heck without you.

Acknowledgments

My thanks to Leslie Gelbman, my editor, without whom this book would certainly never have been written.

Major Joe Leary, New York State Police, retired. I hope I got the flavor right!

Sheldon Taubman, M.D., Director for Pathology Services, Vassar Brothers Hospital, Poughkeepsie.

The family and friends whose daily loving presence—in the flesh and on the phone—pulled me through the hellish end of 1993. Special gratitude to John Flanagan, a literal lifesaver.

This living hand, now warm and capable
Of earnest grasping, would, if it were cold
And in the icy silence of the tomb,
So haunt thy days and chill thy dreaming nights
That thou would wish thine own heart dry of
blood . . .

—JOHN KEATS

CHILL OF SUMMER

PROLOGUE

· · · · · · · · · · · · · · · · · · · ·

THE BEDSIDE LIGHT SNUFFS OUT, SOUNDLESS AS A CANdle—unexpected, since the storm stopped hours ago, just in time to produce a surreal sunset, almost too hectic with color. I lie still, suddenly blind, propped against three fat pillows in my new bedroom. One hand is still poised to use the plastic pen it holds, the other clutches an invisible pile of paper.

In the warm lamp-glow, the room had smelled of paint: the perfume of fresh beginnings. Now, in the sudden blackness, I imagine White Shoulders, my late grandmother's scent. Some ghostly reproach for having taken over her room, for having made it mine?

The light returns. I let out a long, shaky breath and wipe my hands against the fresh cotton of the quilt, ashamed that in a few stretched-out seconds of darkness they've turned sweaty.

This is the country, Emily. This is the way it is up here in summer; sometimes the lights go out. Power failures, remember?

Oh, I remember, all right. My curse is that I remember too many things, not too few. Jagged patches of the past slip at unexpected moments under my guard to flicker like old movies behind my eyes, eclipsing the present totally: power failures of the mind—or the will.

Lately, alarming things have begun to happen here. Given even a hint of encouragement, the apprehensions crouched in the corners of my mind will begin to dart like cockroaches all over the place. I force myself to go back to the script, and pen a quick black slash under a line that gives my character precisely the wrong reaction. This screenplay is quirky, but I like it. I only hope the director will like me; some have found me "difficult"—with reason, I admit.

The light gives a warning waver, but stays on. This time

I wriggle quickly off the high tester bed and make for the brass oil lamp on my bureau, wishing I had a flashlight securely in my hand. I am not alone in the house, but the presence of the man asleep in the bedroom down the hall is no comfort—no comfort at all.

The lamp is filled, oil sloshing heavily in its base, but not a match in sight.

I pull on the long purple tee-shirt draped like a furled flag on the bedpost, and crook my finger through the lamp's keyhole handle. There are matches down in the kitchen, and as I think of it, I recall having seen a cache of flashlights in the basement.

The minute I hit the kitchen, an orange-crayoned stroke of lightning flashes, framed in the French doors to the garden. A second later, thunder rumbles and the lights go out. This time, sixty heartbeats later, they do not come back on. The dark fills instantly with sound: creakings, skitterings—house noises; storm noises. And maybe something more? A chilly shiver prickles at the skin on my back. I tell myself that the new air-conditioning overdid its job before it conked out. The truth is, I've never made my peace with darkness.

I feel for the table and put the oil lamp down on it with special care. I grope around the stove and, with not much trouble, I lay hands on a box of matches. The trouble comes when I try to light the lamp and turn the wick handle the wrong way, right off its thread. I bang the useless lamp down on the table—hard, not caring now whether I break it, hoping I will.

A fresh match guides me to the basement door, but dies midway down the stairs. I grab the banister and manage the remaining steps by sheer feel, an exploratory toe out to let me know when I've reached bottom. Just as I do, I hear the kitchen phone, loud and shrill and harsh. I hesitate just a moment. The phone has rung like this before during these past weeks, at odd hours of the night, a terse click at the other end when I pick up.

After six rings it stops. I light another match, and stand for a moment, trying to picture the flashlights—four of them, I was pretty sure. Where, though? I can't take much more of this. Where? In the cubbyhole above the cabinet next to the wine cellar. *All right!*

I do one more match and start toward them on the run.

Thunder explodes like a gunshot in a cave. Now I run faster. Against all reason, I am a child, and running for my life.

It happens all at once, with the instant flash of long-expected catastrophe. Something trips my foot. I pitch forward, scrambling to stay vertical, the dying match singeing my fingers as it flies from my hand. Pain stabs my upper arm as it bashes against a jut of unforgiving metal. And suddenly, I am tackled by a monster, shapeless, enormous, cold as death. Its crushing weight drops me flat, smashes my face against the stone floor.

"*Nooooo!*" A scream rings in my ears, bounces back at me from the old brick walls, takes over my skull, threatens to crack it. The sound is eerily like my mother, but as it hangs there in the air, I realize that the scream is not hers but mine. "No," I repeat, whispering it now as I struggle to break free. "No." But the word has lost its meaning, and breathing has become difficult. I begin to float, slowly as a feather in the breeze. Magically, the cold wet turns warm against my back . . .

I'm in a shower, big stall shower: one of my favorite places in the world.

"*Hey, my aristocratic friend, only one bathroom here at Chez Hannagan, remember?*" Dev calls through the door, a laughing undertone in his deep voice.

"*I'm an equal-opportunity showerer,*" I call back.

Next thing, there he is beside me under the cascading water, golden skin, black hair, purple eyes, lushly tropical against the stark white tile. What a miracle to love this much!

I reach out to touch his mouth—that lower lip a bit too generous to match his upper one—and with no warning, he disappears. The lack of him etches a cobweb of wounds, thin ice shattering inside my chest.

The shower evaporates in a cloud of steam, and I am again held prisoner on a stone floor by a captor who makes no sound in the blackness. My body shudders against its repulsive coldness: the rank, freezing damp of a meat locker.

I tense my muscles, readying to break free. I give it my best, but a fiery pain in my left ankle cuts my best down to pathetic. I can't move, and all at once, I'm too tired to bother even thinking about it. "Clea," I mumble, but my head aches, and I can't quite get my brain around the syllables. I hear the word at the end of a tunnel, and don't know what it means—just that it's something important . . .

My eyes fly open to the blackness. The meat locker smell fills my nostrils. Have I been lying here, pinned this way, for hours? Or only minutes? Suddenly, my mind clicks on, instantly hyperactive, flashing inside my skull the neon colors of a video game.

I ease my arms slowly out from under me, gritting my teeth against the pain in my right one, and brace my palms against the floor. My ankle complains, and I concentrate on ignoring it. Right arm; left leg: don't depend on those two. Lungs filled with the deepest breath they can manage under the chill, damp burden on my back, I heave abruptly up and over to the left.

For a second, the thing doesn't move. Then it drops with a heavy thunk beside me, and I roll the other way as fast as I can manage, up to a sitting position, before it can climb back on top of me.

It won't, of course. I know by now it is dead.

My hands pad themselves gingerly around the uneven floor stones. I don't want to touch *it*. I want the matchbox I dropped; *I need to see.* I blink my eyes, hoping they'll adjust themselves to the darkness, but the windows are small and high, more like portholes than windows. My head may as well be draped in a velvet hood. I can see nothing. Now I pray for a flash of lightning, but the heavens don't oblige.

Suddenly, my need to know takes firm hold of my hands. They continue to grope—faster now—and not for the matches but for the thing that felled me. Even so, a sharp gasp escapes as my finger lands on what I recognize immediately as a large, bare toe, the nail smooth as polished ivory. I swallow the acid that rises to the back of my throat. *Stay down!* I will not let my gut sabotage me now.

I run my palm quickly over a frozen, hairy leg, and stop abruptly before I get past the top of the thigh.

The power switches back on, soundless but for the burp of air-conditioning kicking in. A rectangle of light, long and slim as an upended coffin, appears in front of me—dimmish, but bright enough to illuminate the naked, dead man lying beside me.

I am shocked without the least tremor of surprise.

I can also see the facts of what has just happened. The things that went bump in the night are no longer supernatural—and somehow all the more horrifying for that.

The light shines out of the cavity of my grandmother's tall, ancient freezer. On my run for the flashlights, I'd stumbled and hit its jutting handle, releasing the door, freeing the frozen body stored inside to flatten me like a cartoon bunny under its dead weight.

A farce. We're playing farce here.

I can almost laugh.

Everything I have known for the past week has just been proved untrue. I have feared the wrong fears, blamed the wrong devils. But as I look at the mottled, bluish face, the darker blue neck, the amazed, bloodshot eyes, I feel nothing but numb, made of rubber or clay. My gut is the only living part of me, and the fears now beginning to put out roots in it are worse than the previous ones. Far worse.

I sit there staring at him, trying to make some kind of sense of his being here. And the sense it begins to make is not anything I want to think about.

You stupid man. You stupid, stupid man!

I try to stand, go woozy with the pain in my ankle, and collapse back on the floor. I try again, and realize almost immediately that it won't work. I have to get upstairs, though. Have to get to a phone. Scuttling like a lobster on a kitchen table, I get as far as the stairs. My ankle hurts like hell. As my hands grab the third step, I stop, gasping. I want to scream—not with the pain, with the frustration.

Suddenly, like an answer to an unformed prayer, I hear the doorbell ring. And I *do* scream. *"Here. I'm here, in the basement! Help meee."*

Another ring, longer, more urgent. I don't even question

who might be doing the ringing this time of night. I scream some more desperate words. The man in the upstairs bedroom will not hear me, nor will he hear the bell—or anything else. The pills he needs to put him to sleep do their job efficiently.

I wait for a third ring. It doesn't come. I am spread out across the stairs, unable now to move up or down. And whoever it was at the door has given up. My yells have stopped being words now, just blurred, elemental fury. I pause for breath and hear the sharp clink of breaking glass.

"Emily?" The voice seems to come from the far end of the basement, through one of the little porthole windows. I want to believe what I hear, but I don't trust my senses now not to play tricks on me. "Emily, answer me!"

The half-taken breath catches in my throat like sawdust.

"Dev?" I manage to grate out. "Dev, I'm here on the steps. I can't move."

"Are you hurt? Look, just stay put." His voice turns guarded. "Are you alone?"

"Yes," I say after a beat. "Yes."

"Then can you tell me a way in here where I won't rip my balls off on broken glass?"

1

....

THE WORN, WHITE BOTTOMS OF HIS SNEAKERS CATCH
the greenish light from the freezer as he slides down through
the old coal chute, and I yelp with something like joy. I am
still spraddled across the stairs, a naked frozen corpse on the
floor not fifteen feet away. But the sight of those sneakers
frees me from inside my head, and with a click I can almost
hear, the world turns real again.

Dev strode past the body with only the smallest pause, and
made straight for me.

"Okay, easy now. I'm going to turn you over and sit you
up. Just go with me."

"Shit! Aaahhh, my arm. No, it's okay."

"Where's a light switch?" I pointed at it, and he turned
it on. After some purposeful palpating of my damaged parts,
he said, "Doesn't look to me like anything's broken. We
ought to get some ice on that ankle, though." He leaned over
and brushed his lips against the throbbing bump on my forehead, while his fingers lightly touched the raw side of my
face. "Were you unconscious at all—even for a second or
two?"

"I . . ." I remembered drifting off, seeing him with me in
the shower. So real. "Maybe."

He turned my face to the light and peered into my eyes
like some comedian aping a hypnotist. Then he gently in-
serted a finger inside each of my ears for a second. The feel
of his breath on my face made me want to pull him close,
hold him there. But I kept my hands in my lap. "Your pupils
look okay. No ear discharge. Feel dizzy? Seeing double?"

"Would you stop showing off, Hannagan? Two years of
screwing a doctor doesn't give you an M.D."

"Fun, though."

I laughed in spite of myself. "I'm not dizzy and there's one of you. One's enough." It was. It was all I needed. Absurd, but I felt my chest expand with simple delight at seeing him.

"Probably no concussion," he admitted as he walked over to the body and knelt beside it for a once-over. "Not a scratch on him that I can see, other than that throat." He stood and turned to me. "He was inside your freezer?"

"Yeah. There was a power failure. I came down to find a flashlight, and I stumbled against the door. He fell out—knocked me flat."

"Do you know him?"

"Yes, I know him," I said, maybe too neutrally.

His eyebrows raised themselves in an irony I didn't appreciate. "New friend?"

The beautiful balloon floating inside me suffered a blow-out, stabbed by a rusty nail of stored anger. "Where the hell have you been?"

"I was away."

"I know *that*," I said poisonously. "Don't you ever check your goddamned messages? Don't you ever call your office?"

"I didn't this time, no." The heat in his tone bounced my own right back at me. "I tried to call you about an hour or so ago, but you didn't answer, so I just came ahead. And yes, I am sorry my troublesome parent landed on your doorstep." He left the body and walked back to me—stood close enough that I felt his breathing again. If either of us were to touch the other now, the touch might be a slap.

"I'm sorry about a lot of things," he said quietly, "but I think they've all just moved to the back of the bus. Let me get one thing out of the way, though. Your message said my father was okay, but I guess that was more than a week ago. Is he still?"

"Sort of. Physically he is. He's upstairs. The doctor gave him pills to sleep. They tend to put him dead out."

"You've kept him here?" That surprised him more than the frozen corpse on the floor—and not without reason.

"Nowhere else to send him," I snapped. "His only known relative was unreachable."

"Here, stand up. Put your arm around my shoulder. That may not appeal to you at the moment, but if you don't, the pain in that ankle will appeal to you even less. Okay, attagirl. Now let's get you upstairs."

"I suppose I have to call the police, but I need to make another call first."

"The police can wait half an hour, and so can anyone else. I want to know what the hell is going on." His professional tone: Hannagan the Investigator.

He looked back over his shoulder at the body. "From the look of him, your buddy here's been a Popsicle for—"

He broke off, silenced by the whoop of laughter that exploded out of me and, once started, refused to stop, each peal of hilarity birthing a fresh one. From where I now stood, I could see what had tripped me in my run across the basement floor: a big, gingham-clothed wicker picnic basket.

Dev's arms were closed around me, holding tight, as though I might fly off into space. And suddenly it was possible I might. "Oh Jesus! Oh God!" Another paroxysm, a wave crashing in my skull. "It is too funny; too awful. Too awfully *funny!*" My face was soaked now with tears that burned acid on my cheek.

"Ssssh, sssh love. It's okay, okay, okay." He waited, held on until I subsided. "What's the joke?"

Hiccup. I opened my mouth to speak, but all that came out was another hiccup. The joke would require some painful explanation. . . .

2

THREE WEEKS AGO. NO, TWO WEEKS AND SIX DAYS, TO be precise. It seemed both longer and shorter. I had come here with no planning at all—right after the last piece of my world fell apart. The movie in my head flashed back, and I saw myself that night, huddling against the wall, in the shadows, while I watched it disappear . . .

The bookshelves gaped empty, grimy and slightly bowed with their books already carted away. The windows were stark, stripped of their flowing curtains; the polished floor, diminished, dingy without its pale green Chinese rug. Each blow of the hammer, crack of the crowbar throbbed in my gut, hard enough to make me bite my lips closed against the possibility of screaming, *"Stop! Don't do this to me!"*

"Hey Emily, whatcha doin' back here? Thought you actor types'd be half in the bag by now, singin' 'There's No Business Like Show Business' to each other." The ornate, carved doorframe, weightless as a sheet of cardboard in his big paws, landed on top of the growing pile of flats and props to be carted away early the next morning. The stagehand grinned at me with confident authority, the small gold ring in his left ear winking rakishly. Why not? He still had a job to do, and he was good at it.

What *was* I doing back here? "I needed to watch it come down, Kenny." I said. The simple truth, and as complicated as most simple truths. This play had pulled me through the last eight months while I watched a woman I'd finally been able to love end her life, and a man I'd just begun to love retreat into his own head.

For two and a half hours six nights a week plus matinees, the world became a safe place. I knew my lines, knew my moves, knew how to make things turn out as they were meant to. In mid-sip of closing night champagne, it hit me that if I didn't actually see the set disappear, I might turn up here tomorrow, slap on my greasepaint and make my first entrance, as though nothing had ended—as though the single part of my life in working order had not just broken down.

I shouldered the orange backpack, bulging with belongings that had accumulated in a pile on the dressing room floor, including—most precious—Dev's book of stories with the *Times* quote on the back hailing "a promising Joycean voice."

Once outside, I stood for a moment in front of the Public, looking at the theater's tall, classic facade. A last look. The billing, the Paul Davis poster were still confidently in place, giving the lie to the mayhem backstage. Tom Stoppard's *The Real Thing,* four actors' names, alphabetical order—the last of them, Emily Silver.

After almost a year of living with the play, I wondered still: What was the *real* real thing? Most people quickly said love. Dev swore it was language, which could at the change of a word—a comma even—alter the reality of anything. But of course, Dev was a writer. Never mind that for the past fifteen years all he'd written were reports on the whereabouts of white-collar thieves and runaway spouses, he was a writer; that was his trouble. One of his troubles.

The air was hot and thick enough to make you conscious of every breath you took, June about to turn into July. I headed for Broadway and started to walk uptown quickly, nostrils filling with the scent of Indian food, eyes registering couple after couple, their heat-damp bare arms around each other, as they chatted and laughed their way past me. My purposeful stride was a lie. I had nowhere to go. Too many toothbrushes in too many places, and no place that really felt like mine. Ironic, since I argued that the realest real thing was home.

My agent, Bernie Clegg, thought I belonged back in L.A., where if I behaved myself, he could get me "some honest-to-God work, not farting around with English revivals in Greenwich Village."

His point was unarguable. It had been a long, hard pull to get Emily Silver onto the big screen. I'd killed my first chance at it with the bludgeon of my own temper, and for six years no one would take a chance on me. Now finally, with one good featured part behind me, I had another shot. "Don't have the bucks for Julia Roberts? Andie MacDowell? Demi Moore? What about Emily Silver, then? Big green eyes; great cheekbones!"

But out of sight, out of mind, eyes, cheekbones and all— and time was not on my side. My thirtieth birthday this past December had not been, Bernie reminded me unnecessarily, the most desirable crossing for an all but obscure actress whose so-called beauty was a key part of the package.

"Maybe you don't want to work anymore," he'd said yesterday into the silence at my end of the line. Knowing chuckle. "Hey, that's okay too. Just let me know. I hear you're suddenly a pretty rich lady."

"You applying for a loan, Bernie?" It came out not jokey, as I'd intended, but snapping with the heat of my confusion.

"Clients like you, I'll need one," he shot back.

Of course he was right about L.A. Except for the past year, my adult life had been spent there. I didn't make friends easily; the few I had were there, and my best one would be as soon as he finished his shoot in Australia. The work was there. My acting coach, whom I sorely missed, was there. Score three pluses for L.A. Dev and I wound things up in a crescendo of defeat. One minus for New York. But something I didn't entirely understand pulled at me like a choke collar: Sit! Stay!

"I'll let you know, Bernie."

He whooshed a reproachful lungful of smoke through the wires at me. "I don't know why I bother with you."

"I don't either," I replied with absolute truth.

"I got a cockamamie screenplay from some Canadian looney tune says she likes your face," he said after a beat. "Artfart stuff. A lot of talk, but no bucks behind it, probably never see the light of day. Oughta be right up your alley. Want me to send it?"

I swallowed hard, but the lump didn't leave my throat. "I'll let you know," I repeated.

• • •

An overly large bunch of keys to doors I wasn't going to open weighed heavy in the pocket of my chinos. At the moment, I felt like flinging it as far as I could.

It took until Twelfth Street to hit me that there was one key on the ring I hadn't considered at all, to a place I owned now. I hadn't seen it in twelve years, but it materialized instantly in my head, every detail sharper, more vivid than the sublet apartment I'd left this morning. My heart flipped an elated somersault, as my hand shot up for a cab.

Within half an hour, a sluggish garage attendant had turned over my big boat of a secondhand Lincoln—which Dev always said I could rent out for low-class funerals, if things got tough—and I was traveling a little faster than the law allows up an empty FDR Drive on my way to Orchards.

I'm a pro behind the wheel. During our nine years together, Mike Florio taught me how to drive the way he did, truckdriver style. And I'd bought myself the Lincoln, hearing his voice in my head ticking off the advantages of a "good, heavy car," though if Mike were alive he'd've called me a jackass for not taking over the Bentley. True maybe, but I didn't want my grandmother's fancy car any more than I wanted her fancy town house, which I'd put on the market two days after she died—or for that matter, her money, which Mike would have called me a spoiled rich brat for not respecting sufficiently.

Mike would have: those words were touchstones of my life now. They rang in my head often—too often to suit Dev, and maybe he was right. I moved into Mike's Santa Monica beach house when I was twenty, somewhere between raw and half-baked, trying desperately to be an actress, screwing up at almost every turn. Mike took me on and, you might say, finished my raising. He certainly taught me a few useful things: to make sauce like an Italian, make love like a grown-up, and above all to trust him. But he didn't teach me any way to stop feeling guilty that he'd gotten himself killed on my account.

One year, four months, twenty-three days ago. The digital clock in my head kept perfect time, and just in case it stopped, clasped on my wrist like a too big handcuff was the diver's Seiko the L.A. police had given me in a plastic bag.

Mike had always said I'd leave him one day; I'd graduate. Now I wondered whether I ever would.

More recently, just shy of three months ago, my grandmother died. She was eighty-two and tired of being sick. The time of death was her choice, and so not untimely for her. But it was untimely for me, unfinished business piled mountain-high between us. She'd been my only family since I was nine, and we'd battled each other almost every waking hour, until when I was eighteen, I'd struck a preemptive blow for freedom: I had run off to Hollywood instead of beginning Vassar.

I had not written or spoken to her again until last year, and by then, it was a little late; she was engaged in another battle. With cancer. Our time ran out too fast. She was gone—unilateral decision, carefully premeditated; plans made, pills hoarded, no help needed, thank you—leaving me with more money and fewer good memories than I needed.

As the Dutchess County sign whipped by me on the Taconic, I switched off the air-conditioning and opened the car window. My face was rewarded by the first fresh breeze to hit it in days. Less than half an hour and I'd see Orchards again.

But why hadn't I taken this drive even once during the past year? Why hadn't I brought Dev up with me? His opinion was that I was "preserving my rose-colored memory like some icon sealed in airtight glass," which would lead inevitably to my opinion of *his* icons, namely the tall, gray typewriter that sat, growing dust balls, on his round oak table. From there, we'd springboard into another brawl, or worse, sink into resentful silence.

The last brawl three weeks ago seemed to ensure that the silence would be permanent.

I pushed a tape into the deck—Bonnie Raitt singing "Come to Me," a warning about hooking up with the kind of man who can't stand a little shaky ground . . . Right, Bonnie, but what if the ground never holds still? You can't build anything on it, is what. By the time I swung off the Taconic at the Route 44 exit, I was harmonizing with her on "Nobody's Girl," the bittersweet junk food truths satisfying as though they had been cooked to order for me. Two fifty-three, according to the dashboard clock. A delicious weariness began to tingle my skin. I could almost feel the cool, smooth pillow, the puffy quilt, each with the smell of Orchards in every fiber: old waxed wood, pine, cut grass, apple trees, well-used fireplaces, roses, rain—all seasons jumbled together in my sense memory.

Orchards isn't anything as grand as an estate—the real Tucker money accumulated a generation later. It's simply a big old white clapboard house with high ceilings, big rooms, deep porches, lots of windows. Many such houses dot the rolling land of Dutchess County, as though dropped there on impulse by a God in a casually generous mood.

In fact, the impulse had been my great-great-grandfather's. Ethan Tucker had had Orchards built in 1862 on forty-two acres, bought for his wife, Jane Ann, just because she'd admired the land while on a visit up here to friends. He'd never shown her the house, or even told her about it till it was all finished, even to the spinet in the music room. Tucker men bestowed; they did not consult.

They also commanded. Ethan's son, the legendary lawyer Samuel Tucker, had vetoed any idea of a marriage between his brainy, red-haired daughter Cordelia and his equally brainy young partner. A smart Jew in your law firm was one thing, in your daughter's bed, quite another. All of this my grandmother had told me in bits and pieces, the part about her marriage not until last year. The bitter spin, though, is purely my own. Steely critic that she was, if she'd ever uttered a word against her father, I'd never heard it.

If injustice, agony, fury screamed inside her, they did so in silence. She abided by his wishes and married someone more suitable, an Otis of the investment banking Otises—a poor choice, as it turned out. My grandfather did more drinking than banking, and made her an early widow when he crashed his car, killing a local storekeeper in the process.

My father, Tucker, six at the time, would grow up to love a drink as much as his daddy did, and would also die young, taking someone with him: my mother, Celia Silver, who could've made it, could've survived, if she just hadn't married Tuck Otis.

Or maybe she could never have survived at all.

Now there was only me. Everything they'd all been had boiled down to merely me. Somehow, I didn't believe the Tucker men would have been pleased, especially the great-grandfather I'd never met.

"Your great-granddaughter's half a Jew, Samuel Tucker! Poetic justice, you old hard-ass. And she calls herself Silver, just like her mommy. How d'you like them apples?" I recited it—an actress, doing her lines alone in her car. But, even speaking the words, I knew the truth: that being a Silver was hardly anything to brag about; that the name on my birth certificate was still Emily Hippatia Otis, and that, as Dev lost no opportunity to point out, more rods of the Tucker steel ran up my spine than I liked to admit.

Those were the thoughts in my head as I turned left between the tall wood posts, driven into the ground almost a century and a half ago, a local artisan's carved cluster of apple trees arching high between them, marking entrance to the property. The satisfying crunch of bluestone under my tires accompanied Bonnie's guitar on "Luck of the Draw." I pulled up in front of the house, stopped the car and sat, inhaling the country summer. I watched the full moon come out from behind a cloud to silhouette the extravagant looping of an old weeping willow against the fluorescent night-white clapboard of my house. *My house.*

My eyes, my nose were so enthralled that it took my ears at least a full minute to realize what they were hearing: though the motor was turned off, Bonnie was still singing. But the song was a different one, and it was not coming from inside my car.

A wave of vintage rage exploded me out of the car. I ran full speed up the front steps. No need even to grab for keys, the heavy red door swung open almost at a touch. Not locked, it was barely closed. Bonnie's voice was coming from upstairs, and I bolted straight ahead blindly up the wide staircase after it, cracking my shin a good one against the top step. Yowling in pain and fury, I chased the sound to the back of the house, and then froze rigid, barely able to breathe, in the lamplit open doorway of my old bedroom. The white-painted twin beds, blue-and-white quilts, high-backed rocker hadn't moved an inch, were just as they always had been. But a naked girl lay motionless, marble-white against the deep blue hooked rug, eyes closed, arms stretched wide above her head, extravagant red-gold curls fanning out as though afloat in a running stream: Ophelia, cut off young.

Then her arms moved, sudden and fast, to shield her face. "No," she moaned. *"Noooo!"*

My legs unlocked in relief and I ran to her. But once I was there kneeling at her side, my temper turned as sore as my dented shin. Melodrama had tricked me into believing it was tragedy: I know a drunk when I smell one. I smelled something else, too: the unmistakable saltwater tang of fresh sex.

After her initial thrashing around, the girl—she looked maybe seventeen—lay still again, small humming sounds coming out of her mouth. Bonnie, still in full voice, was giving out with "Tangled and Dark" from a portable tape player on the floor next to an almost gone bottle of bourbon. As I reached over and pressed *Off,* I heard the sound of a car gunning its motor somewhere behind the house, preparing for a quick getaway. I grabbed the girl's arm and shook her hard. She groaned and her body tried to turn itself over, like a kid not wanting to get up for school.

But I wouldn't let go. "Come on, *move* it!" I shook her again, slapping firmly at her cheek with my other hand.

As her own hand came up to fend me off, her eyes opened—bleary and hostile. "Get off me!"

"No way at all. *Now sit up.*" I yanked and up she came like a stringed puppet. But when I let go, she didn't fall back down. Instead, she sat there hunched forward, elbows resting on long thin thighs, staring up at my face with eyes the color of bottled honey, screened by lashes unusually long and pale. She frowned, as though trying to piece together a particularly tricky jigsaw puzzle.

"Where did he go?" she asked stupidly.

"He's probably home by now, judging by how fast he got his car moving," I said. "This is not a motel, friend. Now get your clothes on and get out of my house."

"Ahh shit." She collapsed back down, slow motion, and promptly snoozed off. I stepped over her and made my way to the adjoining bathroom, where I ran some cold water into a glass. I stood over her, on the point of letting her have it right in the face, when she opened her eyes again and said, "Are you *Emily?*"

Something in her voice as she said my name underscored how young she was. I took her hand and pulled her back up to a sitting position. "Here," I said, holding out the glass, "take this and drink it down." She hesitated for a moment, her eyes considering telling me to go to hell. "And don't you dare spill a drop," I added. "Got it?" She took the glass and poured it down her throat fast. I went back and refilled it. We repeated the drill five times in dead silence.

"I have to pee," she said quietly, sitting there Indian style, the last drops of water glistening on her bottom lip.

"Fine." I picked up the small pile of her clothes and took them into the bathroom. Then I turned on the shower, full blast cold. "Go pee," I said as I walked back in. "Then get yourself into the shower and get dressed."

She got to her legs like a new colt just figuring out how to use them. I wondered why, even given her milky, red-head's coloring, any healthy girl her age would be quite that white in the country in summer. As she turned slightly, the red-gold curls flowing down around her shoulders, she looked like a nymph out of a painting. I wondered about the boyfriend who'd run off and left her passed out on the floor to catch whatever hell was going to come down. "Can I go to the linen closet and get a towel?" she asked, her tone carrying a sarcastic keynote I'd used often at her age.

"Be my guest," I returned in kind. "But then, you're that already, aren't you? I assume you know where the linen closet is."

She ran into the hallway. A moment later she returned, a white bath towel around her neck, and moved quickly toward the bathroom without saying a word. But I saw her sneak a corner-of-the-eye peek at me through the curtain of her hair, and I heard her lock the door.

I sat down on the one of the two beds I'd always considered mine, and before I knew it I was stretched out flat, my eyes beginning to blur with the sweet burn of flickering memory.

I was nine when I first came to Orchards, whisked up here

for a two-month hideout from the flock of reporters and photographers trying to edge each other out to corner the little orphan of "SOCIETY DOUBLE DEATH." In fact, "society" was not exactly what you'd call truth in journalism. My parents' society had consisted of actors and playwrights, like my mother and father, plus directors, set designers, and composers—all about equally successful—people for whom every month's phone bill was a cliffhanger. Of course, since my grandmother was "socialite" Cordelia Tucker Otis, the story was big news.

I'd sat at her side, eyes fixed on my lap, during the ride up here, taking grim pleasure in refusing more than monosyllables to this stiff, old stranger, who'd suddenly taken over my life, held me captive in her touch-it-not town house. If she would allow me nothing—not my tiger-striped blanket, or my Alice in Wonderland, or the photo of my parents dressed up for Halloween as Laurel and Hardy—nothing from my real home, I would pay her back in silence and scorn, no matter what it cost me.

But when the chauffeur turned through the wooden posts up the quarter-mile private road, I inadvertently looked up, glimpsed tree-lined, mirrored ponds, horses grazing on softly rolling meadows, the red, gold, and green of autumn mountains pointing up in the distance, and couldn't hold on to my resolve a second longer.

"Is this it, Grandmother Otis? Is this Orchards?"

"Yes, it is, Emily. This place is part of our family. Someday . . ." But by then I was out of the car, running as fast as I could toward a large brown horse.

The bathroom door opened in a cloud of steam. The girl walked back into the bedroom wearing denim cutoffs and a green tee-shirt which asked across its front, "What part of NO didn't you understand?" Her hair hung in water-darkened corkscrews. The last traces of Ophelia had vanished: she was just a skinny, delicate-featured, kind of pretty, sullen teenager.

"I'm sorry. *Okay?*" The voice was even younger than she was, and it didn't sound sorry. It sounded resentful.

"Not okay. Your boyfriend got down the back stairs and out the kitchen door in record time. The two of you must be pretty familiar with my house."

"Pretty," she said, stepping back into her combat boots, daring me to pursue it.

"How did you get in? Break a window? A door?"

Her face told me she was not eager to answer. "Look Emily," she said after a beat, "I'm sorry. I'm not being snotty now, really. I had no idea you'd be coming up. Mrs. Otis was dead, and the word was that you were living in California, so I thought, what would it matter?"

"You thought wrong. I'm waiting for my answer."

"I took the key from the cleaning service long enough to make myself a copy." Barely audible. "It wasn't their fault." Her voice strengthened in challenge.

"I'm sure that's true."

"Don't tell. *Please.*" The idea that I might seemed to alarm her more than anything that had happened so far.

"Sit down." I pointed to the other of the twin beds. Why I was keeping her here, I had no idea. She paused, looking for a moment trapped and ready to make a run for it. Then she sat. "What's your name?" I asked.

"Why? So you can tell the police?"

"Maybe. If anything like this happens again, you can count on it."

"Clea Held." Her small, pointy chin went up in defiance. "From the book by Lawrence Durrell. My mother adored Durrell." Getting back at me a bit, she watched to see whether I'd know what she was talking about.

"It's pronounced *Dur*rell," I said, the information thanks to Dev, who'd suggested, with one of his smaller smiles, that I read *The Alexandria Quartet* if I wanted to learn why he'd taken to calling me "vain, pretentious, hysterical Jewess." Clea's eyebrows rose just a little. I'd scored a point. "Your mother has good taste," I added, pressing my advantage.

"No she doesn't. Dead people don't need taste." Her face flushed a furious deep pink, which made me know the death was recent.

"Sorry."

"Don't be. No one else is." She stood. "I'm going home." But she didn't move.

"Good idea, it's almost three-thirty."

"My father's been fast asleep for hours. Anyway, he'd probably be just as relieved if I never came back."

Self-pity was an art form I knew as well as she did. "Maybe you're no fun to be around," I said, "especially if you get smashed and pass out every night. So, who does the Raitt tape belong to, you or your boyfriend?"

"It's mine." She stayed put, looking at my face as though it carried the answer to some unknown question.

I got up and stretched in a long yawn. "Come on, Clea, let's go down to the kitchen and see if there's some coffee or tea lying around. And you can tell me how come you're screwing chicken-livered assholes in my house."

3

. . . .

IT MIGHT HAVE BEEN THAT SHE LIKED BONNIE RAITT'S
singing, or that her hair was just the color I remember my
father's being. Or it might have been that she was so obviously a girl out for trouble and in for trouble that it was like
seeing myself in a rearview mirror. Whatever it was, it was
enough so that I found myself pouring refills of Earl Grey,
rather than shooing her out the door.

I cradled the flowered china cup, satisfyingly hot against
my palm, while my other hand ran over the time-smoothed
roughness of the heavy oak table, caressing it absently as
you might an old dog. When I was a child I'd spent little
time in this room—huge, cave-cool no matter what the
weather. Back then, its wood cupboards, tin counters, stone
floors were the domain of my grandmother's longtime housekeeper, who'd disliked me as much as I had her. But now,
a teenaged desperado at my side, I was staking my claim.
Surprising how triumphant it can feel to brew tea in your
own kitchen at four in the morning.

She seemed sober now, or close to it. The whites of her
translucent honey eyes were pinked from bourbon, and the
steaming tea had reddened her small, delicate nose, giving
her the appearance of a child recovering from the flu, or a
delicate white rabbit who, with a nervous flick of its thick
pale lashes, could bolt at any moment.

Between sips, she talked about herself, that small, clear,
girl voice coming in uneven spurts of hot and cold, like a
faucet that hasn't been turned on in a while. She talked about
how she loved to ride, but wouldn't dream of hunting, and
found her father's zest for it barbaric—"Master of the Millbrook Hunt, can you imagine? Yuck!"—about how hot she
was on Scott Fitzgerald, another of her mother's favorite
writers, about how she wanted to be a writer herself, but
never for her father's string of newspapers, inherited from

his father, "dreary little local weeklies, all about building permits and prize tomatoes and old ladies who've started painting watercolors." As she mentioned the Held papers, the name clicked for me. Held was one of those names that were part of Millbrook, like Thorn and Bontecue and Cary and Hitchcock and Tucker.

I'd underestimated Clea's age. She would turn nineteen in September, just two days after she was scheduled to begin Vassar. "I suppose you're wondering why I'm such a retard, a year behind everyone else."

"Hardly. You tell me you managed to graduate from Hotchkiss. I don't think they take retards. No, what I was wondering was, why not go to college someplace else? Vassar's less than half an hour away from home. You seem more adventurous than that."

"I know," she said quickly into her teacup. "I sort of thought maybe I'd like to go to Stanford or Chicago, but my father said it had to be close to home." The curl she put on the word "father" reminded me of the way I used to say "grandmother": the resentment of the rebel straining at the leash, wanting to break loose; too scared to do it. Yet. She raised her eyes up to look straight into mine. "The year I lost, I was locked up at Austin Riggs."

I had the idea I was being given a test. "Uh huh," I said, as though she'd mentioned some Swiss boarding school.

She didn't say anything for a beat or two. Then she shrugged as though answering something she'd asked herself. "Vassar'll be all right. I don't want to go out of town now, anyway. Maybe I'll just skip the whole thing."

"How come?"

"Just because." A smile played around the corners of her mouth, bringing me right back to where I'd found her: on the floor of my bedroom.

"Because of what? The guy who left you lying there naked and drunk?" My tone made no secret of what I thought. It seldom did.

She threw me a you-don't-understand-anything face—that scornful look kids reserve for trespassing grown-ups. I was well acquainted with the look, but accustomed to giving, not receiving it. "You don't know a damned thing about him."

"All I need to know about him is that he will keep himself out of my house."

"Don't worry, he doesn't have your key," she said with exasperated sarcasm. "Here." She reached into the pocket of her pants and slapped a key attached to a paper clip smartly on the table. "I don't have it either anymore. I wasn't going to use it again. I was going to throw it away." So there!

"Thank you," I said blandly, pocketing it. "Austin Riggs, was that about booze?"

"No, that was about suicide." The edge on her voice sharpened on the payoff word. "When he put Mom in, *that* was about booze. My father's great at clapping people into bins. Sometimes I could just murder him. And that's not apocryphal!"

She took a long sip of tea and then leaned in toward me, her face tense. "You know about murder—suicide, too— don't you? Your father. Right while you were there."

In the years after it happened, I'd treated such questions from acquaintances with stone silence, and more than once, I'd bloodied a schoolmate's nose. But the girl across the table, pulse pounding hummingbird-fast inside the thin white skin at the base of her neck, was not indulging casual curiosity.

"No Clea, he didn't," I said after a moment. "I know that's what the papers said, what everyone still thinks—if they think about it at all—that he shot my mother and then himself, but he didn't. And no, I wasn't there, not exactly. I was downstairs sleeping. I . . . I woke up." I stopped, ran my tongue over suddenly parched lips, and knew that it would never be completely over. "I heard it. I didn't see it. I know the truth of what happened now, but three more people died because I needed so badly to find out. Pretty expensive tuition."

"And you blame yourself, right?" She leaned forward, her small chin resting on tightly clasped hands, her mouth tense. "About the other deaths, I mean."

I felt my heart hammer twice. Just twice, then it returned to normal. "Some days more than others," I said after a moment.

"You're just like me. That's the way *I* feel." No games now, just a desolate bell of a voice, as eager for an answering ring as any I've ever heard.

"About what, Clea? Do you blame yourself for your mother's death?" It was a guess, but not really. I remembered the look on her suddenly flushed face as she'd blurted out that dead people didn't need taste.

"Just what you said, some days more than others." She sat up straight, her hands still clasped tight in front of her on the table. "But *he* blames me every day, my father. And the joke is, I loved her; he was the one who wanted to be rid of her. But I was the one who could've saved her. We both know that, and it's there every time he looks at me."

"And that's why you tried to kill yourself?"

It was the wrong question. Whatever had been weaving itself between us snapped abruptly. "No, it had nothing to do with that! My mother only died two months ago." She sprang up, angry that I'd leapt at the wrong conclusion, that I didn't somehow know things I couldn't possibly know. She walked to the French doors that led out to the back meadows, grabbed one of the handles and slammed the door shut. I hadn't realized it was open. She stood there for a long moment, her back to me. "I did it when I was sixteen, *okay?* Right before my birthday. It seemed like a good idea."

I watched her thin shoulders square themselves, a fragile silhouette against the faint morning light beginning to tinge the sky. My eyelids felt glued open, paralyzed with tiredness. She faced me now. "Even after all the shrink hours I've put in, I don't know if I really meant it." She shook her head slowly. "It didn't seem exactly real while it was happening—more like I was looking at myself the whole time, but through broken glass."

She gnawed on her lower lip, and then, out of nowhere, a smile of triumphant mischief took over her face. "I left a great note, though."

"Of course you did." The actress in me smiled back.

"I borrowed from Sylvia Plath, the part where she said that death was an art, like everything else, and that she did it exceptionally well. I didn't do it exceptionally well, though. But then neither did she, really. I did it the same way—put my head in the oven.'' She shrugged. ''It didn't work. Somebody came.'' The last of her smile disappeared without a trace, and her eyes were mournful, the honey clouded. ''I don't read Plath anymore.''

I got up and joined her in front of the doors, careful to leave a good few feet between us, not to invade her space. ''How did your mother die?''

''She fell. From a horse. She shouldn't've been riding. I shouldn't've let her. She was drunk.'' The facts: concise bulletins. The anguish withheld from her voice showed up in her clenched hands.

''I rode with her,'' she said, talking to the floor. ''I could've called my father. I could've called the troopers. I could've knocked her *out,* for God's sake! She wasn't very strong, and I am. I may not look it, but I can lift weights you wouldn't believe!'' Her head jerked up and she looked at me, eyes wide and fixed. ''I just went *along.* I couldn't stand to shame her, treat her like some kind of . . . nutcase.'' She turned away, palms out, gesturing at no one, lashing herself with it. ''So I let her die instead. *That* was an intelligent decision, right?''

You can't keep blaming yourself. It wasn't your fault. Let it go. I'd heard those words myself often enough to know how little help they were. ''I do know how you feel,'' I said. Not all that helpful either, but true.

It was light enough out now to see the back meadows, ghostly in the pearl-gray dawn, but just as lush as I remembered, the blooming yellows and pinks, reds and purples bright as colored lights against the soft misted green. Two young deer were busily breakfasting on azaleas.

At second glance, I noticed a blue Ford, which I took to be hers, and close by, a set of deep ruts the boyfriend's spinning tires had ground into the gravel. ''Your wimpy friend messed up my driveway.''

Her mood turned on a dime, and she burst out in a truly tickled laugh. ''The last thing he is is a wimp. He's like no one you've ever met,'' she added with more than a touch of smugness. ''And he loves me.''

''I've met a lot of people. What does your formidable

father think of him?'' As if there were much doubt about
that.

"You *bitch!* Are you going to go to my father?'' But the
laugh still played in her throat.

"You never know,'' I teased.

"Em-i-*ly!*''

Both giddy with lack of sleep, we'd slipped, improbably,
into a sitcom sister act. Just as improbably, I found myself
enjoying it.

"Cle-*a!*'' I mimicked. "Okay,'' I said finally, "you can
relax. You're nineteen—your life belongs to you. And anyway, I'm not the snitch type. But watch your back. I may
not know him, but I'll still bet he's bad news. Scoot now.
I've got to get some sleep, even if you don't.''

Her lips curved into a smile that looked just short of
happy. "I saw you on 'NYPD Blue,' '' she said. "I thought
you were good.'' And then she bounded out the door, swift
as one of the young deer.

4

....

THE SPRAY DRENCHED MY SCALP, SLICKED MY BODY, cleaned away some of the cement in my brain. The will to sleep had produced only a fitful couple of hours. Finally, I stepped out of the shower and dried myself in the same thick white towel Clea had used hours earlier. With it wrapped toga style around me, I padded barefoot to get my backpack from the car. Going down the stairs, I felt my legs tremble slightly. A sudden, sharp pain descended from chest to gut, where it throbbed dully. I wondered whether I might be getting the flu, until it occurred to me that I hadn't eaten since before last night's show.

I swung open the front door to bad news. The Lincoln sat there, its windows wide open to welcome rain which, by the looks of it, had been coming down for a good few hours. Shit! I started the engine, shut the windows, folded my toga towel into a four-ply blotter and laid it on the driver's seat, while my stomach growled for attention.

I ran back through the house, the damp backpack slung over my naked, wet shoulder, into the kitchen to forage for something edible: a box of crackers, jar of peanut butter, candy bar, years old maybe, but I wouldn't've cared.

Nothing except the package of sugar cubes I'd found next to the box of Earl Grey last night, missing the few Clea had used to sweeten her tea. I popped two into my mouth and walked slowly toward the French doors where she and I had stood side by side at dawn, looking out at the first rays of light. Her misery and confusion spoke to me like an old friend, painfully authentic yet, at the same time, a shadow play, magnified against the wall into a Grand Guignol of misery—a torment truly worth the suffering. But in the next second, I wondered whether it was she I had in mind, or myself.

It was the truck that caught my eye first: a red Chevy

pickup. It had been sitting there who knew how long. I was just too deep into my own head for my eyes to have registered it.

Or the man either. He was about my own age, tallish, strong-looking carved face, blond floppy hair, dressed in a navy tee-shirt and faded denim cutoffs. He stood there next to a bed of brilliant tulips, looking at me, a large clump of weeds in his hand. What was remarkable was the way his body held itself, in a posture of natural swagger, utter easy confidence. That, and the smile on his face: not rude or lewd or menacing, simply a beam of frank pleasure at the naked lady with her orange backpack, munching sugar cubes as she made her way around the stone-floored kitchen.

Our eyes engaged and I felt my skin pucker to gooseflesh. I stood there statue-still, tense as a hunting dog under the command of some soundless whistle, keyed so it was impossible to ignore. My mind struggled to break free, regain custody, call its own shots. Probably it was no more than a moment or two before I was able to force my eyes off him, but that is a long time when you are trapped.

Liberated, I snapped him an Italian hand signal, explicit and universally understood, and made it upstairs on the dead run. When I looked out my bedroom window, he and his truck were gone.

I slipped my clothes on quickly, wanting to be covered, but the touch of them against my skin made me acutely aware of every inch of my electrified body. Turned on by a Peeping Tom in the garden? You are pathetic, Emily Silver!

I knew though, even as I gave myself the requisite slap on the wrist, that this was not just some quirk of mine. There was something about this man—a particular kind of magnetism, rare and oddly exciting. It didn't depend on looks or brains, or even personality. Call it a sexual imperative. I believe my father had it, though I was too young to identify it then for what it was. It did not serve him well, in the end, and it proved disastrous for some who found themselves caught in the gleam of his headlights too long.

I had no idea who the man in the garden was, but I felt certain I would see him again.

• • •

The plastic seat of the booth had a friendly bounce, well broken in but still springy. Other than the fact that the tableside jukebox control no longer controlled anything, the Millbrook Diner seemed blessedly unchanged: a silver-skinned mock railroad car, as at home here at the bottom of Franklin Avenue as it would've been on any avenue in any nice little town in America.

It was just past noon and the place had the same summer Sunday assortment of people I remembered: local families just out of church—round pastel mothers, lean sideburned fathers, scrubbed offspring; stylish weekending couples, dividing up their *New York Times*es, fresh from The Corner Store across the street; college kids, summer-happy, voices a little too loud; trios—they always seemed to come in threes—of old men, faces grave, skin speckled and leathery with sun.

A thick white mug of coffee, poured as soon as I'd sat down, remained untouched next to my right hand. My throbbing gut, teased by sugar cubes, begged for food, rumbled with the almost pleasing pangs and slight nausea of hunger that knows it's about to be satisfied.

"Here you go." The motherly waitress set down my breakfast. "Somebody looks pretty hungry."

"About ready to chew your hand, if it didn't have a plate in it." The sausages sent up a spicy perfume, irresistible as it blended with the sharp, toasty smell of hot buttered English muffin and the grease-rich, almost burnt one of home fries. Twin yolks stared benignly up at me through an over-easy glaze. For just a second I sat there, perfectly still, enjoying the sensual pleasure of anticipation. Then my fork attacked, and I was lost, oblivious of everything but the tastes flooding my mouth, the substance filling my emptiness.

"Emily?" The voice came at me out of nowhere, its melodic sound straight out of a Victorian novel: the self-contained, virtuous heroine—demure, with a touch of long-suffering thrown in. I hadn't heard it in thirteen years, but I recognized it at once—and not only because my ear for the way people sound is highly tuned. For two years of my life, I'd heard it first thing most mornings. *Emily, please get up, you're going to be late. Emily, come on, she'll never let you into class dressed like that. Have you got your math homework? Here, you can copy mine.*

"Ariane." The sizable piece of egg-drenched muffin between my thumb and forefinger popped automatically into my mouth. I chewed voraciously, while she stood there, gracefully still. The moment was, in miniature, our entire relationship as roommates at Fletcher: Emily, overheated, unraveling with some passion or another; Ariane, cool, composed, the model girl.

Everything about Ariane Warburton was smooth as ever: blond hair, coiled now in some kind of braided twist, skin ivory pale, with coral breaking through like the blush of a withheld secret at the top of each softly rounded cheek. Her body, average height and sturdy, without any suggestion of plumpness, was still the body of an athlete, and slightly out of sync with her cameo face. At school, tennis had been her sport; today, white shirt tucked neatly into crisply cuffed white shorts, she looked ready to polish someone off on the courts.

"My God, what are you doing here?" My words tumbled out, food-muffled.

"I just stopped in for a cup of coffee."

Which, of course, was no answer at all, and typical Ariane. She slid her neat bottom into the booth opposite me. "Do you live up here, or what?" I asked impatiently, quite aware that I hoped she'd say no. I didn't want to share my town with her now, any more than, after our sophomore year, I'd wanted to share my room with her. Back then, when I was intent on being an outrageous outlaw, something in her daily presence tended too often to make me feel like a naughty child—a naive one, at that.

"Only weekends, usually. We live in the city—Park and Eighty-second—but we're pretty much up for the summer."

I noticed the band on her finger—a showily broad circle of bumpy gold nuggets—and was surprised she'd picked out that particular ring. Surprised also, for no reason I could think of, that she was someone's wife. "How long have you been married?" I asked.

"Just coffee, thanks." Ariane smiled warmly at the waitress, who filled her cup and topped up mine. "Three years now. You?"

"No." The word hung there, sounding stark. "Do you have any children?" I asked. I remembered the photo on her bureau: a cute, gold-haired boy standing stiff and proud next to a Doberman puppy. Lots about Ariane had been a mystery, but never her almost fierce love for that little brother.

"No. No children yet." I thought I saw a cloud cross her dark blue eyes. "I heard about your grandmother, Emily. I'd've written, but I had no idea where. Everybody seemed to think you were in California." She paused for a moment. "I hope it wasn't too awful. For either of you."

Her features subtly recast themselves into a portrait of radiant kindness. "Nursey," I used to call her when she got that look, as though it were one big bore. But I remembered how, when we were freshmen, I'd come down with appendicitis, and lain for a full week at Yale New Haven after the surgery, head fevered, stomach sore, looking forward to the sight of that face—that look—to the daily visit of the roommate I didn't even like, but who seemed miraculously to know better than anyone else just what word, what magazine, what piece of gossip would make me feel better, whose very presence was somehow a cool compress on a burning forehead.

"Not as awful as it might've been, I guess." And Nursey knew from my tone to let the matter drop.

"I am so proud of your work," she said. As the coral cheeks raised themselves in a smile, I noticed a faintly discolored swelling on the left side under her eye, and then looked quickly away as she noticed my stare. "Sometimes," she continued, unruffled, "I turn on the television set, and—surprise—there you are. But I thought you were especially good in that movie. What was it called?"

"Running Fast." I didn't have to ask her which movie she meant. I'd only made the one.

"You still had your long hair, and you looked so much like that photo of your mother." Neither her face nor her voice gave any clue that the remark was anything unusual, yet she knew damned well that it was.

My heart felt a tweak of something like pity as I recalled two wary fourteen-year-olds, late on a snowy night, an unexpected moment of intimacy in a dorm room. We'd shown each other dog-eared photos of our lost mothers—mine dead, hers run off somewhere remote with a lover—photos normally tucked away in drawer bottoms under the socks, to be looked at only in private. Neither of us had said anything at the time. On my part, at least, it was not lack of curiosity that held my tongue, but the knowledge that if I asked, I'd have to tell. And if I'd wanted a confidante at all, it would not have been Ariane Warburton.

Afterward, in silent mutual agreement, we'd never mentioned the photos again. But I had wondered then how Ariane could know that her mother was somewhere in the world, alive, and not be driven to find her. I wondered now whether she ever had, but not enough to risk asking. I shied away from intimacy with Ariane now, just as I had then, with as little idea of my reason.

"I'm not sure what I think of the short haircut," she said. "It does change you a bit, takes away some of that Wuthering Heights wildness. I didn't recognize you at first."

"I like it," I said, recalling the thrill of liberation as the unaccustomed air first hit my neck. Freed, I'd thought, from the living image of my mother, her vibrant unhappiness, her tense, futile grabs at brass rings just outside her reach. As though the Celia Silver in me could be snipped away as simply as a fall of hair!

"What about you, Ariane? What have you been doing?" It wasn't the question I most wanted to ask, just the simplest one.

"Until we got married, I was teaching English up at Cornell. That's where I did my doctorate. Victorian literature: George Eliot." She smiled, a bit wistfully, as though she weren't thirty but fifty, remembering some foolishness of her youth. "Zach teases me unmercifully."

"Zach?"

"My husband. Thank you so much," she said, acknowledging the waitress, who was again replenishing coffee. "Zach doesn't have the highest regard for George. Too stiff and intellectual, according to him. What I think he really holds against her is that she wasn't pretty.'' She laughed, as though retelling an anecdote about a three-year-old. ''Of course, as he points out, though nobody's writing dissertations on Zach Terman, he beats George Eliot all hollow at the checkout counter.''

''Zach Terman.'' My knowledge of writers was pretty spotty—heavy on playwrights, as you might expect from an actress, and scattered pickup on everything else, as you might also expect, from someone who'd loped through a good old prep school searching for new ways to be bad, and who had never gone to college. ''Zach Terman,'' I said again, almost to myself.

''Oh, you'd never have read him. Zach writes adventure stories for teenagers. Young adult fiction—Y.A., they call it. Good, too, for what it is.'' This round of smile was calm, just short of happy.

''So you stopped teaching? Don't tell me you've dumped George Eliot for the Rover Boys.''

Now she laughed her light, airy laugh, which sounded just like it used to. ''It's a little more complicated, but yes, I guess you could put it that way. Oh Emily, you are still you. Combat boots on your heart.'' The hand with the gaudy wedding band reached across the table to cover mine. ''I am so glad to see you!''

''What happened, Ariane?'' I hadn't intended to ask. Such a long time ago, what did it matter? But the unexpected gesture touched the current chill in my soul with its warmth. ''How come you just disappeared that way after junior year?''

We'd had little to do with each other that year. We no longer roomed together. Besides, while my private war against the adult world was propelling me into the farther reaches of academic thin ice and campus lawlessness, Ariane shuttled between honors classes and tennis courts, and had begun to spend most of her free time consorting with the enemy: our crusty assistant headmistress, the woman known to most of us as Old Bailey.

But late one night just before end of term, sneaking back into the dorm after an illicit date with an energetic Yale freshman, I'd caught a quick glimpse at the far end of the hall of another girl doing the same thing. It had taken a shocked second for me to realize I was looking at Ariane.

Our eyes met, and I caught her smile: a smile of surpassing bliss. A second later, she disappeared into her room. I stood there mulling it—just long enough to get nailed by a prefect. The next day, when I passed Ariane on the quad, she turned away and pretended not to see me.

I did not lay eyes on her again. Not until now.

The following September, she didn't return to school. None of the other girls seemed to know where she'd transferred, and if any of the Fletcher administration did—which of course they must've—they weren't telling. Coincidentally, Old Bailey had left too. For some reason, I'd cared enough to send two letters to Ariane's home address in Chicago, but they were both returned unopened.

"How come you sent my letters back?" Anger, quick-frozen thirteen years ago, thawed, instantly fresh.

The color in her cheeks deepened, but only slightly. Otherwise, there was no outward sign that she was even uncomfortable. I remembered some anonymous classmate referring to her as "the girl who wouldn't sweat in hell." After a moment, she stood.

"I'll tell you sometime. Not now, though." She reached into her purse.

"Forget it," I said quickly. "Let me spring for your coffee." The meeting had been naggingly unsatisfying. It occurred to me that "Nothing Changes" might be a useful motto to post somewhere where I'd be forced to look at it daily.

"Will you be staying at Orchards long?" she asked lightly. Her eyes on my face, looked speculative.

"I'm not sure. At least for a while."

"Good. I'll have you to dinner. Zach enjoyed your movie too. I told you he likes pretty women."

The rain had given way to a sunny Sunday afternoon, and the antique shops that lined Franklin Avenue had opened their doors wide in invitation, festive windows signaling to well-heeled browsers that *this* was the place they'd finally find the ideal table, the perfect quilt, the only possible and-irons: possessions that promised—at least for an hour or two—to transform lives. With respect to mine, that did not seem possible.

On sour impulse, I stopped in at The Corner Store to buy, not the *Times,* but a pack of Pall Mall Gold. I'd quit smoking ten years ago, under heavy pressure from Mike, and last year, during a short bout of backsliding, Dev's pressure had been equally firm. *Screw you, guys! Where are you when I need you?* I lit up and took a deep drag, which tasted as rich as I remembered, but produced a whirling dizziness I didn't much like. The next inhale tasted like dried shit. I stamped the thing out, but shoved the pack in my pocket, resolving another try.

At the very end of the street, across from the library, I spotted a shop, small but conspicuous in its reticence. Draped ivory fabric, seemingly sheer yet, on second look, effectively opaque, masked the windows. The glass of the door was draped too; a small sign, in expert calligraphy, read "By appointment" and included a phone number. The shop was called "Benzinger." I wondered whether I was gazing at the lair of some sort of classy fortune-teller.

I climbed into the Lincoln and spent the next four hours listening to the rasp of Willie Nelson, and saturating my senses in steamy, wet green, with punctuating splotches of flower color. No human being, myself fortunately included, entered my mind.

I followed Route 44 east toward Amenia, and pulled over for a while to let myself be swallowed up in the rolling mountain vista: big sky, eastern version—as ravishing in its way as anything in California. The cosmic tranquilizer of a grand-scale view. I knew from experience it would have little long-term effect on me, and that made every second more precious.

Westbound 44, the road to Poughkeepsie, was an abrupt comedown. It had acquired the pockmarks of small, random shopping centers, and the Cottonwood Inn, which had been a nicely rambling house with a not too tasty restaurant, had sprouted a motel at its side. The inn itself stood half-renovated, the raw wood of odd, awkward new wings pointing like truncated arms to some overextended developer gone bust.

The one change I liked was in Adams Fairacre Farm. They'd added meat and fish departments, a take-out ice cream counter, and a bakery.

As I carried the first two of nine overflowing brown paper bags into the kitchen, I knew how ludicrously I'd over-bought—grabbed up everything that caught my eye: corn and tomatoes, five varieties of green vegetable, four cartons of strawberries, three of ice cream; five kinds of cheese and four different pastas; chickens, cut up various ways; calamari—two pounds. What did I think I was doing? Opening a summer camp? I was alone here. *Alone.*

I finished bringing in the stuff and found myself fumbling, self-conscious, as if I were being watched in an early re-hearsal by some unseen audience. I moved from counter to cupboard to fridge wondering, as I had this morning, about the wisdom of coming here. My icon was out of its glass case now; it hadn't disintegrated or turned toxic. Yet. But was I here to worship the past, or to reinvent it? I didn't need Dev to tell me that one was crazy, the other impossible.

I found my eyes darting, tic-like, toward the French doors. Looking for whom? Clea? Ariane? Dev? Or maybe the man in the red truck? I smacked the tomato in my hand down on the table, where it exploded in a wet splat.

5

THE REST OF SUNDAY AND MOST OF MONDAY HAD passed in slow motion, as I roamed the house and grounds, marveling at how unchanged everything was, how familiar—the ancestors on the walls, books in the shelves, vases on the tables. And yet, the very familiarity had its edge of strangeness. Twice last night, I'd been awakened by a ringing phone and when I picked it up, heard, after a moment, the decisive click of a hang-up on the other end. It seemed to me as though Orchards had been, under its surfaces, living a life of its own. Or perhaps I was simply still spooked by thoughts of Clea Held and her trysts here.

Now, late Monday afternoon, I found myself wandering from room to room to room, as though trying to make friends with a new stage set. I hauled out the Pall Malls for another try. This time I finished the cigarette, but got nothing from it, except for the acrid aftertaste—and the unsettling feeling that Emily Silver might be a freak, incapable of successfully returning to anything, even an addictive bad habit.

The library was a corner room at the back of the house. It opened to the side porch and also gave on the garden patio, as the kitchen did, through French doors. A tufted leather chaise, facing that way, provided a great place to escape into a book, or simply to look out at roses and lilacs.

The large mahogany desk captured my eye, because it looked somehow different. I stared at it for a moment or two before I realized that the difference was the phone. The black round-dialed dowager, which had always sat sedately to the left side of the tooled leather surface, had been replaced with a wavy white number, on a diagonal, smack in the center, as out of place in the room as a surfboard in a Roman bath. When I came closer, I saw the old one on the floor under a window, almost hidden behind the long silk curtain.

This was not my grandmother's phone; she would have

more likely purchased a bikini. I picked up the almost weightless, white receiver and saw the reason for the substitution: a set of push buttons. Clea's boyfriend jumped to mind, and the idea of his cheesy little phone, plugged in so that his sex life here would not interfere with getting his messages, made me want to yank out the cord and strangle him with it.

Instead, I dialed the number of my city sublet and checked my own messages. None. I told myself to stop whining. I was free, rich, and thirty; what could be better? Then I called Bernie's office in Century City and asked his secretary to send me the art-fart script that would probably never see the light of day, and to give Bernie my love if he ever came back from lunch—which he sometimes didn't.

"I knew you had to be here someplace, if your car was," said a small voice behind me. As I spun around to face her, I felt a smile begin to pull at my mouth.

"Hi Clea." She was dressed in tan jodhpurs and a yellow tee-shirt. Her tall boots looked well used and well cared for.

"I came to make you go for a ride with me." I looked for some signal in her face or voice, and didn't find it. But it had to be there: riding could not be just riding for her— not after her mother.

"I don't have a horse," I said. "Not anymore. Didn't you notice the stables were empty?"

There were faint, bluish shadows under the honey-colored eyes. Otherwise, she looked in good shape. "I knew your grandmother sold the horses," she said, "but I have one for you to ride."

"You do?"

"Uh huh. Come on. Put on some clothes and we'll drive back to my house. There're boots and things in your closet." She grinned. "I looked."

"That's no surprise."

Clea lived out past Mabbettsville, about three miles away. The house was a creamy yellow sprawl, of similar age but more random design than Orchards, and somewhat closer to the road. I winced at my instant rush to compare. Here two days, and already house-proud. *You'll turn into a real Tucker, if you don't watch out.*

She drove around the back and parked in front of a good-sized stable. Before she got out of the car, she turned to me for a quick look, but didn't speak. I followed her into the cool darkness, and breathed deeply the sweet, earthy air of clean horse barn. I'd missed it, though I had no idea how much until this moment. A tingle of excitement buzzed at the base of my spine. I hadn't felt a saddle under me in twelve years.

"This is Wilbur. He's mine," Clea said, opening the stall and reaching for a carrot to feed a dark brown horse with a large white mark on its forehead. After his snack, he nuzzled her palm and she stroked his nose. A girl and her horse: perfect love.

"He's beautiful. How old?"

"Five. He was my Christmas present the year I was fourteen. My first horse'd died right after Thanksgiving. He was an old guy—almost sixteen. Wilbur was just a colt. I named him for *Charlotte's Web*."

"I figured. My horse was Birthday. My grandmother bought him for my tenth—a few months after my parents died. It meant a lot to have him." And I'd never told her how much. My joy had been quickly quenched by a crying jag, which neither she nor I had had a clue how to handle.

Clea gestured at the next stall, where a tall black horse stood, powerfully patient as an emperor. "This is Stand Back. He's my father's." She hardly paused at all. "And that one down on the end is Godiva."

I walked over to the end stall to get a better look. The horse was a fine-looking white mare. I glanced at Clea and saw her face close in on itself for just a second and then open, quick as the flex of a muscle. "You're going up on Godiva. She hasn't had enough exercise the past two months."

The rhythm of the ride came back to me, but jerkily. My knees were no longer used to the grip of posting a trot, and my butt bounced around like a beginner's. No surprise. But

Clea's riding technique *was* a surprise—steady, relaxed, I guess mature is the word. I'd expected flash. Tension. Showboating. I'd expected, I admitted to myself, that she'd ride the way I did when I was her age.

After a long, satisfying canter we slowed down to a walk. I glanced over at her. The fast rush of July air had whipped her face damp and pink, and pasted wet ringlets of hair to her cheeks. She looked happy, radiantly happy. Weeks later, I'd remember her face right then, and it would break my heart.

We didn't talk. I knew this was a ceremony: her first real ride after her mother's death, and she'd chosen to take it with me. Some bond forged in my kitchen at dawn was strengthening itself, and right then neither of us was about to risk wrecking it with a wrong word. We traded knowing smiles, then I eased Godiva out into full gallop and spun off into a glorious blur, where the horse and I and the summer countryside were one. And where nothing else existed.

By the time we got back to the Held stables, the horses were well cooled down in an easy amble, but Clea and I were soaked in sweat, shirts plastered to our backs.

"Thank you," I said with the formality suitable for an important occasion. "I loved it."

I slid myself off Godiva's back and felt my knees almost buckle as my feet hit the ground. I'd be pretty damned sore tomorrow.

"Clea." The voice was dry, dry as snapping twigs. I turned to see a tall, thin man in blue seersucker pants and a white business shirt with sleeves rolled up a notch and striped tie at half mast. My instant impression was that he was old, but a second look made me wonder why I'd thought so. He was not stooped; his face—less pale than Clea's, but far from vivid—was unlined, except for twin deep furrows that stretched like parched riverbeds from the sides of his nose to the corners of his mouth; his hair, blond blended with some white, was soft-looking and plentiful. He couldn't be more than fifty, yet his light gray eyes had a defeated look, as though they'd failed to find something lost after too long a search. And there was something in the way he held himself that seemed played out.

"Clea," he repeated. "I'm glad to see you . . . here." His smile was tentative, but looked real. "Did you have a good ride?"

"Yes," she said, the word managing to sound clipped. Her eyes slid over in my direction. "This is Emily Otis . . . Silver, I mean. Emily, this is Barnet Held. My father." *My father: chronicler of prize-winning rose gardens; Master of the Millbrook Hunt; clapper in bins of his wife and daughter.*

"Hello, Mr. Held." I dried a hand on my pants and held it out.

"Hello, Emily," he said, taking it for a surprisingly vigorous shake. "Please call me Bart. I'm not that old." Which made me wonder whether my mind was open for reading. "Your grandmother was an extraordinary woman. We'll all miss her." Had the Held papers used those words in her obituary?

"Extraordinary is the word," I said. "And so will I."

His attention returned to his daughter. "Will you be in this evening?" The anxious look he leveled at her said more.

"No. I'm going over to Orchards. Emily's asked me for dinner." She gave me a bland glance. "That's where I've been the past couple of nights," she added, chin going up. I answered Barnet Held's questioning look with a small nod, and felt my face turn hotter, having nothing to do with the weather. She'd taken the gamble that I'd lie for her. She'd been right—and I'd been used.

"Oh fine," he said, accepting with relief the respectable explanation, which I'd just validated. "That's fine, then. I'll have Malvina fix me a quick bite before she goes home. I have to get back to the office for a few hours."

"He *always* has to go back to the office for a few hours," Clea said mockingly. I felt their tug-of-war, and knew instantly that however much she wanted to break free of him, she also wanted something else: she wanted him to fight to keep her.

His mouth moved slightly, without sound, and then his face turned martinet-harsh. "You are to be home at a decent hour, Clea," he said in a tone that would have provoked mutiny in a self-respecting twelve-year-old.

"I may sleep at Emily's again," she responded stonily.

They entered an eye-to-eye wrestle. After a five-second standoff, she won the point.

"Maybe tomorrow night we can have dinner together," he said wearily. It was obvious how little the prospect appealed to him.

"Maybe." She shrugged dismissively. "Come on, Emily, let's go have a shower. I'll lend you some clothes."

I waited till we were back at Orchards to say it. "Don't ever do that to me again." Her eyebrows rose. "And cut the wounded innocence; I'm the actress, remember?"

"Well, I *was* here Saturday night, wasn't I? It was half true." Her small smile teased with an edge of malice. "I play head games with my father. Sometimes I even win."

I wanted to tell her the game wasn't worth the injuries. There was so much I wanted to tell her that it whirlpooled inside my head, reduced itself to processed advice-column sermons. "I don't want you to play head games with me," was all I said.

We were in the kitchen. I wore a tee-shirt and shorts borrowed from Clea, a pretty good fit as long as I didn't button the waist of the shorts. I was a little taller, and on the skinny side, but she was skinnier. "Do you like calamari?" I asked, the afterglow of our ride together now almost totally gone.

"I guess. I'm not much of an eater, though, so—"

"*I* am. And I feel like cooking. Since you invited yourself here, you can damned well join me." I got a couple of cutting boards out of a cabinet next to the sink, searched around and finally found the right knives and started slicing the squid into rings. "Here, chop up some of this garlic and basil."

She gestured at the liquor store carton, open but unpacked on the counter. "Could we have some wine while we chop?"

That sounded good to me, too—and then I wondered. "Do you have a problem with booze, Clea?" I asked it straight. If she lied to me, it would have to be a straight lie, not the slippery kind she'd palmed off on her father.

"No. That was my mother. *Remember?*"

"I've got an excellent memory, thank you," I zinged back.

"Wonderful Wendy. Well, she was almost wonderful, my mother. That's a lot more than most people are. I always called her Wendy, like we were girlfriends." She began to chop fast but unsteadily, like someone who'd never done it. Then she stopped, her hand holding the knife as though it were someone's supporting arm. "It was so awful, the two of them. God, I'm never going to marry a man like my father! I remember one night she was sitting at her dressing table getting ready for some dinner party. I can just picture her brushing out her long red hair. It was darker than mine, much more . . . glamorous. Yeah okay, she did have her bourbon there, but she wasn't drunk, and we were laughing together about something or other. And then he came rushing in, late from his precious office. And Wendy swiveled around and said, 'If it isn't the late Mr. Held. To quote Dorothy Parker about Calvin Coolidge, how could they tell?'

"Then, out of nowhere, he swooped over and smacked her across the face. Then he grabbed her glass and threw it at the mirror, and the mirror broke into this long, diagonal crack. I was facing it, looking into it, and the crack went right through the middle of my face. Funny, none of the bourbon got on her or him, but it splashed all over me. And I didn't do anything. I should have helped her. I should have . . . But all I did was stand there smelling the bourbon all over me and staring at how I looked in the broken mirror."

"How old were you, Clea?" I asked.

"Eleven, I think. Old enough to get the pun about late, but not old enough to know who Calvin Coolidge was. And not old enough to help my mother. You know, Wendy just laughed after he hit her. She just laughed, and finished brushing her hair—and they went to the party. But she wouldn't let him get the mirror fixed for years. That was her way of punishing him. It was so Wendy!

"Sometimes when I was really bummed out about something, I'd go in there alone and just look at myself, broken up in that mirror."

"Was that the way it seemed when you tried to kill yourself? You said it was like looking at yourself through broken glass.''

''Yeah, it was. But of course the mirror had been replaced by then.'' She smiled and I felt my eyes sting. ''Brand new. Not a scratch on it.'' She split a clove of garlic with a karate chop of the knife. ''So, I guess we were just the typical American family.''

''I guess so. Amazing anyone gets out alive, huh?'' I reached across the table and brushed a curl back from out of her eyes.

She put the knife down and looked at me. ''I don't drink all that often. And that's the truth.''

''Okay, we'll have wine.''

''I wish you were my sister, Emily.''

''Your sister,'' I repeated, the words fizzing husky in my throat.

I hid an unexpected rush of powerful emotion under the business of rummaging for a corkscrew and opening chardonnay. ''We'll have red with the food,'' I said, my voice returning to normal. I poured the cold wine into a pair of proper stem glasses and handed her one.

''Sisters,'' I said, wanting to try out the sound of it again. The glasses struck a pure tone as they touched.

''Sisters.'' Her voice rang as clear as the crystal.

I put pasta water on to boil, while I chopped tomatoes and sautéed them with the garlic and basil in a large black skillet, dish towel wrapped around its handle. Pot holders. I'd have to buy pot holders.

''Do you have a husband, Emily? Do you have a lover?''

''Had,'' I said, tipping the skillet and moving the tomatoes around. The movie behind my eyes started to screen. I saw Dev walk into the kitchen with that rakish roll his slight limp gave him.

''And now?''

''No.'' But a second later, the ungarnished no wasn't enough—not enough to fob off on a sister. ''I lived with a man in L.A. He died a little over a year ago. And then, I met another man, a friend of his. No, more than a friend—almost like a son, even though they were only about ten years apart in age. Years ago, Mike, the man who died, kind of rescued Dev from his real father, who'd knocked him down and smashed his hip. When Mike died, Dev paid back the favor by helping me find out the truth about my parents.'' And it would have been better if we'd both just left it at that. Mike did for him; he did for me. Debt paid in full. I put the pan down and drank a bigger mouthful of wine than I'd intended.

''What *was* the truth about your parents?'' She was tearing lettuce now, but stopped, motionless, and leaned in toward me to ask her question.

''The truth was,'' I said slowly, ''that no one was completely guilty, or completely innocent—not my father or my mother or the others. No heroes, and no villains either. That was hard, so hard, to accept.'' I felt my throat go dry. ''And I don't want to talk about it anymore.''

Her eyes continued to look straight into mine, but she didn't press me. This time it was she who reached across the table and touched my hand lightly with only the tips of her fingers. ''Tell me more about Dev though,'' she said. ''What kind of a name is Dev? Is he very handsome?''

''No.'' *I can do this. See, I can talk about him, if I want to.* ''I don't know if he's handsome. Probably not. His name is Paul Eamon De Valera Hannagan. The Dev is for De Valera. Most people call him Paul, though. He's half Irish, a quarter French, and one of his grandmothers was Algonquin Indian. He kind of looks like all three, so . . .'' My gears ground to an abrupt halt, jammed by a clutch of feeling I could barely stand. ''What about your . . . friend?'' I used the quick switch to cut off incipient tears. ''Give me something to like about him.''

''He's dark and handsome.'' That at least knocked out the sexy blond man with the red truck. ''And a little crazy. He's completely free, not one bit ashamed to be romantic. When the two of us are together, it's like there's nobody else alive. We have a special place, just for us, and when we're there—''

''Shit!'' Not an editorial comment, though it might have been. While she talked, the water had begun to boil, and just as I began to drop the pasta in the bubbling pot, the phone rang. I was certain it would be another hang-up, and considered not answering. Then I dashed to grab the receiver from the wall on the fifth ring.

"Oh hi, Emily. I was just about convinced you weren't there. This is Ariane."

"Oh." Beat, beat, beat. "Hi, Ariane."

"Do I have you at a bad time?"

"Sort of. I was just making dinner." *And I am not glad to hear from you.*

"Well, dinner's what I'm calling about. I wonder if you might be free to join us Friday evening."

"Friday evening's fine," I said after a small hesitation, sensing that if it weren't, some other night would have to be. "Where do you live?" She gave me the name of a road I couldn't quite place. "Is that in Millbrook?"

"No, not exactly. It's Salt Point. Right off Salt Point Turnpike. Make a right and it's the second mailbox. You can't see the house from the road. You'll see the name on the mailbox; Terman, remember? Eight o'clock all right?" I said that it was and got off. I found a stubby pencil and jotted down her address and new name on a hunk of paper towel.

"Who was that?" Clea asked, her back to me, putting the salad greens in a bowl.

"My old roommate from school. I bumped into her yesterday at the diner. Seems she has a place in Salt Point. I'm going to dinner there Friday." I turned up the light under the garlicky tomatoes. "Now when you do calamari, the trick is to only cook it about thirty seconds or so. Otherwise, instant rubber bands."

We ate. Mostly, I ate. Clea picked. She didn't drink much either—sipping at the Barolo I poured like a sparrow at a birdbath. Her mind had flown off somewhere else, and when she asked whether she could use the phone, I knew exactly where, and was instantly sorry that, in my eagerness to get off Dev, I'd brought him up.

"Help yourself," I said, indicating the one on the wall.

"Could I use the phone in the library?"

"You mean the one your boyfriend put in?" I was irritated, and didn't bother to hide it.

"What?" Puzzled outrage. Who did she think she was conning, her father? "I don't know what you're—"

"Give me a break. It's past ten. When are you going to meet him, midnight?"

"I didn't *say* I was going to meet him."

"Right, you didn't!"

"I don't *need* this. All I asked is if I could use the *goddamned phone!*" She turned and stomped off.

I started to slam plates into the dishwasher. Great pair we made, both of us ready to swivel our moods at the drop of a word. *Clea Held, you could have picked yourself a better sister. I am a little too screwed up and much too selfish.*

When she returned five or ten minutes later, her eyes were glassy and pink with fresh tears. "I'd better go home," she said, not looking at me.

Something clicked in my mind then—something from my first two years in Hollywood, the time before Mike. Tense, unhappy calls: *Can you get out? You promised. Why not?!* I could almost hear the voice slithering the excuses into Clea's ear: *It's my wife's birthday. The baby has the sniffles.*

"He's married, isn't he?" She nodded, but didn't turn to face me. "Come on, Clea, just go ahead and stay here tonight," I said. "You're nineteen. You can do what you want. I've got no right to muscle you. In your place I wouldn't like it either."

She shrugged and ran water into the pasta pot. I slammed the dishwasher shut and turned it on. Then I refilled the wineglasses, and held mine up in a tentative toast. "If you're going to adopt a big sister, you'd better be prepared for some bossing around. But not tonight. Promise."

"Turn it off. I'll call Chris," was Clea's response, and I didn't understand what she was talking about—not until I followed her eyes down to the puddle of water quickly spreading in front of the sink.

6

. . . .

Banging noises were coming from downstairs. I
tried to sit up, but my body weighed like lead and wouldn't
move. It creaked from shoulders down to knees, my rear end
a focal point of soreness. Well, ache away; the ride was
worth it! A shaft of morning sun coming through the window
played a circle of spotlight against the floor.

Since I'd given Clea my bedroom, stopping short of a jibe
about how she ought to feel at home there, the master bedroom had seemed the logical choice for me. Nevertheless,
I'd hesitated in the doorway, catching—or thinking I
caught—a whiff of White Shoulders. This was my grandmother's room. It looked precisely the way it had when I
was nine, the walls papered in rose-colored flowers, the tester
bed spread in pink just a bit darker than the plushy rug that
covered most of the wideboard floor. Pink was not a color I
liked. Mike's watch said it was almost eight. I groaned myself out of bed and took a long stretch and a deep breath.
White Shoulders: it was still there.

I slipped on last night's tee-shirt and shorts and got myself
quickly down the back stairs.

It was him.

He was on his knees, crouched in front of a dismantled
dishwasher. He caught me out of the corner of his eye and
stood to face me. If he'd smirked, twitched even the beginnings of an intimate smile, it would've been over. I could
have dismissed him as a crass small-town jerk, told him to
get the hell out of my house, and gotten some other plumber.
But his seawater eyes were sober, the cast of his face scru-
pulously professional. Okay, fair enough. Let's ignore the
whole thing, start from scratch. He shifted the screwdriver
he was holding to his other hand and reached out to shake.

"Chris Held, Ms. Otis. Glad to meet you." He sounded
like he looked: natural—the best of natural—as though body,

face, voice had chanced to come together in a harmony so perfect that it was barely noticeable. "My cousin called me about the leak."

"Emily Silver," I said automatically, my mind working on the word "cousin." "Emily'll do." I looked for a family resemblance, and found only the slightest one—not to Clea, to her father.

"Sorry about the dishwasher," he said. "I wish we'd've caught it for you, but"—he shrugged gracefully loose as an athlete—"no dishes to wash, so we didn't need to run it."

"We? I don't think I follow you."

"At Home. We take care of your cleaning—do your garden, too." His arm gestured at the French doors. "Sometimes I stop by myself, pull a few weeds, take a look." *At any naked women who happen to be sashaying around.* His face remained blandly pleasant. I tried to keep mine the same, but I couldn't swear I succeeded. The cleaning service. No challenge at all for Clea to have gotten hold of the key; it suddenly made perfect sense.

"How often do you come?" As my words hung there, I felt my face redden and controlled an idiot urge to laugh.

I thought I caught a ripple of something on his face— amused satisfaction, or merely recognition?. But a second later it was gone, and I wondered whether it had been there at all.

"I stop by three, four times a week," he answered, entirely straight. "My cleaning crew comes Tuesdays and Fridays. Should be here anytime now. That was the agreement I had with Mrs. Otis, and she never changed it. I was sorry to hear about her—tough lady, nice though. Course, she must've wanted to go at the end." Now, how come he knew that and I hadn't?

I saw a surprising flash of shrewdness quickly enter and leave his eyes. "Well," he said after a beat, "the bad news is that you're going to need a new machine. Wouldn't be worth it to repair this one. What is it, twelve, fourteen years old? Should I go ahead and put one in?"

"Sure."

"Be about four hundred. Maybe a little more."

"Okay."

"I can put it in Thursday, maybe even tomorrow."

"Fine."

The exchange was like a time step, or the vamp of a song: filler on the way to the real thing. Was that the real thing, after all? Sex? I had no idea whether four hundred was a good or bad price for a dishwasher, and he damned well knew that. We were checking each other out. Any exchange of words would have done. It made no difference at all.

"Nine in the morning too early for you?" His turn.

"No, that's fine."

"Two days be enough for you with the cleaning crew?"

"Sounds good."

"I can get you someone full-time, if you want."

"Good God, no!" I saw myself taking over my grandmother's life—housekeeper, chauffeur. What would be next, committee meetings? "Tuesdays and Fridays are fine," I said more calmly.

The screwdriver shifted to his other hand with a jaunty bounce, the little juggling move club singers make with a mike. "Anything else I can help you out with?"

I made it a point to look right at his eyes. "I'll think about it," I said.

"See you later, then."

"There *is* something," I said, propelled by the sudden recollection of my night with White Shoulders and pink-flowered wallpaper. "I'm interested in some . . . redecorating—you know, painting, wallpaper, things like that. Can you recommend anyone?"

"Me. I can take care of that for you." He glanced at his watch. "I'm running late now, though. Mind if I make a call?"

"Go ahead."

He picked up the receiver and listened. "Off the phone, blabbermouth," he said after a moment, "I have to make a *real* call." He hung up and threw me a knowing smile. "You want to watch Clea. She'll take over your life."

"Look Chris, why don't you go do whatever you have to do. This is hardly an emergency. We can talk when you come back with the dishwasher."

"Rightio." *Rightio.* Was it possible to be this turned on

by someone who said "Rightio"? The sexual imperative knows no shame! He smiled again. I watched him walk out the door: entirely comfortable inside his skin. No self-conscious strut, no macho thrust. Chris Held didn't need devices. He was a natural.

As I poured a large glass of orange juice, I noticed that last night's dishes and pots had been hand-washed and put away. Meticulous Chris. Shrewd Chris. Sexy Chris. I wondered how it happened that Bart Held's nephew had become a plumber.

"*Good* morning!" Clea's voice floated down the stairs, almost singing. When she hit the kitchen, she glanced around and her face came up disappointed. "Where's Chris?"

"Gone. The dishwasher's dead. He's going to bring a new one tomorrow."

"You didn't tell him, did you? About the key? He'd kill me."

"I'll bet he would," I said. "No, I didn't tell him."

She helped herself to some juice. "I've got to go." Judging by the upswing in her mood, maybe the boyfriend was taking a sick day. Or maybe he worked nights.

"Off to your special place?"

Her fingers made a quick lock-and-key motion against her mouth, while her eyes grinned at me. "Wouldn't you like to know?"

"No, as a matter of fact I wouldn't. If you're lucky, he's just a flu shot—inoculate you against a more serious case. I'm more interested in knowing about Chris."

"Ohhhh." She grinned. "Isn't he the *best?* My mother thought so too," she said, enjoying it. "And my father, of course, can't stand him." The playing smile left her face. "Chris saved my life. The Chinese say that means he's responsible for the rest of it—or maybe it's the Japanese."

"So he was the one who walked in and hauled you out of the oven?"

"Uh huh. He's strong. So cool, nothing ever gets to him. But that time he was mad, I mean really mad."

"At you?"

She nodded. "See, it happened right after his mother died. Emphysema. God, that's an awful thing to have! She had to walk around with an oxygen tank all the time, and even then she could hardly breathe. But the thing was, she tried so hard to live, and she couldn't make it. And here I am, sixteen, in perfect health, trying to die. He just went ballistic. He took me outside and shook me till I thought my head would come off.''

"I get his point."

"Oh, me too. But in some way, I really envy Chris. He's had to work hard for everything he has, and it's made him so strong. My cousin isn't afraid of anyone, doesn't take shit from anyone, especially not anyone named Held. And no way would he ever have worked for their tacky newspapers, even if they'd begged him—which of course they never would. Grandpa Held liked to make believe Chris didn't exist. The bastard grandchild. Isn't that Victorian? And his mother called him Christopher Maddock Held the Third. Threw it right back in Grandpa's face!'' She refilled her juice glass and downed it in a gulp. "Is he better-looking than your Dev?''

I wasn't going to touch that one. "Actually, he looks a little like your father.''

"Are you *nuts?* Chris is . . . Who he really looks like is his own father: the blackest black sheep in the Held flock. I only met Uncle Christy once, when I was a real little kid. There he was in our living room, but he was right off a T.V. screen—ten-gallon hat, lizard boots with stars. I was so impressed. He came to get money of course; he owed a lot of it.''

"And did your father give him money?''

"Oh sure, and then shook in his shoes that Grandpa Held would find out. Actually, Wendy was kind of mean to him about it. 'I'll tell your daddy.' God, I can hear her sort of singing it at him.''

Good old Wendy! Almost wonderful, was she? *Have I got news for you, Clea.*

"Uncle Christy died a couple of years ago somewhere out West. Chris went to get him buried, even though he never did a damned thing for Chris in his life.'' She put down her glass and shot me a sudden grin. "Will you still be my sister if I get to be the blackest black sheep?'' Without waiting for an answer, she bolted out of the kitchen toward the front door.

A moment later, a white van with a large green "At Home" printed on its side pulled around behind the garden. Four people—three trim males, one pretty, rounded female—climbed out. All of them wore neat white pants, tee-shirts with the green At Home logo, and pleasant smiles. Not one of them looked a minute over twenty. A quick round of introductory hi's and Peter, Vince, Sam, and Lisa dispersed, crisply as a crew under its captain's eye, to begin work. Looked like Chris ran a tight ship.

Alone in the kitchen, I massaged the back of my neck and felt, for the first time in my life, old. Suddenly, the aches in my body screamed for action. I ran upstairs, changed Clea's tight clothes for my own looser ones, and tied firm double knots in my sneakers. Then I was out the kitchen door.

Down the winding paths I ran. Past the neatly pruned apple trees that Ethan Tucker named the place for, past padlocked stables where Birthday used to greet me with a delighted snort, past the studio built for a great-grandmother who liked to paint watercolors, past the tennis court where my grandmother and her father had delivered slashing serves to each other, and to the less worthy. Forty-two acres of total Tuckerness all around me, and no ghost of my own parents at all.

Third time by the big swimming pond, I stopped, flame-faced and panting, in the dappled shade of a low-weeping willow. Then, without thinking about it, I plunged like a sizzling skillet into the dishpan-warm water.

Many hours later in the library, my eyes opened to the dimness of late twilight; the little white phone had a train whistle ring. My bare legs peeled off the tufted leather like Scotch tape off a roll, as I struggled to get up out of the chaise and whatever dream I'd been dreaming there.

"Hello." Irrationally, or perhaps left over from the unrecalled dream, I felt certain it would be Dev.

"Emily, this is Bart Held." I could hear the uncomfortable sound of his breathing. "Is Clea with you?"

Now all I was aware of was the equally uncomfortable sound of my own, while I squashed my heart's impulse to cover for her. "No. No, she isn't, Mr. Held . . . Bart."

"Do you know . . . ?" *Don't ask me,* I begged silently. And he didn't. "Never mind, Emily," he said, voice tight. "Sorry to have disturbed you." I was grateful for the quick click.

I stood there, hand still on the phone, stomach souring, as the grandfather clock in the corner bonged nine times. I'd given an honest answer to the only question he'd asked. There wasn't a reason in the world for the guilt I felt. Worse was a sudden sense of being a beanbag, tossed from Held to Held to Held in a game whose rules nobody had bothered to tell me.

7

....

THE NEXT MORNING, WHEN I HEARD THE CRUNCH OF tires on gravel, I threw open the kitchen doors and saw, to my disappointment, not Chris's red truck but a smoke-gray Audi. A small woman slid out from behind the driver's seat. She could've been forty or fifty, but as she walked toward me, what struck me most was her complete absence of color. Tip-tilted brown sunglasses masked her eyes, but everything else—her cap of hair, her skin, even the uniform-plain pants and shirt she wore and the large satchel on her shoulder— was all one or another shade of beige. And yet she looked in no way meek; a certain quality in her walk suggested a Siamese cat.

"Hi," she said in a voice quiet without being soft. "I hope I'm not too early." She came into the kitchen and put out her hand. "I'm Jane Benzinger." I shook the hand be- cause it was there, but she must've seen her name not reg- ister. "Chris told me you were interested in making some changes. That's what I do. Chris and I, we work together." The accent was on the flat side, but I couldn't quite place it.

"Benzinger." It was a belated take. "I saw your shop in town. The one with curtains all over the windows. Yes, I do want to change a few things . . . I think," I amended with an instant, uncomfortable vision of Orchards disappearing into a sea of beige.

"Chris told me to tell you the dishwasher won't be here till tomorrow," she said. "I don't know whether you have anything specific in mind about the redecorating, but I have a few ideas."

"Uh huh. Jane—I don't know—this is hard. I wanted some things to be different, but not all *that* different. I grew up here, and . . ."

"This is a wonderful house," she said with a note of something that sounded like passion. She took off the sunglasses then, and I saw her eyes: a deep gray, which gleamed with a brightness especially startling in that bland, ageless face. "I see this house; I understand this house," she said slowly, almost like a benediction. "Maybe if we just walked around together a little, I could tell you some of the things I've been thinking about."

"Thinking about since yesterday?"

"Oh no. Since I first saw Orchards." I wondered when that might have been, but didn't ask.

We began with the master bedroom. "See," she said, "this is a room for morning sun." She ran a hand, an unusually large hand for a person of her size, along the wall. "I don't know what the original paper looked like, but whoever put all this pink in here in the fifties was not right."

While she spoke, Jane reached into the satchel on her shoulder and pulled out a square of ivory and yellow wallpaper with stylized, old-fashioned flowers and just a few pointy green leaves. "This is a mid-nineteenth-century pattern, just about the same age as the house. I think the furniture is lovely. That inlay on the armoire is unusual in American furniture, and the burl on the dresser's wonderful. See, with this paper and a different rug—green, like the leaf in the paper and the vine on that quilt . . ."

As we walked the rooms, Jane used the word "see" a lot. And I *did* see, because the power of her vision made it impossible not to. I was in the hands of an artist, her own colorlessness as ideal a backdrop as a jeweler's black velvet for the swatches of rich texture and color she pulled, one by one, like a magician, from her bag of tricks.

"Good Lord," she said as we walked into the library, the final room. "Chris's phone does look absurd on that desk, doesn't it?"

"*Chris's* phone?" For a surprised second I thought again of the late-night phantom calls my first two nights here, and wondered wildly whether the separate life I'd fantasized for the house really belonged to Chris Held. Had the whole damned Held family appointed Orchards its sexual headquarters?

"Yes." She gave me a look that could only be described as appraising. "Chris hates to be out of touch with his answering machine.'' The faintest smile—maternal-flavor—touched her lips.

She started toward the offending object like Lady Macbeth going for the daggers, but I stopped her. "Leave it for now. I agree it's not a design triumph, but I've got a machine in the city, and from time to time I like to be in touch too. I'll go buy a better phone, I promise."

"I'll pick it up for you," she said quickly. "A simple, square black one, I think." She gave the room a scan, nodding almost imperceptibly as she took it in. "This room really needs nothing." Which was also her verdict on the kitchen and my old bedroom.

"Let's talk about how all this will happen," I said, propping my rear on the corner of the desk. "I guess it'll take more than a wave of your wand, but I don't want to have to move out or anything."

"No, no, you won't. We'll just cart away the things that need to be re-covered or replaced, but there's enough furniture here so that shouldn't bother you any. If the house was empty, Chris could get a crew together and do a good job fast. But since you want to stay, it'll be less disruptive if he does it himself, room by room. That will take some time, of course, but the work will be perfect." She gave "perfect" the same reverent weight as she had when she'd pronounced it about the oval chestnut dining table and the small Constable landscape in the living room.

She sat at the end of the chaise. "There's a pair of chairs at the shop I'd like to show you for the music room, and some tapestry pillows."

"Fine. I'll bet everything in your shop is . . ." I hesitated before appropriating her word, not wanting to mock it. "Perfect."

"Yes, it is. You see, I know how things ought to be. Flaws, misuses, even in something beautiful—especially in something beautiful—make me very angry." She sounded so deadly serious that I wondered whether she might be exercising an offbeat sense of humor. But, after a look at her face, I didn't think so.

8

· · · · · · · · · · · · · · · · · · · ·

THE NEXT FEW DAYS TOOK ON THEIR OWN PROGRAM.
Mornings I ran, and then surfed Jane's wave of swatches and
paint chips, rugs and cushions, while the old dishwasher gave
way to a new one and Chris's At Home crew did whatever
they did; afternoons I rode Godiva, and then swam; evenings
I spent with Clea. In between times, I tried without much
success to keep myself from snapping too many mental pic-
tures of Chris Held, bare-chested and moist from his wallpaper steamer. And right upstairs . . .

By the time Friday came around, I might have forgotten
entirely about the dinner at Ariane's except for Clea's re-
minder. That afternoon, she and I drove up the Taconic to
the Rhinebeck shops, where within fifteen minutes I acquired
wide-legged white linen pants and shirt, a black set just like
it, black espadrilles and shoulder bag, and, at Clea's insis-
tence, a wide black woven belt. Shopping for clothes is not
my sport.

I spotted the Terman mailbox and turned the Lincoln up a
rise of S-shaped driveway, wondering irritably as I swiveled
the steering wheel back and forth what the point was of so
many apparently needless curves. Then I saw the point: this
was the entry to somebody's idea of a castle: a Tudor-style
house in dark red brick, with pointy slate-topped turrets
sticking out all over the place. The twisty road was a modern
stand-in for a proper moat and drawbridge. In Beverly Hills,
where building to suit the fantasy of the moment passes for
normal, this would've fit in fine, but here in the land of
clapboard and shingle it was an unwelcome intruder.

Ariane stood in the large rounded doorway, regal in a
long, sleeveless silk shift of pale lavender, a heavy dull-gold
shield hanging from a linked chain around her neck.

"You had no trouble finding us, I hope," she said. Her eyes scanned me; I passed inspection. "The white is wonderful on you, Emily, and those pants make your legs a mile long."

"I figured if I showed up in torn jeans, you'd think we were back at Fletcher. You look like a queen, and your house is extraordinary," I volunteered. No lie there. I thought I caught a wry twist to her lips, which I couldn't recall ever having seen before.

We bent into one of those awkward kisses that women of different heights exchange. Hostess and guest: a pair of well-brought-up young ladies out of a good girls' boarding school. Perhaps what bothered me about Ariane was simply that she took me back to bad times. I handed her a bottle of the California cabernet Mike had favored, and followed her into the living room.

Where I found myself staring into the face of Bart Held.

My astonished bark of a laugh was met by a smile that looked calmly assured—nothing like the strained, tentative one he'd worn the first time we'd met.

That little bitch! I'd been mildly surprised that she had remembered my dinner date here, been so interested in what I was going to wear. No wonder. She was probably giggling her head off right now, picturing the egg of amazement all over my face. Nothing was at stake, of course, but I felt stung that she'd played with me in a way that came too close to the way she played with her father.

"Nice to see you again, Emily." He put out his hand, and I was struck by a resemblance I'd noticed before. If Bart were able to shed fifteen years of strain and add the swagger of sex appeal, he'd look a lot like his nephew. "It looks as though Clea didn't get around to telling you that I'd be here."

"Looks that way." I tried to relax into a smile.

"She does love her tricks," he said, the subject of his daughter beginning to visibly tense his face. "Teenaged girls . . ." His hand pantomimed the generic unpredictability of them. Not much conviction to the gesture.

Ariane chimed in. "Don't despair, Bart dear. Emily and I are living proof they do get over it." She turned to me.

"Bart told me how you've befriended Clea, Emily. She and I barely know each other, but from what I've heard, you could be just the right person for her after all she's been through."

Or just the opposite. "Clea befriended me, actually," I said, more coldly than I meant to. I wished we could get off this. Fast.

"Welcome." The new voice behind me had almost too much resonance to it. "If Ari isn't going to do the honors, I'll do them myself. I'm Zach Terman."

The hand he extended had on its back enough dark fur to suggest a paw. As I took it, the house, the driveway, the nuggety gold band on Ariane's finger, and the shield she wore around her neck now all made sense. This was his castle; she was his queen maybe I'd read the wryness in her smile correctly. Beauty and the Beast, except that the beast was very good-looking. Handsome in the way of a middle-aged movie star: largish, noble head, topping a short, slim, perfectly proportioned body. His face was deeply tanned, features solid and assertive. He wore his hair Roman style—short and brushed forward on a forehead higher than it must have been ten years ago. One button too many was open on his shirt.

"I'm sorry, darling." Ariane gave him a small squeeze and me a small smile. "Ever since we saw that movie of yours, Emily, and I told him we'd roomed together at Fletcher, Zach's been dying to meet you. So when we bumped into each other at the diner . . . well: kismet."

"What to drink, beautiful lady?" Zach asked, flashing very nice white teeth.

"Scotch," I said, though I'd planned to ask for white wine.

As soon as we'd seated ourselves, Bart picked up a conversation he'd obviously been having with Ariane before I arrived.

"The point you make about Eliot and Wharton is intriguing, Ariane. But wasn't Dorothea, in her way, as trapped as Lily?"

"No," Ariane said, leaning in toward him. "Dorothea would never have given up in the way Lily did. She has her core of aspiration, and that makes all the difference.''

"But if Casaubon hadn't died, would she have stuck by him?''

"She would have," Ariane said slowly. "Yes, she would have. Eliot doesn't give Dorothea the same liberties she took for herself, I'm afraid.''

I remembered *Middlemarch* barely well enough to recognize the characters' names, so I had no opinion on how Dorothea felt about Casaubon. But Bart Held's feelings for Ariane were crystal-clear: he was crazy about her. He did not touch her, or even sit very close to her on the red sofa, but for him there was no one else in the room. His eyes never left her face, and when she rose to go to the kitchen to get more hors d'oeuvres, he was on his feet to help before she'd taken her first step.

"Bart and Ari," Zach said to me, shaking his massive head. "Listening to them go at it, you'd think George and Edith were the hottest numbers out there.'' He shifted in his armchair to give them his back and me his full face. The evening, I realized, was going to be one of couples. "So, when's the next movie? You flying back to Hollywood anytime soon?" he asked, moving his chair closer.

"I'm not sure.'' The questions were not out of line, but I damned him for asking them.

"My new book's just been optioned by Disney.'' He grinned. *"Mucho dinero.''*

"Congratulations. Usually writers complain about not enough *dinero.''*

"Isn't that the truth. Well, I'm enjoying the hell out of it. I did my time with five-thousand-dollar advances—didn't begin to really break out till *Panning for Gold.* That was my fourth. The rest is history,'' he added with a smile that was halfway toward disarming.

But halfway was not far enough. Since I was stuck for the evening, better to ask questions than to answer them. "Tell me about your books, Zach. Boys' adventures, right?''

"Girls read them too. They take place in the 1880s and 90s out West. These two brothers, Clint and Tad—orphans— they get into all kinds of things. They even fall in love.'' The white teeth flashed in a suggestive grin.

"And if they're well-behaved boys in that kind of book, they don't do much about it," I said primly.

"True. Squeaky clean." His eyebrows raised and lowered playfully. "So, how're you liking it back up here? Big old house, all that land—all yours now."

"I like it fine." Every word out of his mouth chafed like sandpaper against a sunburn, and yet the brashness had about it a quality of exuberant innocence. "It's not a castle, of course."

"Aha. The princess approves my castle?"

"Let's say she *appreciates* it." I was reaching dizzying heights of tact. Better watch my balance.

"I met this architect Scandura out in L.A., used to design movie sets. He copied this from the castle in *Robin Hood*— not the new one, the old one with Errol Flynn. Even the way the floor's laid. See that pattern around the edges? Not bad for a *De*Witt Clinton boy."

"A what?"

"Public high school. The Bronx. I forget that Fletcher preppies like you and Ari never would've heard of it."

Fuck tact. "You know the name of the public high schools in Poughkeepsie? Kingston? Rhinebeck?"

He grinned, his face suddenly boyish, almost charming. "Touché, Princess."

Just then, Ariane announced that dinner was ready, and Zach led me into a large, candlelit dining room with a stone floor. A big Oriental rug glowed, red as fresh blood, under the dining table. I wondered if the set-designer–architect had designed a castle for Macbeth, as well as for Robin Hood.

Suddenly, I thought of what Clea had said about Chris, about people who'd started with nothing and made it on their own. Everything in this house—every overdone bit of it— was aimed at making a single point: that a boy from the Bronx can make it big. Maybe it was a point worth making. *Here's looking at you, Zach Terman!*

The four of us grouped at the center of the long table. Megaphones would've been required had we used the whole thing. I sat opposite Bart and beside Zach. Ariane had laid on a full-course meal, from prosciutto and melon to salmon to roast beef. Heavy stuff for a warm night, but no lack of air-conditioning in this place. Just short of chilly.

The food was excellent. As an admiring Bart reported, she'd done her own cooking. She served and cleared herself, too—no hired help for this queen, and no help allowed from either guest—while Zach kept rare French wines, and his commentary about them, flowing freely. Bart and I talked of Millbrook, of horses, of families with names I remembered and faces I didn't. He did not mention Clea again, nor did I. I was surprised to find myself having not a bad time. "Did you always plan on going into the family business?" I asked.

"Good Lord, no," Bart answered, glancing first at Ariane in a way that suggested this was a topic talked of more than once between them. "My brother was the one who was supposed to run the papers. I expected to have what you might call second-son freedom. I was going to teach Victorian literature." The smile on his lips, the flush of wine in his cheeks gave a glimpse at a different man in a different life.

"Your brother? That would be Chris's father." I hadn't forgotten Clea's words about her father disliking Chris. I suppose I was, in the spirit of the evening, playing a mind game of my own.

"Yes." Bart's smile disappeared, leaving the color in his cheeks looking mottled and dull. I'd knowingly stepped on a corn, and now felt tongue-tied. I glanced at Ariane, hoping for help, but she was absorbed in the food on her plate.

My host broke the silence. "Ariane and Bart: a pair of schoolteachers. The two of you are straight from the same pod." Zach leaned over, bottle in hand to top up Bart's glass. "But it's *opposites* who attract, Bart." He added with a touch of malicious enjoyment, "Now, you've read enough Victorian literature to know that."

Ariane continued eating—small, even bites, like the lapping of a secure cat. In a face suddenly stone-hard, Bart's eyes ignited with a flash of searing anger.

"Where does your brother live, Ariane? Jamie, isn't it?" I asked quickly. "Still out in Chicago?"

"No, he's not—and how nice that you remembered his name. Jamie's pretty close by."

"Really. Did he move up here because of you?"

"Come on, Ari," Zach cut in, "you're not talking to a

stranger. Brother Jamie is not all there, Emily. He—''

"Stop it," Ariane almost whispered.

"He gets shipped around like her tennis rackets wherever big sister—"

"Stop it!" She did not raise her voice, but something in it silenced him: a distilled fury, sudden and impressive as heat lightning, and over just as quickly. "Jamie is autistic," she said evenly. "I was able to find a residence in Union Vale. Are we ready for salad?" she asked, back in social voice, as though the last moments hadn't happened. "Come on, Bart dear, give me a hand, would you?"

"Want to go out on the deck for a little fresh air?" Zach asked as soon as they'd left the room.

Not with you, you clod. "No, I don't think so," I said, looking straight ahead. Reflexively, I raised my hand to bat away a gnat tickling at the back of my neck. It wasn't a gnat, though, it was a finger. "What the hell do you think you're doing?"

"Touching a princess's nape." He put his two hands on my face and turned it toward him. "Ever been kissed in a castle?"

I pulled his hands away. *"Stop it!"*

"Is that all they teach Fletcher girls to say?" He was having a wonderful time.

I might have answered him with a fist or a foot, except that Bart walked in right then carrying a large cut-glass salad bowl, followed by Ariane with a plate of cheeses. Somehow, we got through the end of the meal. I was all but silent.

The surprise was that the other three all seemed restored to the previous convivial mood.

After Zach left the table to fetch some "port a lot older than I am—wait'll you get your mouth around this one, Bart," I excused myself and went to find the royal john. It was off the library and, in fact, looked like an extension of the library: wood-paneled, the toilet cunningly concealed under a French chair with a hinged caned seat, and the sink sporting golden hardware shaped like a dolphin. As I turned the creature's tail and started to splash the cool water that poured from its mouth against my hot cheeks, I heard a telephone begin to ring, and then heavy running steps, which seemed to be directly over my head.

"Terman." Zach's voice, clipped and businesslike, interrupted the ring. I heard him clearly through the bathroom ceiling, amplified, I suppose, by pipes or vents. "Hi Princess." Aha, another princess, though he didn't sound all that pleased to hear from her. Short pause. "Look, have a heart." Longer pause. "Let me up! Don't do this to me—to *us*." Almost no pause. "No, that's not gonna be good. Okay, okay, that's a better time. See you then." Loud smooch noise. "Did you catch that? It was a biggie." The phone clicked into its cradle.

He was almost too awful to be taken seriously. Almost.

The car drove itself toward home, while I pondered what lunacy might have drawn Ariane to Zach Terman, what worse lunacy kept her with him. I knew it couldn't be money. Unless something had changed drastically, Ariane came from a far greater wealth than I did.

The deer was on my bumper with no warning at all. By nothing but blind instinct my foot slammed at the brake. I lurched crazily forward and up off the seat, then whipped back the other way, the jerk of the belt curtailing my flight through the windshield. In the instant when the car hit his body, I shut my eyes.

I opened them to see the deer as stunned as I was, peering at me through the glass, standing utterly still, unable to move. But standing. After an interminable moment, he lifted his head and took off like Pegasus across the turnpike.

I walked in the front door to the ring of a phone, which seemed at first to be coming from inside my own head. Once more, I was certain Dev would be on the other end, and made for the study on the dead run. But when I picked up the new black receiver, it buzzed into my ear.

9
. . . .

A FIST CLENCHED AND UNCLENCHED INSIDE MY SKULL, threatening at any moment to begin punching in earnest. It had not been easy to fall asleep. My gut—always the most vulnerable enemy within—had been shaken by the close call with the deer, soured by the evening at Ariane's. I awoke to find the turmoil risen to my throbbing head. I'd come here pining after an idealized piece of the past: safe, simple—a sheltered place, where I could stop time and make myself a home. Another motto to hang on the wall: Nowhere is safe; nothing is simple.

I hunted up some aspirin in the front hall bathroom, and as I was fiddling with the childproof cap, I heard a car pull into the driveway and stop in front of the house. Chris, I thought, before I remembered that it was Saturday and he wasn't working today, though he did plan on seeing me "bright and early" Sunday morning. Even if he'd changed his mind about today, six forty-five seemed a little earlier than early. Besides, he always drove around in back. I pulled aside the bathroom-window curtain to take a peek, and saw a deep red Jag I didn't recognize. I gulped three tablets with a handful of water and ran downstairs, but by the time I opened the door, the Jag's rear end was disappearing down the driveway.

Whoever it was had left a fairly large rectangular package wrapped in shiny gold paper sitting smack in the center of the doorstep. I scooped it up and kicked the door shut. The way things had been going, I probably should have checked to hear whether it ticked. I carried it into the kitchen and put it on the table. As I began to tear away the bright wrapping, I saw it was a wicker picnic hamper. I lifted the lid and groaned out loud.

A collection of items lay there before me, swathed in what looked like a red-and-white-checked tablecloth: a bottle of

Perrier-Jouët, festive white flowers painted up its side; a pair of tall champagne flutes; a loaf of Italian bread and a book—the *Rubaiyat,* just in case I didn't get the point. On top of it all rested a slightly crushed branch of dogwood blossoms, a thick white card taped to it.

"Only thing missing is thou beside me singing in the wilderness."

The note ended with a P.S. apologizing for the supermarket bread, and explaining that only Grand Union was open this early. It was signed "ZZZ"—as though one Z were not more than enough.

Jesus. Oh Jesus!

I stared down at the lovers' picnic, more disgusted even than angry. I tore the note to pieces and tossed them in the trash barrel. Then I grabbed the hamper off the table to throw it in, too. It didn't come close to fitting. For a moment I stood there helplessly, holding it in my arms, a cloying adolescent parody of love. Then, because I didn't want the damned thing anywhere I had to look at it, I ran down to the basement, threw it at the floor and sent it skidding. I raced back up the stairs, closing the kitchen door hard behind me.

Head pounding, I considered going back to bed, but decided to make coffee instead. Coffee helped aspirin work better: one of the bits of medical lore Dev had acquired from a doctor he'd recently lived with, I remembered with an unpleasant—and, I reminded myself, now unwarranted—spurt of jealousy. She was right, though. By the time I'd finished my first cup, the waves of pain had receded into low tide. As I was thinking about pouring a second, the phone rang.

It was Clea, sounding altogether chipper. "Let's go riding later. Want to?"

Normally, the answer would have been a quick, enthusiastic yes, my surrogate sister an instant antidote to the brackish taste left by ZZZ. But this morning, her voice produced its own brackish taste.

"No, I don't want to, Clea. Why didn't you tell me you knew Ariane? Why didn't you mention yesterday that your father would be there? Not that it's that big a deal, but I told you not to play your mind games on me. Remember?"

"Oh come on, Emily, don't be mad at me. I just . . . didn't know how to say it, but now I can ask you. What do you think of my stepmother-to-be? Has she changed a lot since you knew her in school? Do you like her?"

I couldn't hold back the laugh. "Your *stepmother?* You mean Ariane's going to leave that jackass? Well, her judgment's better than I thought."

Silence on the other end. "Anyone who'd marry my father can't have very good judgment," she said finally, her voice suddenly subdued, almost resentful.

It came through to me how wrenchingly hard this must be for Clea: her complicated weave of love and guilt about her mother; the equally complicated battleground she occupied with her father. And now, here he comes, obviously smitten with someone new, barely two months after the violent end of his miserable, punishing marriage. No wonder Clea had been ambivalent about how to tell me, when her own feelings must be twisted into figure eights.

"Hey little sister, I just got over being mad at you. And if you want to know what I think, I think your father and Ariane seem perfect together. I also think that once he's happier, he'll be easier on you—and maybe you'll be easier on him too."

"Do you like her, though?" Clea would persist until she got an answer. I didn't want to lie.

"I'm not sure," I said. "Let's just say I've never understood her. I think I still don't."

"Would you mind if we skipped riding today?" she asked, her voice extra young, the way I'd learned it got when she felt on shaky ground. "I know I asked you, but . . ."

"It's fine," I answered, relieved. Today I craved solitude. "You okay, though?"

"Yeah, big sister. Don't worry about me."

10
....

AFTER A HOT RUN, A COOL SHOWER, AND A LONG NAP, I put on an old cotton bathrobe and stretched out on the library chaise with a bowl of green grapes and the screenplay Bernie had sent me. It was a modern-day knockoff of *As You Like It,* which, with the determined optimism of an actor toward a script containing a meaty part, I was trying to like better than I did. My character, Rozzie, was an investigative reporter with the flashy physical skills of Wonder Woman. I could do it, I thought. Just. I'd have to get back into fencing and acrobatic dance class, but . . .

It took a while before I responded to the tapping on the glass of the French doors, before I even noticed it. When I looked up, I saw Zach Terman, silhouetted against the evening sky, smiling his shiny teeth at me.

He pantomimed a broad greeting, little wave of the hand. I considered just turning my back, leaving the room, and going upstairs. I also considered hollering as loud as I could for him to get his sorry ass off my property before I called the police. But instead, I got off the chaise, wishing as I stood that my robe were longer and the fabric heavier. I turned the knob and slid through the semi-opened door, shutting it quickly behind me. About one thing I was determined: he wasn't coming inside.

"Hi Princess." His dark eyes narrowed with his grin. I wanted to punch it out. And I'm not sure why I didn't.

"I have some things to say to you, Zach."

"She looks so serious! Summer's no time to be serious. I thought we might have a little picnic, sip some of that champagne."

"Well, you thought wrong. Hear me: You do not interest me one bit. Not a millimeter."

"You break my heart."

"Keep this up and it'll be your head."

"If it's because of Ari—"

"It really has nothing to do with Ariane." *And it certainly won't after she dumps you for Bart,* I added silently. I could have taken the high road and said that married men were off limits for me, but I wanted Zach Terman to know that I was rejecting him. *Him.*

"Well why, then?" His actor face was truly puzzled.

"I am not attracted to you." I spoke with exaggerated slowness. If he couldn't hear me, he could read my lips.

"Ah Princess, say it isn't so." He clapped his hand over his heart in mock pain.

"Believe it. Maybe you'll have better luck if you call back the other princess—you remember, the one you blew off on the phone last night."

"What?" I'd confused him.

"I heard you through the pipes. Sounded like you were right there in the bathroom with me," I added. " 'No, that's not gonna be good. Don't do this to me. To *us.*' " I'm a damned good mimic, and I hoped the needle stuck him hard.

No such luck. "Do I detect a little jealousy there?" he asked playfully. Then he turned earnest. "She's over. I swear she is. She doesn't know it yet, but it's true. Cross my heart." His finger drew a little cross on the left-hand pocket of his ivory shirt.

I looked at him in disbelief. "You didn't understand a damned thing I said, did you?"

"I understand that we strike sparks for each other. You know it and I know it. We're not going to just ignore that, are we?"

"Sparks? In your dreams! Look, I don't care how many simpleminded books you write for pimply-faced boys—"

"Wait a minute!" No mock pain this time—the scream was one of outrage. Now I had him where he lived. I watched his hand rise in threat.

"Don't even think about it, asshole. I'm a black belt and I'll boot your balls so hard they'll replace your tonsils." A line straight from a movie I'd auditioned for, and hadn't gotten.

His arm fell slowly to his side, and after a moment, his face smiled again. But it looked forced. "Except that it's a cliché, I'd say you're beautiful when you're angry."

"Get off my property right now," I said, my voice suddenly hoarse, clogged with fury. "I am going back inside my house. If you make one move to follow me, I will kill you. As you may have heard, I am not a very well balanced person, so believe me."

I walked back into the library, and locked the door—symbolic only: the house had other doors, which would open at the turn of a knob. I stood there giving him my back, flimsy robe or no. Curiously, I was not in the least afraid of Zach Terman. A minute or two later, I heard his Jag start up and drive away. Then I quickly locked all the doors, went into the kitchen, and poured myself a fairly stiff scotch.

Once upstairs, I peeked into what was on its way to becoming my bedroom, damp and warm despite the open windows. The metal of the steamer machine shone silver in the moonlight, against mottled, denuded walls. No more pink wallpaper; no more White Shoulders. I breathed deep and caught, or thought I did, clean sweat with a dash of lemony spice: the echoing scent of Chris Held.

Chris and I had said few words to each other that didn't have to do with paint, wallpaper, or appliances, and when he talked about these things, it was with the easy professionalism of a good doctor. But conversation was no major element between us. What was going on was foreplay. Our first sight of one another through the French doors remained the loaded gun lying in plain sight on a stage set mantelpiece. The ever-present question was, when will it go off?

I noticed the beginning of a tingle in my back, and felt it make its tantalizing way down between my legs. I pulled the door shut with a slam and ran back to my old room.

That night, I dreamed of Dev for the first time in weeks. We were floating naked side by side, hands clasped together. Lazily, I turned my head, and saw that everything around us—water, sky, shore—was stark white, as though we were figures painted on a clean page.

11

. . . .

EARLY-MORNING SUN FOCUSED ITSELF THROUGH THE window glass against my shoulder. For the first few semi-dozing minutes, I felt reborn into a world where anything I might want was possible. Then I woke up the rest of the way, and inflicted a suitable punishment for having fairy-tale dreams about something impossible: I forced myself to re-member, line for line, the reality of the last time Dev and I had been together.

More than three weeks ago. Tuesday afternoon. Dev's for-tieth birthday, and hours yet before I had to show up at the theater. Tense times for us. Forty: though he claimed relief at finally "hearing the gates of 'promising' clang shut" be-hind any writing he might do, his recent moods had given new dimension to the term "black Irish." To be fair, my own temperament had been far from sunny. The impending closing of *The Real Thing* loomed as threatening as a step off the edge of a flat earth.

Against those odds, the day had turned out better than good. We'd downed a bottle of celebratory champagne and followed it by some even more celebratory sex. I was break-ing him up doing old Monty Python routines, and he'd just begun musing about how we might go to France together after my show closed, how he'd love to show me his favorite parts of Brittany. Then I'd said something about wondering what Mike would think. Why I said it, I don't know—maybe just to destroy a moment too good to be trusted. Once it was out, I could see the explosion coming, but I couldn't stop it.

"Hear me, actress." His monk's mouth ground out the words through almost closed teeth, while his purple eyes glared hot. "I am not Mike. You loved him. I loved him too. But Mike is dead. Why can't you let him be dead?"

His face rearranged itself into a faraway, stony quiet that I always thought of as his Indian look. He shook his head very slowly, a chunk of aggressively straight black hair escaping onto his forehead. "For some unknown damned reason, I think I love you, Emily. I'll give you the words, whatever they mean, but I don't know that I have much else to put on the table."

"Shut up. *Just shut up, will you!* I don't need your words, if that's all they are. Why don't you *write* your words?" Dangerous ground, but what the hell did it matter?

"Clever." His lips thinned to a stark, straight line. "I do not write, because I am not a writer. I am a tracker-down of embezzling bank tellers, check-forging brokers, runaway husbands—poor bastards."

But I couldn't stop; didn't want to. "Come on, that's what's really at you, isn't it?—the books you're not writing. That and your goddamned father."

"My father is my father," he said, his voice chill. "The truth is the truth. And it doesn't go away."

"Right." My fists clenched.

The week before, Liam Hannagan had shown up twice—unannounced, as always—with a face as glazed as his carefully shined, heavy old oxfords. It went the same way it always did. Dev, his face tight with strain, poured the drink his father asked for, but refused to join him. We sat, a captive audience, while Liam talked of years past, tears of regret making their way down his ruddy cheeks. I hated his tears; he had no right to them. And I hated what the visits did to Dev.

"His apologies are too late and too easy," I'd said when he left finally, after protesting the forty dollars Dev pressed in his hand for a cab from Brooklyn Heights to Washington Heights—but taking it anyway. "Some things are just not forgivable."

"Forgive is your kind of verb, not mine. Simplistic." His ultimate epithet. "Do I *forgive* him after thirty years? What the fuck is the difference whether I do or not? He. Is. My. Father. And he's alone now. Ethne left him last month—went back to Ireland with an IRA fund-raiser or some such. He'll never be able to manage the bar by himself. He's a pitiful old reprobate, but he's my old reprobate."

"He's a wife beater and a child beater. He's left his mark

on every step you take, for the rest of your life. Simplistic? *He broke your hip for Christ's sake!''*

''So speaks the daughter of impeccable family.''

''So speaks the daughter of dead family.''

''Well, that makes it nice and simple, doesn't it? You can forgive or not, whatever suits your mood that day. Perhaps I should kill him off.''

Just then the downstairs buzzer bleeped, and my heart dropped. Dev pressed the answering bell. We stood, facing each other, listening to heavy footsteps climb the four flights of stairs. The thing was, I knew what was coming and he did not. Not until the UPS guys carried in the big boxes and he saw what was written on them: ''IBM''; ''Hewlett-Packard.'' My birthday present to him. And it was going to be a disaster.

Dev signed the delivery receipt. Once the men had gone, he looked at me and laughed, not pleasantly. ''For the record, one thing I do not need is a benefactress. Auditioning, are you, to play your late grandmother issuing grants to defunct writers? I don't care how many millions she left you, the role doesn't suit.''

''You son of a bitch!'' My hands grabbed my own hair and yanked hard. I was glad for the pain. How could I have done something so stupid? Planned it, relished it—so goddamned excited about my surprise that I never once questioned whether he . . . I was sick of myself, why shouldn't he be? But even so, I wouldn't back down. I couldn't. ''Look at that dinosaur sitting there. Nobody fucking *uses* typewriters anymore.'' My throat stung as though attacked by hornets; my eyes burned with tears I was not going to shed. ''No wonder you have writer's block! You—''

''Stop blathering about what you don't understand. Stupid fucking term—'writer's block.' Is it something like housemaid's knee, tennis elbow?!'' His tone mocked, but his eyes were dark with anger. ''My writing,'' he said, clipping off each word, ''is not blocked.'' He strode over to the round oak table and rolled a sheet of paper into the old machine. ''See? Writer's block is bullshit.'' Furiously, he typed the words as he spoke them. ''I can write chewed-over, dressed-up banalities by the ream and maybe even get them published.'' He stopped, his fingers still splayed out on the keyboard, and looked at me, his face unlike any way I'd seen it before: skin stretched tight, as though pulled from behind by a powerful, invisible hand. ''But I can't write the way I want to, so I'm not going to do it at all.''

''Yeah, you'll show us!'' My hands itched to slap, to punch, but I held them resolutely at my sides.

Suddenly, he turned to the IBM box and kicked it hard, breaking the brown cardboard with a gunshot-loud crack. Then turned his back and walked fast to the other side of the room.

Any last shred of control melted down in a fury that clouded my eyes in red haze. *''You want to kick it? Let's kick it!''* I bashed my foot against the Hewlett-Packard box—once and again, and once more. And then I did what I'd been wanting to do for months. Before he could stop me, I lifted the heavy typewriter in my two hands, just high enough to send it with a satisfying crash to the wood floor. And then I kicked it hard, exploding into a howl of pain as the damned machine retaliated by almost breaking my foot.

My limp as I bolted out the door was a lot worse than Dev's.

The shrill of the phone brought me back to Orchards. I grabbed it like a weapon. Jane Benzinger, admitting that it was awful to call anyone at eight A.M. on a Sunday, but wanting to let me know not to expect Chris today. She sounded like a mommy phoning school. ''Emergency plumbing call, no telling when he'll be finished. He'll see you tomorrow morning.''

''No problem,'' I said, probably more relieved than disappointed. A Chris Held hormone rush was something I thought I could do without today. ''Doesn't he ever get a day off?''

''Chris isn't much for days off. Neither am I, really.''

That was for sure. She'd been here at least once every day since we'd met. If I happened to be in, I'd glimpse her quiet magic in progress. If I was out, I'd find surprise treasures when I returned: a pair of graceful eighteenth-century candlesticks perched on the sideboard; a vivid tapestry fire screen in the living room.

Now, I heard that telltale excitement creep into her usually colorless voice. "Look, I know we didn't discuss redoing the dining chairs, but I've come across some fabric that would work a lot better than what's on them. Okay if I stop by and show it to you later?"

"Sure." The prospect of a challenge as straightforward as deciding about a piece of cloth to sit on was appealing. "Give me a couple of hours, though. Ten?"

"I'll be there."

I put on my shorts and sneakers, ran a few miles' worth, and tried to empty my mind of any and all men. By the time Jane showed up, I was showered, dressed, and depressed.

She was right, of course, about the fabric. The crewelwork on ivory homespun looked as though it had been created for no other reason than to cover those particular chairs. "It is perfect, Jane. How do you know these things? Did you always?"

"I think I did. In school, the teachers would accuse me of dreaming, but I wasn't really—just seeing things. How would the classroom look painted yellow or red, instead of green? What if the windows were arched and the desks moved around? Funny quirk for a backwoods kid."

"What backwoods were those?" I still hadn't placed her accent.

"Montana, about fifty miles north of Missoula, best hunting in the world. I was the only girl in the family, but my father taught me anyhow. Every October I was out there with him and my brothers."

"Do you hunt here?"

"No, not really, aside from hotline calls. After elk and bear, white-tailed deer's not exciting."

"What are hotline calls?"

"Wounded deer." Her face turned fierce. "I'd shoot sloppy hunters instead, if I could. They walk away from their messes and don't give a second thought to what they've left behind. If you can't make a clean kill, you shouldn't be allowed to own a gun."

"How did you happen to wind up in Millbrook, Jane?"

She hesitated for a second before answering, as though the question were overly personal. "Oh, I came east for the paintings, sculptures, tapestries—to learn about them, work with them. But I couldn't breathe in New York City. It was so closed in, locked up, ugly. I hated it." The beige of her face seemed to bleach sallow with the memory.

"One day, I just got on a train at Grand Central and took it to the last stop, which was Poughkeepsie. It was fall. The ride up the river—the water, the trees. Of course, I had to stay, and . . . here I am." She stopped and lowered her head for a second in punctuation. "Do you want to go ahead with the chairs?" Back to business.

"Yes. They'll be great," I said absently, wondering about the quiet woman beside me, her personal colorlessness concealing a blindingly bright passion for beauty. I thought of a flame burning strong inside a brown paper bag—and realized after a moment that the image made no sense: the bag would be gone in about two seconds.

"Good." Her large, capable-looking hand ran lightly over the chair's curved back, enjoying in advance the transformation to come. "Maybe we'll have Chris lighten this wall, just half a shade," she said, squinting up at it.

"You and Chris make a good team."

"Yes, a perfect team." She turned away, and quickly began to gather up her things, as though to ward off any possibility of my picking up on that and asking another question.

The front bell rang then, and sent me running, as eager to end the conversation as she was. When I opened the door, the person who faced me was Ariane. Even behind her sunglasses and under the brim of her hat, I could see the bruises.

Jane's voice as she emerged from the dining room and walked toward us: "Well, I'd better hustle. I've got to meet the twelve forty-six. I have a dealer bringing up some good pieces from the city." Ariane did not attempt to hide her face from the stranger's view, but I could see her jaw tighten.

"Jane Benzinger. Ariane Warburton . . . uh, Terman." Jane had put on the big brown glasses she always wore. Behind both their tinted lenses, I couldn't tell whether the two were even looking at each other, much less what either might be thinking.

"Nice to meet you." I was struck again by how little Ariane had changed since school days. That gracious social voice was so much a part of her she'd've used it to greet her executioner.

"Yes," Jane said, as though in response to something else, and promptly headed the other way, toward the kitchen door.

"I needed to . . . to talk to you," Ariane said, removing her sunglasses. "I needed to talk to someone." I recognized the tentative shakiness of an actress walking through a part for the first time. Then it occurred to me that what I might be seeing was the girl who wouldn't sweat in hell on the edge of shock.

Wordlessly, I led her into the living room. The north light through the front window outlined the puffiness in her left jaw. It had begun to discolor, not nearly as dark, though, as the purpling under her right eye. I remembered the slightly discolored swelling I'd noticed when we met at the diner. No mystery now. I didn't have to ask who.

"I hope you have a suitcase in the car," I said. "If you don't, just tell me where to find the clothes you want, and I'll go get them. You can stay here as long as you need to, unless you'd rather stay with Bart."

She sat herself at the end of the one sofa that hadn't been removed for reupholstering. "Bart?" It was as though she'd never heard the name. "Emily, please sit down and talk to me."

Incongruously, in the battered face, her slightly swollen mouth gleamed with fresh lip gloss: pink icing on a damaged cake. I wanted to scream. I wanted to club him to death. But I didn't want to sit down and talk to her. "Do you want some tea? Coffee?" I asked as ungrudgingly as I could manage.

"No, nothing." She reached up and removed the hat. I sat next to her on the sofa, but kept my distance. "This doesn't happen often," she said, a slight apologetic smile on the lips.

"*Often?!* You're an English professor; you know about language. So I take that to mean it's happened more than once or twice before." She didn't speak; she didn't have to.

"What is it you were waiting for him to do? Kill you?"

Something crossed her face. Alarm or straight surprise, I couldn't tell. "He would never do that," she said, sounding short of sure. I watched a swallow make its way down her throat. "Zach is different from what he seems."

"You're right about that. He seems like a garden-variety self-important, childish, bullying bore. But really he's a *brutal,* self-important, childish, bullying bore. Makes all the difference." The heavy sarcasm was serving little purpose—except maybe keeping me from physically shaking her the way Chris had Clea after her try at suicide.

"He is childish. Child*like,* really. Perhaps, under everything else, that's what I fell in love with. Emily, I want you to understand this, and not to forget it, no matter what," she said carefully. "I love Zach Terman. You must understand that. I'm not blind or stupid. Perhaps I'm just a caretaking sort of person. And Zach needs that, maybe more than anyone I've ever known—in some ways, even more than my poor Jamie." I thought of the flash-fire storm I'd seen over her autistic brother. Could it be that Zach had simply been jealous? "I know he can be hard to take—so full of himself, all that bluster, the lack of polish—but Emily, you should see him hunched over his word processor. Sometimes, when he's working at home, I walk in and find him with such a rapt look on his face, tongue off to the side between his teeth, like . . ." Her voice failed her for a second. "Like an earnest little boy." I saw tears overflow her eyes, slower to get out of the swollen eye—the one he'd blackened.

I didn't get her at all. If I'd had to play her on a stage, I wouldn't have had a clue how to get inside that character. I thought suddenly of Bailey Hutchison, the assistant headmistress she'd been so close to at school. Maybe Old Bailey had understood her. Maybe Bart Held did now. "I know Zach must have his appealing side," I said carefully, "but I'm glad for you that you decided to leave him. Was that what set him off this time? When you told him?"

She looked at me, uncomprehending. "Leave him? Where on earth did you get an idea like that?" She sounded and looked too shaken to be lying.

I hesitated. Had Bart spilled his wishful thinking all over

his daughter? Or could it be that Clea had simply spotted her father's feeling for Ariane, just as I had, and filled in the rest with imagination?

"No, I'm not going to leave him. I'm afraid he's going to leave me, Emily," she said, the words rushing unaccustomedly fast out of her. "I know he has someone else. In the past, that hasn't mattered. He's gotten over it after a while, but this time, I think it may be something special for him."

"Let me get this straight. You are not intending to leave him; you are afraid he's going to leave you. Is it that you like being smacked around?"

"I know you must think I'm crazy, but this isn't . . ." Her hand rose from her lap to touch her face. "It isn't what it seems. You see, Zach . . . oh God, I feel so disloyal even saying it . . . Zach and I don't always have an easy time in bed. I know it's hard to believe—with all his passion, that swashbuckling look of him. It surprised me, too."

Ariane continued, visibly composing herself, as though to complete a difficult recitation in class. "The truth is, he sometimes can't. And then he works himself up into kind of a frenzy. The violence . . . it helps him make love to me."

Her face was damp now with tears. She had never been a crier, not as I remembered her. All at once, I was puzzled. "I do think you're crazy, as you knew damned well I would," I said. "Why are you here, Ariane?"

"Because I need a friend."

A friend. It took me back to age thirteen, two new girls at Fletcher, looking up from our stacked luggage to make eye contact. We'd recognized each other immediately: girls shaped wrong to fit in—misfits, each in a different way. Instinctively, we'd drawn together, but not as friends.

"Bart is your friend," I said deliberately.

"You're right. Bart is dear. I love him very much, but he would never understand." She began to say something more, then stopped, then decided to say it after all. "And he might . . . might hurt Zach."

"Bart?"

"Yes," she said simply. "Bart." A smile that looked as though it couldn't help itself began to curve her lips. "Appearances are often deceptive.''

"And more often they're not. Who is it you think your childlike husband is going to leave you for?"

"I don't know, but yesterday I heard him leave the house very early in the morning. I pretended to be asleep, and when I looked outside, I saw him putting the picnic basket into his car. Well, Zach has very romanticized notions about picnics, and—"

"If that's all that's bothering you, you can rest easy. He was bringing the basket, complete with his romantic notions, here.''

"I see," she said slowly.

"No, I don't think you do. He was not invited or expected or welcomed. I would sooner join a leper colony than screw your husband, much less run off with him. And you can tell him I told you that. In fact, I hope you will.''

She smiled. "Not in precisely those words, I think. Though you do turn a phrase as pungently as ever.''

"By the way," I said, "I hadn't intended to mention it, but when I was in the bathroom at your house, I overheard him on the phone with some woman.''

"Yes?" Her body tensed in expectation.

"That's it. I think he made a date with her for sometime or another. I have no idea when.''

She rose, her damaged face looking oddly at peace. Before I realized it, she'd leaned over and brushed her lips against my cheek, leaving a waxy feel of pink gloss. "Thank you, Emily—for being you.''

12

LATER THAT AFTERNOON, CLEA AND I WENT RIDING, but we barely spoke. Since I wasn't prepared to slash and burn the fantasy of her father's romance, I couldn't tell her about Ariane's visit. But neither could I get my own mind off it. And Clea, a small curve of smile fixed on her lips, seemed off in a fantasy that had nothing to do with her father.

I spent an aimless, solitary evening. I tried to enliven it with a brandy and one more pass at a Pall Mall, which succeeded only in ruining the taste of the brandy. Shortly after nine, I threw the pack in the trash and the remnants of the booze down the sink and went to bed.

Just before daybreak, I awoke tossing and twitching, bare body damp and itchy against the sheets, unable to go back to sleep, unable to make myself get up. Sex seemed to saturate the warm air, an epidemic, a kind of crazed *Midsummer Night's Dream.* At dawn, I pulled on an old, stretched-out swimsuit and fled the house for the pond.

I floated on my back, eyes closed against the faint sun beginning to brighten a milky sky. Then I flipped abruptly, with a spanking splash, onto my stomach and swam fast—back and forth, going nowhere.

I hauled myself out of the water to be hit in the eye by a beam of early sunlight bouncing off a shining red truck hood. I walked back to the house slowly, sneakers in hand, feeling chilled despite the heat. He was not in the kitchen—probably already at work upstairs. I constructed coffee and munched a peach, staring at the percolator, waiting for it to brew.

"Morning, Emily." I whirled around. Chris was just coming up from the basement, which put me oddly off balance. "Measuring for the ductwork. Should have that A.C. in by the end of the week. Sure gonna be able to use it, heat keeps up like this." His eyes looked cool as he talked about heat, more decisively green than blue today: ice cubes from the sea. "I thought you were still asleep."

"No. No, I went for a swim."

"Good way to cool off."

"Feel free to use it anytime." The not-quite smile on his lips made me remember his jaunty white phone in the library, and wonder how much of Orchards he had already used—and with whom. Pretty, round, dark-haired Lisa, the girl on the cleaning crew, would certainly be a willing partner, judging by the glow on her face whenever they were in the same room.

A trickle of peach juice made a slow, winding path down my chin. I brushed it away with the back of my hand.

Suddenly, I was acutely aware of the lemon clove salt smell of him. I turned to the stove to fiddle with a skillet—or anything—and felt the pins and needles tingle in my butt, the dampness flood my crotch. I took a deep, uneven breath.

"I guess I'll go upstairs and get to that bedroom," he said.

I nodded, without turning to look at him, and after a moment, heard his steps mount the stairs, slowly, one by one, laying down a trail of sexual breadcrumbs for me to follow. Deliberately, I poured more coffee, buttered toast, and consumed my breakfast.

Then I just stood there, radiating enough wet heat to melt the faded blue flowers right off my swimsuit—a comic figure: thirty years old, fumbling around like a teenager in a cat-and-mouse sex game with a plumber she barely knew. From upstairs came high-volume music—a group I didn't recognize doing a song I'd never heard. A mating call.

I climbed the stairs, the beat between my legs keeping time with the music, echoing shock waves down my legs. There he was—as expected, yet at the same time, astonishing—standing in the hall, not five feet from the door to my room, stripped to the waist. A triangle of fair hair gleamed gold on his damp chest. The music behind him had switched, I noticed dimly—another unfamiliar song, but with the same insistent beat.

He didn't speak; neither did I. We had nothing much to say to each other in any circumstance; nothing at all to say now. I took one step toward him. He covered the rest of the ground and put his hands on both my arms. I felt my skin pucker in an exquisite near-pain, my wet hair turn to dry ice, burning into my scalp. The pounding in my ears would have drowned out gunfire. We walked slowly into my bedroom, me going backward, as though being led in a dance step. Our bodies touched only lightly until I felt his erection hard against my leg.

He stepped back and began to unbutton his shorts. My heart skidded past its normal beat and stopped for a split second, stark still as a trapped lizard. I watched, fascinated, as he drew a condom out of his pocket, unwrapped it and rolled it on—all one easy move—as his shorts drifted to the floor, slow motion.

Then I peeled down the swimsuit, and my mind disconnected, circuits knocked out flat by pure sensation. Locked together, we sank down on the blue and white quilt of my childhood bed. I came quickly in hard, jagged firecracker bursts. He withdrew slowly and then took his time, moving his mouth over my body, as though measuring it with his tongue, which finally thrust deep inside me, over and over until I yipped with the ache of pleasure. At just the right moment, he was in me again; in me, but not *with* me—off in some universe where I did not exist. Suddenly, he came, shuddering as if from a lethal jolt of electricity.

"Put your pants on, boyo, and get the hell out of here!"

I recognized that almost-brogue, and refused to believe my ears. But when my eyes snapped open, I had to believe them. Dev's father stood in the doorway of my room, fisted hand raised as though it held a weapon. Chris rolled off me, cock still stiff enough to hang a flag from, and stood perfectly still, facing the unknown intruder with his usual ease. What the hell did it take to shake him up?! I stayed where I was, unable to catch my breath, and flipped the quilt over me. All of this in stretched-out seconds.

"*Get out of he . . . re!*" I half hollered, half panted, fury and embarrassment combining to crack my voice in mid-word. And then, in an instant, it all flooded away in a tide of raw fear, corrosive as lye, as I looked at Liam Hannagan's waxy face. "What is it?" I managed to get out. "Has something happened to Dev?"

"I thought he was here," Liam said truculently. He threw a contemptuous look at Chris, who had efficiently rolled the condom off, knotted it at the top like a miniature garbage bag, and was now leaning over to pull underpants and shorts back up his legs. "Just you get rid of this strutting fancy boy, before I have to kick his arse down your stairs."

"You're dreaming, old man," Chris said almost nonchalantly, as he tucked the neatly sealed condom efficiently into his pocket. Meticulous Chris. "If anybody's ass gets kicked—"

"And take that bloody so-called music with you," Liam cut in. "Damnable noise—wouldn't fook to that noise if they paid—"

"Shut up!" I bellowed, "and knock off that goddamned phony brogue. You were born in *Boston,* for Christ's sake!" But my anger at Liam Hannagan was interrupted by a brain flash of unmistakable truth.

"Chris," I said, his name rasping sore in my throat, "it'll be better if you do go."

He nodded at me slowly, the expression on his face as relaxed as the now smooth front of his shorts. "Yeah." Our eyes met in perfect understanding. Our moment had happened, urgent as a giant sneeze, after a week-long tickle of buildup—and just as satisfying. Now it was over. Liam's amazing, untimely arrival was an embarrassment, but it hadn't really ruined anything, and we both knew it. "You sure you're okay with this old guy?"

"I'm fine." My head felt light—light and large. "Look, this is . . . I'm sorry," I said. "I hope you'll be able to come back tomorrow. To work."

He smiled—a smile cool and businesslike. "To work."

I watched his finely shaped back as he sauntered down the hall and disappeared around the corner, and felt a twinge of regret in my relief at what the sight didn't do to me. The fever had passed, quicker than I'd imagined possible.

"Get out into the hall, Liam," I said, hardly loud enough to be heard over the music, "and shut the door behind you. I don't need you gawping at me while I get dressed."

As the door closed, I heard the tape stop in mid-wail, and knew that Chris would be gone when I emerged. I threw off the suffocating quilt and retreated to the adjoining bathroom, where I gratefully let the shower rinse his spicy smell off my body and down the drain. I'd just been performed upon by a virtuoso—Yo-Yo Ma, trying out a new cello—and I'd responded like an overtuned instrument, unplayed for too long a while. Nothing personal about it. On either side.

And Liam Hannagan was not going to make me feel guilty, I promised myself as I dried off and pulled on shorts and shirt. When I opened the door, Liam stood gazing down the hall—blue serge legs apart, white-shirted arms folded: the rogue male, entitled to plant himself anywhere he wanted.

"You old bastard," I said, "you barge into Dev's place whenever it suits you, and for some reason he doesn't throw you out. But that's him, not me."

"I didn't barge, you know," he said, as though defending his record. "I rang your damned bell, then I bashed at your front door for a good five minutes. Weren't for that bloody noise, you'd've—"

"Beside the point. This is *my* house, and I'll play whatever music I want; I didn't invite you. Hey, how did you even know where . . . ?"

"Where your house was?" He chuckled, proud of himself. "Dev's not the only detective in the family. I asked after you last time I saw him, and he said you were probably at your grandmother's place upstate. When I couldn't find him, I figured that's where he must have gone off to." I saw his face sharpen with pride as he warmed to his tale. "So I looked up her obit there in the public library. 'Of New York City and Millbrook.' Piece of cake. I got off the train in Poughkeepsie, told the taxi fella Millbrook. All I had to do in the town was ask at the shops. Second one I went into knew just where the Otis place was. Orchards, isn't that what you call it?"

So Dev had guessed where I was, and had chosen to keep his distance. In the circumstances, it made little sense to feel devastated by that knowledge, but I did. "I don't know what drunken, brain-scrambled idea got you here," I said, fighting to hold myself together, "and I don't care. I'm telling you to go."

He didn't move. "I'm not drunk," he said quietly. I

looked at him hard. It occurred to me that I'd never before seen him in daylight. All those times, late at night in Dev's apartment, his face had seemed painted with a light coat of rosy shellac, eyes glittering like moist cobalt glass. Now his skin looked yellowish-pale and dull, and the eyes dry and faded as old paint. But the square of the jaw was sharp—as sharp as Dev's. His hands—not entirely steady, I noticed— were nicked with newly healed cuts. He did not look well, but he did look cold sober.

"I came to find Dev," he said, taking a step closer to me, the brash posturing of moments ago gone. "He's not been home for more than a week; I figured he must be here. So if you're lookin' for a brain scramble, that's the brain scramble. I have . . . things I need to say to him. I've made a decision, an important one. The decision of a lifetime, you might say." He laughed suddenly at a private joke, which he seemed to be trying to let me in on. "I'll be going away. I want to see my son."

My son. *He. Is. My. Father.* Well, walk into the fucking sunset together! "Dev isn't here."

"I see that, yes," he said dryly. "But I thought . . ."

"Whatever you thought is many weeks out of date. He isn't here. And he won't be." Liam's faded eyes looked at me as though I were a kid spouting foolishness. "As you see, I have other interests," I said deliberately.

"Ah Emily, that boyo's not an interest. I know what he is; so do you."

"*Get out of here!* You haven't any right to—" I saw him breathe in sharply, almost a gasp. He reached quickly into his shirt pocket for a vial of pills, got hold of one and stuck it under his tongue.

Reflexively, I ran to his side and grabbed him as he staggered. It was the first time I had ever touched him. The arm beneath its damp starched sleeve was firm, strong with stringy muscles—the same muscles that had tensed in drunken fury, the same arm that had shot out and crippled a ten-year-old boy. I dropped my hands.

"I'm okay now," he said, his face smoothing itself out. "Do you mind if I sit down?"

Yes, I mind. I mind everything about you! "Go ahead."

He lowered himself carefully into the white rocker: fragile cargo.

And then, without a sound, as though at the touch of some inner switch, he collapsed, head rolling crazily forward onto his chest, upper body jackknifed in the chair.

In the second it took to register, I understood his private joke, his talk of leaving.

I held my hand under his nose and felt a faint warm puff of breath. "Liam," I said urgently in his ear. "Liam!" I grabbed both his shoulders and forced them upright, afraid he wouldn't be able to keep breathing folded over as he was. As I did it, his head snapped backward, heavy as a bowling ball, and I thought I must have broken his neck. But the breathing continued—loud now, almost a gasping snore through his open mouth.

My own breathing wasn't working so well either. I reached for the phone and dialed 911. The calmly sympathetic woman took the information and said an ambulance would be there shortly.

Was he dying? Heart attack? Some kind of alcohol withdrawal fit? The loud staticky breathing continued, but less regular in its rhythm. I knelt down and removed the thick polished oxfords from his feet, which, encased in their black socks, felt marshy-damp. I loosened the green tie and unbuttoned the first two buttons of the sweat-soaked shirt. After a moment's hesitation, I undid the buckle of his worn black belt and opened the waist fastener of the heavy pants. The acts felt unpleasantly intimate.

I punched in Dev's number and felt my heart dip sickly when I heard his machine. "Your father's here. He is sick— passed out. *Call me as soon as you get this.*" I recited the number through gritted teeth and slammed the phone down. Liam gave a pair of small moans, as though somehow, wherever his mind was sleeping, he'd heard.

At that moment, the phone rang, and I dove at it.

It was not Dev. "Emily." Ariane's voice, mournful as a day-old funeral bouquet. "Zach is gone, and I don't . . . think he's coming back." Her breath caught in her throat, but the delicate sound was obliterated by a volley of staccato knocks and rings at the front door.

"I can't talk to you now," I said with a cool firmness that sounded like someone other than me, and hung up.

"Heat exhaustion, Ms. Otis." The small, young doctor's mustache looked like it had been stuck on with spirit gum, and not enough. It wobbled as he spoke. Liam lay on a gurney in the emergency room at Vassar Brothers Hospital, stripped of his unseasonable clothes, covered now only in a thin blue and white open-back gown. He was awake but stonily silent, raising his head periodically to dispense eye-to-eye poison to anyone who happened to notice. The doctor addressed him now in that uneasily loud, overly familiar way his profession reserves for the old and feeble. "Liam, looks like you haven't been eating much, huh?"

"Mr. Hannagan to you, twerp," was the growling answer. I made myself not laugh. My grandmother would have used different words, of course, but the tune would have been the same. "I passed out with the heat, is all. I'd've woken up on my own hook without all this fancy bullshit. If you'll just give me my duds, I'll be on my way, thank you." So he knew quite well that he was not fatally ill. The grandstanding about going away, saying goodbye, had been a different idea of dying.

"No, Mr. Hannagan, I don't think so. You're on heart medication, aren't you? Nitroglycerin for your angina? What about diuretics?"

"Die you wha'?"

"Pills to get rid of water, swelling. They make you pee a lot." The little doctor was moving toward exasperation.

"Yeah, what about 'em?" Liam snapped.

"You have to eat and drink when you take them—and when I say drink, I don't mean alcohol—especially in this weather. Speaking of alcohol, how long's it been since you had your last drink?"

Liam's glare upped its wattage, and turned on me.

"Stop acting like a twelve-year-old," I said. "You are pissing me off. There are about twenty things I'd rather be doing than chaperoning you through this hospital. He's asked you a legitimate question. Answer it."

"Ten days," he mumbled, as though ashamed.

"Good for you. We've got A.A. right here in the hospital, and I can give you a list of—"

"Forget it, quack! Not interested." The doctor backed off, with a meaningful glance at me.

"Are you married, Mr. Hannagan?" he asked.

"No," Liam said, the syllable harsh. "No, not anymore," he said quietly.

"Do you have a job?" the doctor asked.

I cut in, irritated. "If you're concerned about the insurance, doctor, I told them at the desk, I'd be responsible for . . ."

"The business office has its questions, I have mine," he said testily, studying Liam's hands and arms. "I want to know what kind of work this man does. These scars are what, a month or so old? Did you get them on the job?"

Liam gave a short hoarse laugh. "You might say so." He swiveled his head to look at me. "I guess Dev didn't tell you, the bar is gone. I couldn't run The Troubles on my own, and once Ethne left, I didn't even want to look at the place."

"Are you saying you sold it?" That damned place up in Washington Heights had been Liam's monument to himself—the place where he could be the host, pour the drinks, tell his lies—vivid stories of a country he'd never even visited.

"Yeah, I'm saying that. And to answer your question, sawbones, before I turned it over, I broke it—every piece of glass in it. For some of that, I used these hands." I wanted to clobber his outthrust chin. The old bastard was enjoying the hell out of playing Sean O'Casey for a country doctor. But would he kill himself as part of a performance? Would he, if he thought it was the only way to get Dev's attention? I couldn't say whether the lump that rose hard in my throat was one of fear or anger.

"You like to break things with your hands, don't you, Liam?" I asked, pouring cold spite over both of us. I saw my words hit and sting.

Now the doctor turned his scraggy mustache on me. "I want to admit him. Hydrate him. Nourish him. Reregulate the medications. Get that blood pressure down. Has he got a doctor in New York?''

''Have you?'' I asked after a beat, when no answer was forthcoming.

''Some clinic—Dev took me. Group of names like the United Nations. Wouldn't know the one from the other.''

''Dev is his son,'' I explained. ''I'm trying to reach him.''

Liam tried a lurching move off the table, yanking at the I.V. tube attached to his arm and almost toppling the tall pole it hung on. ''I'm not staying here in this tatty nightdress with my arse flappin' in the breeze.''

The doctor, stronger than he looked, managed to get him back in place, and looked to me to make him stay there. ''You. Are. Staying. Here,'' I grated, one word at a time. ''Because if you don't behave, and do exactly what they tell you, I will not lift a finger to find Dev for you.''

13

....

On the way back from the hospital I swung by the Terman castle, and was let in by a bulky gray-haired woman in a flowered smock, who introduced herself as Winona and asked me with sharp-eyed suspicion whether Mrs. Terman was expecting me. "She called me earlier today," I said, in no mood to explain myself.

Winona sized me up frankly. I squeaked by. "They're on the patio," she said. "I suppose it'll be all right for you to go on out." Her voice stopped me midway down the corridor. "You want to be careful, now. She's feeling ... poorly."

The other part of "they" was Bart Held, who sat decorously across the glass-topped table from her, suited up in blue and white for the office, a bulging briefcase at his side. A large platter of triangle-cut sandwiches and a pitcher of iced tea, both as yet untouched, stood between them.

Ariane didn't seem all that poorly. She looked cool and composed in a bare-shouldered green-and-white-striped dress that flattered her firm tanned tennis arms.

Her hair was neatly chignoned, and no protective or concealing makeup attempted to hide her face. The swelling on her cheek and eye had receded somewhat, but the bruises—beginning to turn brownish—were somehow even more startling outdoors, sharing the brightly impartial summer sun with an exquisite riot of flowers.

Except for that battered face, the scene was civilized as a Coward comedy.

Bart began to rise, but I gestured not to bother. "Sorry I hung up on you, Ariane," I said, and then explained about Liam: the expurgated version, edited to state simply that the father of a friend had come to visit and been suddenly taken ill.

"What a shame. I hope he'll be all right." Ariane gave a

small laugh. "I did wonder at how you were on the phone. I thought you might just have had a bellyful of Zach and me, and our problems. Which would be more than understandable."

Amen, I replied silently, and took a couple of eager steps back toward the house. "Well, it looks as though both of you are in good hands, so I'll be on my—"

"Please don't go," she said, reaching out for my arm in time to capture it in her cool hand. "I wish you'd stay and have some lunch with us." Bart nodded tentatively, obviously wishing just the opposite. "Please, Emily," Ariane insisted, holding on firmly, a flicker of pain crossing her face. "You see, I . . . don't know how I feel just now—how I *should* feel, what I should do." Now she removed her hand from my arm and left it up to me.

"Sure," I said after a moment. "I don't have any wisdom to contribute, but I'll stay for a little while, if you want."

Over crustless tuna and turkey, and tall iced glasses of strong, pleasantly minted tea, she told me that Zach had not come home last night.

"I knew it was different this time, Emily. I told you it was, remember? Not that Zach's never stayed away before. He's done it four—no, five—times. Five times in three years." Her expression seemed to say that surely that wasn't so bad. I bit back any comment. "But each time, he's called me the next morning—very early, before whoever she was was awake—to tell me when he'd be home, and that he . . . he loved me." She put the sandwich she'd been holding, two neat bites already gone from it, down on the plate and flicked her tongue around her lips: no pink gloss today. "He was like a naughty little boy, checking in with his mother—apologizing—and yet keeping it a big secret from his playmate, so she wouldn't think he was a mama's boy."

I sneaked a look at Bart's face, which was trying to hide whatever was going on behind it. "But this time he didn't call Mama?" I asked, trying not to lash out my disgust.

"No, he didn't. And after a while I did something I never do. I went into his office to snoop. But I didn't have to look far. He'd left a note for me, left it lying right across his keyboard where I couldn't miss it. 'It's over, Ari. I'll never stop loving you, but don't try to come after me. You won't find me.' And he signed it 'ZZZ' the way he always does." She rested her forehead on her fisted hand, and I watched her head move slowly back and forth, as though telling herself that what she'd just said hadn't happened.

"And have you tried to go after him?" I asked, with a glance over at Bart, who was drinking glass after glass of the tea, but had not touched one sandwich, or spoken a word.

"Yes and no," she said softly. "I drove into the city. I just got back an hour ago. I checked our apartment, the garage, his little office studio right around the corner—sort of a garret, where he lived when he first started to write, before his great success. He was still living there when we met." Regret, loss, held her face for a moment in a grip painful to observe. "Anyway," she went on with a forced brightness, "no trace of him, and nothing gone that I could see, except his laptop computer. I called his agent and his business manager, who's also his oldest friend. Nothing."

"Is he in the middle of a book or something?"

She laughed. "Wouldn't that be convenient! Unfortunately not. He signed off on the page proofs for his latest one only last week, and that Disney deal he's so thrilled about is signed too. His manager . . ." Her voice thickened into a sob. "His manager told me he'd probably be home before I knew it, with his tail between his legs." Her smooth head dropped forward onto both hands, and she wept in earnest.

Now Bart leapt to his feet and wrapped his arms around her shoulders from behind. "Darling, don't. He isn't worth it. He's worth *nothing*." On that last word something in him caught fire, and his grip tightened on her bare shoulders. When he let go after a moment, the red marks of his fingers lingered briefly, before they disappeared into her tan.

He might hurt Zach. Appearances are often deceptive. Did Ariane really believe that of Bart? Did I?

"Emily," he said, his voice bone-dry the way it had sounded when I'd first met him, and I knew he was about to mention his daughter. "I wonder if you'd be able to have Clea over this evening. I had planned to go out to dinner with her, but . . ." He gently touched Ariane's smooth head, which shone gold in the sunlight.

"No problem," I said. Of course there was a problem. I wondered whether at any time in her life, Bart's daughter had come first for him.

The secretary at the law firm Dev investigated for said she had no idea where he was or when he'd be back. She and I had met a few times. I remembered a large, casual woman who looked as though she had an interesting after-work life, and was having a frankly hard time coping with a newly smokeless office. "He does that from time to time, you know," she said, her voice kind, just short of commiserating. "Year and a half ago, we got this case—embezzler, bank wanted him found quick before the story got out. Everybody in this office was hollering for Hannagan, and he was nowhere to be found. When he turned up couple of weeks later, Vince Everstall, one of the newer partners, hopped on his back, I mean right there in the reception area. Well, our boy just eyeballed him and said, real quiet, 'You rent my ass, friend, you don't own it.' " She let out a deep, appreciative chuckle. "Made my day! Artistic temperament, Emily, or maybe just Irish."

I called two of his male friends, neither of whom had anything to tell me, and then I started on the females: the photographer, the doctor, the caterer. During each uncomfortable and useless call, I thought I detected a complicit smile, imagined the rustle of sheets in the background. The sexy Italian NYPD sergeant was unreachable at home or work. Finally, I dialed his machine one more time.

"Your father is up here. He got sick and passed out. He's at the hospital now. They say he'll be okay." I spoke like a robot. And then exploded. *"I hope you're having a ball, you son of a bitch!"*

Zachary Terman; Paul Eamon De Valera Hannagan: two worthless men missing. As far as I was concerned, they could both stay that way!

• • •

Wednesday morning I picked Liam up and took him home with me. There was really little choice. The doctor strongly recommended "an eye on him" for the next week or so, and mine seemed to be the only one around. No wife, no son— not even any drinking buddies left to qualify as friend. And, unless I was way off base, the man intended to kill himself. So I filled the doctor's prescriptions, bought a random stack of men's summer clothes that looked the right size, and took him home.

"About the A.A. meetings," I said, once we were in the car, "it'll make it . . . easier on you, and—"

"I don't want it easier," he growled through gritted teeth. "I want it hard—hard as it can be." We exchanged no more words on the drive back to Orchards, but twice our eyes met unexpectedly, like strangers in an elevator, and the second time, I swore I caught a flash of amusement in his.

14

It was Monday: a week to the day since Ariane had found Zach's note; a week to the day since Liam had appeared at my bedroom door searching for Dev. Zach was still missing. Dev had not turned up. And Liam and I had settled in together. Uneasily. More accurately, Liam and Clea and I. Virtually the moment they met, something—the lilt of his phony brogue, the planes of that hard-used face, those scarred hands—had reached inside her and struck pay dirt. She still rode with me, joked with Chris, but it was obvious that Liam Hannagan was the reason she spent most of her time here now.

I came down this morning to find Chris working in the dining room, and Liam drinking tea with Clea in the kitchen. It was the fourth day in a row that had begun the same way. I realized with a buzz of annoyed surprise how fast the dailiness of anything becomes normalcy. By that standard, I saw before me a normal household: a displaced actress rooming with her ex-lover's appalling father, while her most recent lover applied fresh paper to her walls. A mercurial teenager had all but moved in, too. Oh, we mustn't forget the beauty-obsessed decorator who wafted in and out, bearing rare objects. And in the wings, making the occasional drinks-and-dinner appearance, were the teenager's love-struck father and his fair lady, on whose face a close observer could still spot the last of the fading bruises inflicted by her runaway husband.

That about covered it.

I gave Liam a wide berth, not all that difficult in a big house. But occasionally, I'd come upon him in the music room tooling out some melody of love or revolution on my grandmother's Steinway, or in the library dealing a solitaire hand onto the inlaid wood of the game table. Always at his side was a can of Coke or a cup of tea. He did not smoke, or a cigarette surely would have been fixed between his fingers.

I could only imagine what hell it must be to give up drinking, especially when your life lies in shards at your feet, and I wondered where he might have found the resolution—and why. A problem for me was that I'd find myself on the brink of admiring Liam for sticking with it. Even more dangerous, I'd totter on the edge of liking him, and something deep in my core would pull back reflexively to save itself from the fall.

But Liam did not languish in my neglect; he basked in Clea's attentions. Spurred by her cajoling, teasing, scolding, he had actually taken walks, eaten full meals, consumed his pills on time, even swum in the pond a few times. When he looked at her, his faded blue eyes kindled and his face took on an expression of relaxed enjoyment that I'd never seen there before.

As far as I was concerned, Clea had scraped the bottom of the barrel for a father substitute, but I could certainly understand her craving for one. The coincidence that she couldn't get enough of Liam's company and that I was relieved to have him off my own back kept my tongue still.

The day lazed its way into late afternoon, warm and thick. I'd spent most of it holed up in the library with the *As You Like It* screenplay. The air-conditioning system Chris had installed was up and running—and not a moment too soon. Finally, I summoned up the will to consider braving the heat outdoors for at least a short jog, my minimum daily commitment to getting in physical shape to play Rozzie, in the unlikely event the filmmaker actually ever did get her financing—and liked me well enough to cast me.

"Oh now tell me, Sean O'Farrell, where the gatherin' is to be. At the *old* place by the river, right well known to you and me . . ." Liam's rusty tenor rolled down the hallway from the music room. I poked my head in the doorway, and saw Clea leaning in close, elbows propped against the polished mahogany of the piano, her mouth moving slightly, as though she were trying to memorize every word he sang.

". . . at the risin' of the moon," they finished together with a flourish, Clea a tad out of key. "That one's good," she said to him, ''but 'Brennan on the Moor' is still the best. You know, if you opened a bar up here, it'd be packed. I mean they'd be waiting two miles down the road to get in, to hear you sing, tell those stories about Ireland in the old days. You could call it The Troubles, just like your other place. Or maybe Troubles Two.''

''Wouldn't Dev like that?'' he asked himself with irony, knowing quite well the answer. He'd named his bar after Dev's book, copies of which supposedly adorned one wall. Dev made no secret of his loathing for the gesture. He had never set foot in the place; nor had I, but I'd harbored a secret desire to burn it to the ground—only partly to see whether its obliteration would let Dev write again.

''Nah pet, my salooning days are over.'' He gave Clea a smile of restored sunniness. ''Barkeep, barfly: they're over. You're my best audience.'' Now he spun on the piano bench and held out a beckoning hand. ''Come on, Emily. Join us. Sing a song with us—any one you like.''

Instinctively, I began to back out into the hallway. ''Not just now. I think I'll get some running in and reward myself with a swim.''

When I returned a couple of hours later, the sun had begun to set, and Clea was just leaving.

''Not staying for dinner?'' I asked, jogging past her.

''Can't,'' she said in a tone bubbly enough to turn my head toward her. The expression on her face looked slightly out of kilter: excited, secretive, spiced with naughtiness—a look I remembered but hadn't seen for close to two weeks. The boyfriend look.

So he was back on her scene, sneaking a night out. I wondered if he'd had to line up a babysitter, or whether his wife was on duty.

''Have fun,'' I said, the curl of my sarcasm hanging heavy in the steamy air.

Unenthusiastically, I fixed Liam and me an early, light supper of omelette and salad.

''Go on, have yourself a glass of wine or something, why don't you?'' Liam said as he popped open a fresh Coke and sat himself down and watched me beat up some eggs.

"I don't want anything to drink," I lied, the whisk in my hand punishing the already sufficiently whipped eggs.

"Doesn't trouble me one way or the other," he persisted.

"Leave it alone. I told you, I don't—"

"Have a fookin' glass of wine, for Jesus' sake! It won't send me into a bottle, or keep me out of one." He leveled his eyes at me in combat.

"Fuck off, I don't want a drink!"

He broke into a sudden grin. "You're a tough girl, Emily. There's fiber to you. You're a fighter." The smile closed in on itself like a quickly shut umbrella. "Dev's mother, Mim, she could've done with some of that—would've been better for us all. But she'd just get lost, disappear into her head."

"Don't you dare blame her! What would've been *better* was if you'd kept your damned hands to yourself."

"That, too," he said quietly, his tone reminding me painfully of the way Dev would have said the words. "I haven't hit anything alive for thirty years, Emily—just in case that's of interest to you. What's really on my mind is Clea, though. She's not like you, you know."

I cut the omelette in two and eased the halves onto a pair of plates. Without looking at Liam, I retrieved a half-empty bottle of Merlot out of the back of the pot cupboard where I'd hidden it yesterday, and pulled out its cork.

"What is it you're saying?" I asked, pouring myself a healthy glass.

I'd taken two sips before he got around to answering. "She brings back Mim, just a bit."

"Nonsense, Liam!" I fought a temptation to cover my ears like a child. Instead, I filled the air with the sound of my own voice. "Dev says his mother was a depressive, that she used to sit for hours not saying a word, just staring. Clea . . . Clea isn't that way at all. You see her every day. She's vibrant. She's . . ." I stopped cold, my denials not truly persuasive, even to me. "How is she like Mim?" I asked finally, not eager for an answer.

"Put it this way. If three people were singing a round of 'Three Blind Mice,' she couldn't hold on to her part to save her life."

"Lots of people can't."

"And usually they know it, and stay away from that kind of thing. Clea volunteers for it. She jumps into one part, then another and another and another, till she's dizzy with it. She loses herself in people the way Mim did in the spooks in her head. You never do that. You may be an actress, but I bet you don't get lost that way in any part. Dev's lucky to have you. And you him, of course."

"I don't have him," I snapped. "He doesn't have me, either. And as soon as he gets back from wherever the hell he is, I'm sure he'll come for you and take you home with him."

"I am not a parcel, or a dog boarding in a kennel, Emily." His voice was bleak, edged with outrage. "I don't need to be called for and taken home."

"I'm sorry," I said slowly, surprised at how much I meant it.

He rose and turned to leave the room. "Maybe things work out for the best," he said, facing away from me. "Maybe it's just as well that Dev wasn't here just now. I think that as soon as Clea gets back, I'll thank you for your hospitality and be on my way."

"And do what? Make some grand show of killing your—" I stopped myself abruptly, as his words hit me. "What are you talking about?" He continued walking as though he hadn't heard me. *"Gets back from where?"*

That turned him around. "Slip of the tongue. Don't let it trouble you."

"Where?" I suppose I shouldn't have been surprised that she'd confided in him in ways she hadn't to me, but I was— and nettled, too.

"Mum was the word, but I guess I've blown it. Clea's gone off for a couple of days."

"With that scummy boyfriend of hers?"

"I'm surprised to hear you talk that way, what with your own taste for—"

His first out-and-out mention of Chris and me, and I wanted to hit him with the almost boiling teakettle. "Don't even *think* about finishing that sentence! Now, where's she gone?"

"I don't know where. I don't know who. And if I did, I wouldn't tell you." He strode out of the room, the spring back in his step.

I turned the flame under the kettle off. If I needed a refresher for my dislike of him, I had it. And yet, as I played them back, his observations about Clea chilled me. *You want to watch her. She'll take over your life.* That's how Chris had put it, but Liam saw it turned the opposite way entirely: she didn't take over people's lives; people took over hers—one after another. A scary idea, but one that rang too true for comfort.

15

· · · · · · · · · · · · · · · · · · · ·

MAYBE IT WAS THE PICTURE THAT LIAM HAD PAINTED of Clea as a straw in the wind. Maybe it was intuition, whatever that truly means. But, unreasonably, I wanted Clea to be home and safe; wanted to hear her voice. Around the edges of anxiety, it occurred to me that if I were this overprotective of a nineteen-year-old surrogate sister, I'd probably be a disaster as a parent. I felt an unlikely flash of sympathy with Bart Held.

I waited until nine the next morning to call, when Bart was sure to be gone and I wouldn't have to lie to him. Perhaps Liam had gotten it wrong; perhaps she'd just been showing off with her talk of going away; perhaps she was up in her room right now, sleeping off a night in paradise.

Malvina, the housekeeper, told me that Clea wasn't home, and that she'd assumed she was here at Orchards. Just as I was hanging up, Chris's truck pulled in, followed a moment later by the large white van with the cleaning crew. I watched absently as the three boy-men in their spandy green and white At Home tee-shirts marched like a National Guard unit toward the kitchen doors, and noticed pretty Lisa hanging back to walk with Chris, her shoulder brushing against his arm. They traded smiles, and I saw his hand reach out to give her butt a casual, apparently welcomed pat.

Since our leap at each other last week, the sexual pull between Chris and me was about as strong as between a pair of freshly altered cats, and that lack drew my heightened attention to the coolness in his eyes, and a calculating look I'd catch occasionally in his finely carved face.

When his path crossed Liam's—as Liam, with his keynote perversity, made sure it did more often than necessary—the static of mutual dislike electrified the air. Chris would saunter past in silent disdain, while Liam muttered under-his-breath taunts along the lines of, ''Now what's the fancy fella up to today?'' or, ''Pants a little roomy there round the cock-a-doodle. Oysters, boyo. Oysters make it grow.'' I'd threatened Liam with bodily harm, but when it came down to reality, there wasn't a thing—short of throwing him out—that I could do, except try to ignore the whole thing.

I waved a good morning at everyone, and interrupted Chris on his way to the dining room, which he'd prepped for papering yesterday. ''Chris, could I have a word with you?''

''Sure thing.'' He poured himself a cup of coffee and propped his behind against the table. ''Shoot.''

''It's about Clea.''

''Uh huh.''

''She's gone off for a few days with a lover . . .'' I stopped for a beat in sheer embarrassment. Damn it, I *wasn't* a prying gossip, but that was the way I reflected back at myself in his eyes. I speeded up and got the rest of it out. ''Look, this guy is married and . . . I'm worried about her.''

''Why?''

''I'm not sure,'' I admitted. ''Do you have any idea who he is?''

''Not a clue. And I'm not a bit interested. She's nineteen. She's got a right to have a life.'' He and Liam agreed on one thing, at least.

''That's not the point.'' And if it wasn't, what was?

''Let me give you a piece of advice, free of charge.'' He put the coffee down and leaned across the table, his weight resting on arms caramel-tan against the faded blue of his shirt. ''Don't worry about Clea,'' he said. ''She's a lot stronger than she looks. People have been worrying about that girl all her life. That's what she knows how to do, get it? She makes people worry about her.''

''You saved her life. She loves you, Chris. Do you know that?''

''She doesn't even know who I am,'' he said slowly, with a half smile different from any I'd seen on his face. ''To her it's romantic to grow up the way I did in a town like Mill-brook, right? A bastard with a father's fancy name and a mother working extra shifts at the restaurant to pay the oil bill. For Clea, it's like something she read in a book, or some story her boozed-out mother told her.'' He stopped on a dime, and the smile relaxed into one I recognized. "Hey, sorry about that. I'm coming off a lousy night's sleep. But really, you can chill about Clea. Sometimes I think a solid kick in the butt would be the best thing in the world for her.''

Clea wasn't here to feel betrayed, so I did it for her. "And who ought to give her this kick? You? Her father perhaps?''

Now he laughed. "Bart? She gets in a lot more licks at him than he does at her. My uncle couldn't swat a deerfly while it was biting him.''

"Why does Bart dislike you?" The question had been in and out of my head for weeks.

"Why don't you ask him?" His face reset itself in a way that reminded me of the first time I'd seen it, looking at me naked through the French doors. He left the room quickly, and a few minutes later, the music from his tape player floated in from down the hall. Old Johnny Cash songs; the lonely grit of them made me want to cry.

Alone in the kitchen, I felt an onset of the waiting jitters— an acute case. It seemed to me suddenly as though all thirty of my years had been spent waiting like this, tensed and expectant, for someone to come, or someone to leave. I couldn't bear it right now: to will the phone to ring, hoping it would be Dev; to listen for a car in gravel, hoping it would be Clea. And I didn't want to spend the day rattling around the house, avoiding Liam in one room and Chris in another.

"Will you be okay if I cut out of here till tomorrow?" I asked Liam when he came down for his tea.

"You mean will I stay with the tea and Coke, not go for anything stronger?"

"No, that's not what I mean." I spoke carefully, the words a narrow path of slippery stones, perfect for tripping on. "I mean will you give me your word that you'll eat and take the right pills, and *be here* when I get back?"

He nodded almost imperceptibly, in discussion with himself. "I will, yes. I'll be here.''

•   •   •

I drove north with a tape deck full of Bonnie and Lenya and Pavarotti, stopping randomly in any town that looked white and green and invulnerable. The point was to be away. I got as far as Brattleboro, Vermont, where I stayed the night at a bed-and-breakfast. Next day, on the way back, I bought a brass bed warmer which the antique shop owner said was eighteenth-century. I liked its shape, and wondered whether, when winter rolled around, I'd need to use it for its original purpose.

The sky had turned dark when I got home. For some reason—probably for no reason—I pulled the car around in back, instead of leaving it in the front crescent as I usually did. When I got out, I noticed the red of Chris's truck, behind a clump of white birches, halfway to the swimming pond. It was almost ten. Odd that he should be here this late.

If I'd approached the truck from another angle, I'd have seen them sooner. As it was, I got pretty close before I saw the bare legs—four of them—sticking out the open door. The lovers didn't notice me at all, which was no wonder.

So the pretty girl in the cleaning crew had gotten her wish. *Enjoy, Lisa,* I said silently. *He's terrific. Enjoy it and get over it.* Just then she sat up, head thrown back, breasts pointing sharply north.

When her face turned sideways, I saw that the woman I was beaming good wishes at was not Lisa at all.

She was Jane Benzinger.

16

....

FOR A MOMENT I STOOD THERE, REELING FROM THE
sleight of hand of a magician's trick, wondering if I'd have
spotted the rabbit in that empty hat if only I'd been looking
more carefully. I'd noticed her feeling for him, but had mistaken it for a sort of motherly concern. Jane and Chris. It
had simply never occurred to me. Why? Because she's
beige? Older? *What a shallow twit you are, Emily!*

Liam was in the library, playing cards with himself and
washing down the last of a ham sandwich with a cup of
milky tea.

"Hi," I said. "I didn't expect I'd be this late. I'm glad
you fixed yourself something to eat." I made myself not ask
whether Clea had come back.

"Ah yes. Well, I am the big boyo, amn't I?" he said, a
touch of sourness in the mocking.

I made a face. "I don't know what you get out of that
ridiculous vaudeville brogue," I replied, just as sour.

"Don't you?" he asked, suddenly gravely earnest. "It's
the last scrap of my act. Forty years, now. Longer—forty-
five. The booze, the stories, the songs, the talk, in the beginning they helped me get through. The factory was death on
a stick, day after fookin' day slappin' paint on the bowels of
submarines. And Mim to come home to, but her not there at
all really. A man needed something to hold off the devils.
Of course, the joke is that I didn't hold them off at all, I
invited them inside.

"But the act's a part of me now, don't you see? Tattooed
under the skin. Then when I hooked up with Ethne and
opened the bar, I even had a stage. You're an actress, you
can see what that meant." He gathered up the cards and
rapped the deck against the table. "It's over now, Emily. I'm

about played out." The lilt thickened, as though to demonstrate the truth of what he was saying. Now his face turned harsh. "So leave me my songs and stories, would you? And get your fookin' foot off me brogue, there's a good girl."

"Got it," I said tersely, my cheeks flooding with the shame of having marched with thick-soled boots into his skinless private region. "I'm going up to bed." I turned and took the stairs two at a time. I couldn't wait to close the door and dive under a quilt.

The glasses didn't fit. They kept sliding down my nose, and I kept pushing them back up, even though when I looked through them everything turned upside down. I shoved them back into position one more time, because I wanted to walk on the sky, but now I began to whirl, while everything else stood still. I hurtled through space, flipping and turning, my arms flailing uselessly, trying desperately to stop the fall, to gain control, to . . . Suddenly, everything shattered in a piercing howl.

My hand, unconnected to any other part of me, reached out of the nightmare and grabbed the phone.

"Mmmh," I grunted.

"Emily, Bart Held. I need to speak to my daughter." To chew her out, from the sound of him.

"Your daughter isn't here," I croaked hoarsely, adding an unspoken *So there!*

"Where is she?" The crisp executive, used to having his questions answered.

"I have no idea," I said with an exaggerated coolness, fully awake now, and aware from the bedside clock that the time was close to three. "Clea is nineteen years old. She's free to go where she pleases."

"Is that so? Well, you can tell her for me that unless I hear from her pretty smartly, she can go where she pleases on foot." So he was going to pull her car, ground her. God, he really was a stiff-necked prick. I waited for the rest of it. "I've just heard from the Poughkeepsie police. They've got her car. It was in the train station parking lot."

"I don't think I get this. What's it got to do with the police?"

"They caught some kids vandalizing it, trying to steal the tape deck. They say the car's been there since last night." Then he switched into high gear. "It's a bit much, don't you think? All this irresponsible running around she does. I suppose she's in the city. Fine. I'm pleased that she has friends, but she might have let me know she was going, where she's staying. Common courtesy, I believe it's called—far too common for my self-styled bohemian of a daughter. I blame myself. Spoiled, it used to be called. *My* father would have kicked her behind for her and made her get a job and pay for her car."

That made two men—her only living family—who wanted to kick Clea's behind, which only intensified my desire to protect it, and perhaps to kick theirs.

"It wasn't Clea's goddamned fault that her car got vandalized. You're just embarrassed about losing face with some cops. And by the way, how do you know she's in the city?" I added for spite. "She could've caught the Amtrak to Canada."

"Just reasonable assumption," he said, the professor now. "Likelihood. I must say I'm disappointed, Emily. I'd hoped you'd be the right kind of influence on Clea. Ariane thought the relationship would help—"

"Ariane's thoughts on relationships don't impress me, not after a look at hers with the brutal creep she picked to marry." Pow! It was a low blow, but I wasn't sorry I'd dealt it.

"I mean what I say about the car," he said through what sounded like barely moving lips.

I hung up without a goodbye, and after a long minute of indecision, pulled my chinos and shirt back on and made my way down the hall to Liam's room, where I was surprised to find the door wide open and the bed smoothly made.

I found him just where I'd left him—in the library, dealing himself yet another hand of cards. He didn't lift his head to look at me. I sat myself down across the table and took a deep breath.

"Liam, I need to find Clea."

"Ah, get off it, Emily."

"No, really. Her car's been vandalized at the train station, and her father's mad enough at her to take her wheels away. Is she in the city?" He gave me Dev's stoniest glare. I reached across the table and grabbed his arm. "I am *not* prying. I am *not* planning on tying her up in a sheet and dragging her home. She needs to know about her car. I just want to tell her."

He pulled away hard enough to make my chair rock back, and stood, his face furious. "That poor sod's not going to take her car away. Even if that was the right thing, he wouldn't have the balls. Let the girl enjoy her couple of days with her prince in his garret."

It felt like a mallet coming down square on my head. For a moment I couldn't make a sound. Then I managed a whisper. "What did you say?"

He was half out of the room. "You heard me well enough," he grumbled.

"No, *stop!* Is . . . is that what she said? About the prince and the garret?"

"What if it is? Past my bedtime. I'm going up to sleep."

"Oh my God. Oh my God. Oh my God." I repeated the mantra under my breath, as though it could counteract the truth that had just exploded into my brain.

The garret. The prince. The princess. The castle. Dark and romantic. Oh my God! This was no sleight of hand like Chris and Jane; this had been out there in plain sight for weeks! If only I'd had the sense to look. I'd been blinded by just what Liam pointed out the other night: my idea that Clea was somehow me at nineteen. I'd known the lover was married; I'd known he was bad news, but I'd pictured her with a dark-haired version of Chris—someone *I'd* have picked.

Clea and Zach Terman.

Now, behind my eyes, I saw his hairy body covering her white one on my blue rug; saw him jumping up like a springed toy at the sound of my car, jumping into his pants, barreling down the back stairs to make his getaway. Then I saw something else: his fist swinging back, to shoot out at Clea's startled face—once, and again, and again.

I felt the way I had after Mike's murder: ready to kill.

The blood chilled under my skin, my beating pulses slowed down. *Good,* I told myself. *Good. Think, damn it, think!*

He'd left more than a week ago, and his note to Ariane seemed to say it was for good. Had he really gone to that much trouble to blow smoke over a few illicit days with Clea? Maybe he had, with his taste for drama. And hers. From the beginning, Clea had loved the dramatic secrecy. Part of the thrill for her.

But what if it wasn't just a few stolen days? What if Clea had lost herself for good in Zach Terman? The chill inside me deepened. The two of them could be anywhere, but anywhere is a big place, so I was going to bet that wherever he'd been since last Sunday night, they were up in that Manhattan hideaway of his now—reading Omar Khayyám to each other, and melting candles into Chianti bottles.

Where the hell was the place? Their apartment was at Eighty-second and Park, and Ariane had said this was right around the corner. If that was literally true, it would be somewhere between Madison and Lexington. Hell, maybe it was even in the phone book, though somehow I doubted it. And a look proved me right. But I'd find the damned garret, not a second's doubt about that.

Okay, Zach Terman, watch out. Here comes your worst nightmare!

17

·····················

I<small>T WAS JUST STARTING TO GET LIGHT AS</small> I <small>PULLED INTO</small> a space on Lexington near Eighty-second. I locked the Lincoln, wondering whether it would be on its way to a chop shop when I returned, and decided that was the least of my worries.

Eighty-second is a block of brownstones mixed in with more recent apartment buildings. Walking west, I mounted the stairs of each of the brownstones, checked the tenant names next to the buzzers, and hit it lucky on the seventh one, south side.

One-twelve East Eighty-second had seen better days. As I gazed at it, a piece of memory bittersweet as a jagged chunk of dark chocolate stirred inside me: voices, extravagant in their emotion; hugs, offhand and passionate; tears; laughter. My heart was seeing not this house but a house very much like it, miles downtown and west, where I'd spent the first nine years of my life.

With a single difference: perched on top of this one, higher than its neighbors, was an afterthought—a peaked garret. I stepped down off the curb and threw my head back, staring up at it, as though my will could command a view through the curtained windows. They could be in Tahiti, of course, or Paris. But Clea's car had been at the station; she'd been unable to resist telling Liam about the garret.

The street was still dawn-deserted; a pink tinge to the sky promised good weather. I checked my watch: six thirty-five. You're here, smartass. What now?

I walked up the six steps to the front door and checked out the buzzer list. Terman was 5. My finger halted an inch shy of the button. No—too easy for them to just let it ring till the intruder went away. At the bottom of the list was Kolonsky, Supt. I shut my eyes for a full minute of pre-scene concentration, and then pushed Kolonsky's bell. I counted

thirty heartbeats, louder by far than the faint rumbling of
trucks a couple of avenues away, before I pushed again, long
and hard this time. Fourteen more beats, then the static of
an intercom and a sleepily belched "Yeah?!"

"Emergency. *Emergency!*" Nothing. Maybe the sound of
his name. "Mr. Kolonsky, please! My brother may be dying
upstairs!"

"Wha'? 'Kay. Right up." I felt a tear trickle warmly
down my cheek, and had the gall to pause for a moment of
professional pride. Then the door opened just wide enough
for me to see half of a massive, dark-haired Russian bear in
a rumpled green cotton bathrobe, under which one barefooted
leg stood rooted like a hairy tree trunk.

"Oh Mr. Kolonsky, thank God!" I slipped myself
through the stingy opening into the vestibule before he could
change his mind. And saw that he wasn't a he. "Sorry,
I . . ." Shit. *Go on, Emily!* Now I began to pant as I spoke,
the effort rushing blood hot into my cheeks. "I ran all the
way from Seventy-second Street. My brother Zach. He called
me. Then I think he passed out!"

Not yet fully awake, she stood planted there, a hostile
sequoia between me and the stairway.

"Mr. Terman on five. My brother. I *must* get to him." I
grabbed onto her wide shoulders as though preparing to
climb her. "Insulin shock. He . . . He's a diabetic." She did
not knock my hands away, or even seem to notice them.
"He's sick. Very sick."

I watched her small dark eyes focus sharp on my face,
the last vestiges of sleep replaced by suspicion. "I call," she
said sourly. "I call the nine-one-one. They send ambulance."

Oh Jesus! "No. No, *no.* There isn't time. We need to help
him now! See, all he needs is some sugar. Orange juice. He
has it right there in the apartment. *And he could die while
we stand here!* Do you have a key? In case he's unconscious." My body itched to dart to the left and run around
her, but I knew she could—and well might—flatten me.

I saw her face weigh it. She shrugged. "You go try knock
on door," she said at last. "I get key."

I took the stairs at a dead run.

The door at the top landing was painted a deep blood red:

Zach's color. I put my ear to it and listened hard. Nothing. Not even seven yet—they'd be sleeping. So much the better: element of surprise. "Zach," I hollered, banging at the door. "Clea. *Clea!*" I bashed at the door with hands and feet. *"I have the police out here!"* A stirring? Did I hear it? I leaned over again, ear against the door. Yes! A rustling, shuffling sound.

"You are liar." Kolonsky's voice was close enough to tickle my ear. She loomed huge behind me.

What the hell. *"Clea!"* I gave the door one more bash before her hand caught hold of my arm and held tight.

At that moment, the door opened. Clea stood there like a corpse propped vertical. Her sleeveless yellow dress was stained with purple, smudged with black. Her face was white, blank as a peeled boiled egg, and her hair was ropy and tangled. She smelled rank with old sweat. Behind her was chaos, destruction: furniture upended, cushions slashed open, remnants of food scattered randomly on the floor—everything covered with a snow of torn white paper. I took a step inside, my captor right there with me. The large room was stifling, the soggy air saturated with the stink of rancid pizza and stale wine.

She's killed him. A surfer's wave of nausea swept me. "Clea," I said almost soundlessly. I yanked free of Kolonsky's grip and enclosed Clea in a tight hug. "It wasn't your fault," I said into the matted red hair.

"I call police now." Kolonsky moved into the room, and began to search for a phone.

I stepped back and looked more closely at the room. As far as I could tell, all of the studio was right there to see; even the bathroom door was open wide. "Clea," I said, my hand holding on to her shoulder, which felt cold despite the hot room, "Where . . . Where's Zach?"

"Dunno," she mumbled dopily. Hard to tell how much of her haze was alcohol. "Not here."

"Not here?" I asked, my voice soaring with tension and hope. She shook her head, which then dropped to her chest with the effort.

I let out a long, ragged breath. *Thank you, God. I know you don't exist, but thanks anyway.* I spotted Clea's shoulder bag under the desk and scooped it up. "Look," I called over to Kolonsky, who'd finally retrieved the phone from the debris on the floor and was readying to use it, "wait a second. I *did* lie to you. I'm sorry. This . . . this is my sister. She's sixteen. Zach Terman is a rat bastard. He seduces girls. Uh, you know what seduces means? He takes them and—"

"I know what means," she growled impatiently. "I know what means. I know Terman." Her mouth looked ready to spit him out. "I see this girl here lots of times. Other girls, too."

"Please." I wasn't acting now. "Please just let me take her home. She's . . . You can see the shape she's in. I'll give you anything." I reached into my bag, laid hands on my wallet and pulled five twenties out. "Please," I repeated.

"I not believe you before. I think you some stupid girlfriend trying get in. So, let her in, I say to myself. Let her see." The small, bright bear eyes looked at me with something in them I hadn't seen before: compassion. "Take your sister. Go away." Her hand, which I now noticed was surprisingly small for her size, almost delicate, reached out and took the bills from my hand. "I take your money; I can use. And I clean up, don't worry. But is not really the money why I let you go," she said. "He is not good man, Terman."

18
. . . .

"WE'RE GOING HOME, CLEA. WE'RE GOING HOME now. It's over." I kept up the sound, as much for myself as for her, till we were safely in the car.

"I'm proud of you," I said determinedly as I pulled out of the space.

She looked at me, uncomprehending, as though I'd told a joke she didn't get, and then suddenly burst into tears. "Zach. He . . ."

I patted her shoulder with my right hand and kept driving. "I know, I know, honey, I know." She never dreamed he'd do it to her. She'd seen Ariane's fading bruises—wouldn't talk about them, and now I understood why—but he would never hit his Princess Clea: he *loved* her. "Looks like you defended yourself better than Ariane did. I'm so proud of you," I said again.

The crying stopped as abruptly as it had started. "You think he *hit* me?" she yelped, her fog cut by surprise. "He didn't hit me. He just never came. And he *promised*."

I'd started to change lanes and then didn't follow through, earning an angry pair of honks from the car behind me. If I had surprised Clea, she had astounded me. "I think you'd better tell me," I said carefully. She didn't speak. "*Now, Clea!*" Good old anger, always there in cold storage for me when other ways to feel became too complicated.

"This was our place," she said, "our special place. We took an oath in blood and wine, and Zach said that would fix the magic just between the two of us. He lived there when he first got back from Paris, and he said he'd keep the garret for the rest of his life, no matter how rich he got, because it reminded him of the Left Bank, and because it reminded him how far he'd come with nothing except his own imagination. You know, he was completely poor and nobody ever gave him anything." Her voice quavered as it caressed each part of the fairy tale. "We'd have Chianti in baskets and melt candles in the empty bottles. We'd order up pizza and sandwiches and have picnics on the floor, and the streetlight would shine in the triangle window like a private moon. We'd read to each other . . ."

I concentrated on not screaming, forced myself not to mention the wrecked apartment. "Clea, tell me about this time. What happened?"

"He didn't really want to come, but I got him to. I can always get him to do things." I gave her a quick glance and saw that secret I-am-woman smile on her face. "I knew that if we just had a couple days together, it would all be okay— back the way it was. And he *said!*" The woman vanished. She could have been eight, and furious at missing the circus.

"But he didn't come."

"No."

"How long did you intend to wait for him? How come you didn't bother to call your father, tell him some convenient lie?"

She sighed, finishing on an exasperated note. "You know I like to torture my father, don't you?" Sarcasm was back. It made her sound more normal. But only for a moment. "What day is today?" she asked in a small, bewildered voice.

"Thursday."

"I don't . . . I don't remember. I got here—Monday night, I guess it was—and I let myself in. I have the key. He's never given it to anyone else. He said he'd be there by nine, ten the latest, but he didn't come. I waited till midnight, then I opened some wine and had it myself, and then I guess I went to sleep."

Ariane and Clea, ladies-in-waiting, both of them, for a crazy overage adolescent who hit women to stiffen his cock and favored oaths in blood—and who by now was probably somewhere in the south of France with his new princess.

Clea continued with no prompting, but she still sounded only half there. "The next morning, I called his house, but she answered, and I hung up. I called the apartment, but all I got was a machine. And then . . . I was so mad. I guess I broke things. It kind of got strange after that—broken mirrors; broken glass. I don't know." Her voice trailed off into a yawn. "I'm tired," she said.

"Well, why don't you just lean back now and let yourself drift off." A few minutes later I heard soft snoring sounds, like a child getting over a cold. My own eyelids felt stiff, their insides gritty. I couldn't imagine closing them, or wanting to.

I'd accomplished my mission: gotten Clea out, somewhat the worse for wear, but safe—that was the thing. I should have been elated; what I was, was uneasy. She seemed balanced precariously on a ledge, ready to leap at any moment. Talk of broken mirrors; broken glass: the way life had looked to her just before she'd tried to end it almost three years ago.

I thought of Bart Held, right this minute probably shaving his face for the office, still angry with his incomprehensible daughter—not expecting the news that would rip his careful life apart. I'd seen flashes of a better Bart, as he argued literature with Ariane—one civilized intellectual to another—reasoned opinions bouncing back and forth between the two of them. No broken mirrors there; more to his taste than his turbulent late wife, his turbulent daughter.

I touched Clea's shoulder gently. "We're back. Wake-up time."

Her eyes opened fast and wide, like a doll's, and just as unseeing. "Wendy?" She blinked a few times. "Emily," she said carefully, as though making herself remember. She opened her window and stuck her head out. "It's a beautiful day, isn't it?" she asked sadly.

"I brought you to Orchards first. I thought you might want to get cleaned up before you see your father."

Her face focused itself sharp, and for a second I had the idea she was going to tell me again how much she liked to torture him. Instead, she fingered the wine stains, stiff and purple on her yellow dress. "I don't want to see this dress again. Ever," she said.

As I opened the door, the sound of Chris's tape player assaulted me. Of course he'd be here.

"Turn that damned thing down!" I blasted, louder than whatever group it was; louder than necessary. The music stopped dead, and he sauntered in from the dining room, dressed decorously in red tee-shirt and cutoffs. He did not work bare-chested any longer, at least not here. Clea's face broke into the relieved smile of a lost child spotting Daddy, and she ran into his open arms.

He looked at me over her head, his eyes registering something I'd never seen in them: alarm. After a moment, he moved out of the hug and gave her a slow once-over. "Hey Clee, what's up with you? You look like shit, and you stink!"

"I don't remember," she said after a beat. "I want to wash my hair." She started up the stairs.

"What the hell happened?" Chris asked me.

"You thought she needed a kick in the behind?" I snapped. "She got one. Over eighteen or not, she picked the wrong playmate."

I followed Clea upstairs, and gave her a set of clean clothes—the same ones she'd lent me after we'd gone riding that first time. While she was in the shower, I took the ruined dress and shoved it into the deepest recesses of the trash barrel. But before doing even that, I swiped the key to Zach's garret from her purse. Why, I couldn't have really said. Then I called Bart's office.

"Clea's with me, here at Orchards."

"She came back." The words were flat and resentful.

"Not exactly. I went and got her. I think you'd better get over here right away."

"I'm just going into a meeting, and—"

"And I am telling you, get here *now*."

"Is she . . . ? Has she . . . done something?" Stiff righteousness vaporized into terror.

"No, she's all right," I said fast. "But she's had a bad time."

"I'll be there in ten minutes." The voice was clipped, resigned. He did not know what had happened, just that somehow one more battle with his daughter had been concluded—and again he had lost.

Clea was still upstairs when Bart arrived. I took him into the living room and shut the door. Neither of us sat. The only way to say it was to say it. "I found Clea in Zach Terman's studio."

He stared at me. Just stared, while his face whitened and began to shine with a sudden sweat.

"They were having an affair."

"Clea?" he murmured, having difficulty with its syllables. "Zach with Clea? Did he . . . hurt her?" His lip began to tremble, readying to cry.

"No. No, he didn't hit her. He didn't even see her. She was supposed to meet him there, and he never showed up. She kind of fell apart."

His Adam's apple worked and then took a lurch. His hand went to his lips and pressed there for a second. "Could you excuse me?" he asked from behind closed teeth. "Where's the . . . bathroom?"

I opened the door and pointed him down the hall. It took him about ten minutes to return. When he did, he seemed back in control—shaken, pale, but a Bart Held I recognized.

"That man will not get away with this," he said evenly.

"I hope not," I said, with no clear idea of what I meant by it.

"Did you know about them?" He rounded on me with a quiet fury that made me doubt Chris's assessment about his uncle and biting deerflies.

"Cool it! I know you're looking for someone to blame, but I'm not it. *No one's* it! No, I didn't know about them, not till after you called about the car." I tried to take my own advice about cooling. "Look Bart, Clea's going to need some gentle handling right now. I'm worried about her."

"Join the club," he said bitterly. "Have you spoken to Ariane yet?" he asked.

Always Ariane for him. "Ariane can wait. We're talking about your daughter here. Wherever Zach is, he's still gone, and not with Clea. That's what's important. Maybe Ariane will be lucky and he won't come back," I added.

"Maybe," he said grimly.

Just then, Liam came down for breakfast. And, through the kitchen door, Jane, to measure something or another. All of a sudden, the place was full of people.

"Clea's upstairs," I said. "Let me go get her for you."

But I didn't need to. As I turned around, there she was, looking almost normal.

"Hello, Clea," Bart said, his mouth held tense with all the things it wasn't saying.

"Don't expect me to say I'm sorry."

"I don't expect anything at all from you," he said.

I remembered, crystal-clear, the disdain in my grandmother's face as she looked me in the eye and said, "You have not been worth it." I'd been close to Clea's age at the time. I had cut and run for L.A. two days later.

Bart started for the door. "Come on," he added without turning around, as though to a puppy who'd just soiled the rug. Clea followed behind him obediently, her face blushed pink with the effort of holding back tears.

"Poor kid," Liam said as the front door shut behind them. "If there was a God, he'd've arranged a different dad for her."

"He'd've arranged different dads for lots of us," I said.

Unexpectedly, he laughed. "Right you are. Why don't you get yourself a little sleep, girl. You look like you could use it."

For once, I had no argument with him.

19

"So that's it," I said to Dev. "I brought Clea back yesterday."

I lay on the library chaise, my death-damp purple shirt changed for a crisp, dry white one and shorts, my bad ankle wrapped in ice and dish towels. I'd been talking for what seemed like a long time. I hadn't told Dev precisely all of it—I'd skipped the parts about Chris Held and me—but I'd told him most of it, and if he sensed any censorship, he didn't say. And he hadn't interrupted to ask a single question.

I struggled to sit up, the alarm in my gut reawakened by hearing myself. I knew what I needed to do now—and I knew I couldn't do it on the phone.

"Dev, I need to do something. I need you to help me." I felt his hands warm on my shoulders, propping me up to sit.

"Wait a minute. Who's your frozen friend? The father or the lover?"

"Zach Terman."

He nodded. "Just making sure."

"Look Dev, before we call the police, I've got to go and see—"

"Emily. No. You can't do it."

But he didn't take his hands away, and with their support, I managed to pivot on my rear end and get my feet on the floor. I winced, but it was bearable. "You don't even know yet what it is I want to do."

"Sure I do. You want to go see your Clea." We exchanged the looks of a pair accustomed to viewing the same thing in opposite ways.

"What time is it?" I asked.

He checked his wrist. "Quarter to six."

"We can be back in an hour. We've waited an hour already. What the hell is the *difference?*"

"You've got to kick the habit of asking questions whose answers you don't want to hear. But now I'll ask you one. Do you think she killed him?" He knelt beside me, those purple eyes not letting me off the hook.

I stared straight back at him. "I don't know. And honestly, I don't think I care. I just want her to be safe." I stood up, leaning heavily against his shoulder. He stood too, and didn't let me fall.

"She's not safe, as you damned well know. Not any way at all. And you can't fix it for her."

"I am going to drive over there, Dev, with you or without you. You'll have to knock me down to stop me. I need to do this."

I watched his jaw muscles bump and grind as he made up his mind to go against his own grain. "Come on," he said finally. "I'll drive that hearse of yours, give you a bit more legroom than my car."

The Held house was dark. I was about to rouse the sleepers to disaster, and the knowledge stilled my hand on the bell push. Then when I began ringing, I couldn't seem to stop. After what seemed too long, I saw a light go on upstairs, heard stirrings. When Clea opened the door, my stuttering finger was nudging the chimes into one more falsely upbeat toll.

Her hair, backlit by the hall light, was a fiery halo. She wore her "What part of NO didn't you understand?" shirt and nothing else, her barefoot girl-legs extravagantly long and slightly bowed. I'd never noticed that little bowing before, but seeing it made me want to cry at her vulnerability. I took a deep breath and tried to gather up my own strings.

"This is Dev," I said.

Briefly, her face broke into a smile. "Of course it is," she said, eyes not fully open, still gummed with sleep. "What happened to your face, Emily?"

Before I could speak, Bart appeared in a neat blue robe, his blond head office-neat. Had he combed his hair before coming downstairs, or didn't it rumple, even when he slept? The skin around his eyes was rumpled, though.

"Emily, what is it?" he asked, everything about him quickly braced for a crash.

I couldn't make the words come. I wished hard to be back in my basement, where I could wrap that frozen thing in a sheet, and dump it someplace no one would ever find it. I saw myself tying strong knots at the ends of the fabric, hoisting the bundle up through the old coal chute. *Why couldn't you have just stayed gone, Zach? Why did you have to make someone kill you?*

Oh God, let it not be Clea. Please!

I took a step out from under Dev's arm—the pain in my ankle for the moment outranked by less specific pain—and put my hands on her shoulders, wanting to steady her against what she was going to hear; knowing it wouldn't do much good.

"Zach Terman is dead," I said.

Horror and hope fought for custody of Bart's eyes. "You?!"

"What?" For a second I didn't get it, and then I did. My hand went involuntarily to my face. "No, I didn't kill him. He's been dead awhile, I don't know how long. His body knocked me down, face first. It fell out of my grandmother's old basement freezer. I was looking for flashlights in the blackout."

I felt Clea's body tense under my hands, and saw on her face the panicked confusion of a suddenly trapped squirrel. "I didn't," she blurted. Her head turned toward Bart. *"I didn't, Daddy!"* I'd never heard her call him that. And it cracked my heart.

Instinctively, my arms wrapped themselves around her tight. "I've got you. We'll get through it. It'll be okay." I murmured those things you murmur to a loved child, while your own gut screams doubt that they are true.

"I didn't," she said loudly over my shoulder.

"Come inside." Bart's dry voice was at the point of breaking. "Clea . . ." Saying her name did it. He turned to me. "Is this a trooper?" he asked, noticing Dev finally.

"No, he's a friend of mine, a close friend."

"His name is Dev," Clea said, with the disconnected sound of a ventriloquist's dummy. "He's Liam's son."

"Mr. Held. Bart, is it?" Dev said. "Could we sit down someplace and talk?"

"Yes. Good idea." Bart's mouth tried a man-to-man smile, and gave up almost immediately.

Clea squirmed in my grip, and I set her free at once. My mother, coiled permanently inside me, tended to surface at unpredictable moments to grab at people, hold them too tight.

Each of us chose a separate chair, no one wanting to risk a sofa's potential for closeness. A flowered ginger-jar lamp cast a dim, nervous light on our faces.

"I haven't called the police," I said. "I came here first, before anything else."

Bart looked at me—suspicion, seasoned with a pinch of hostility. "Why?"

Clea's eyes were on me too, and I looked back at her as I spoke. "I wanted to make sure you were going to be okay," I said.

"Do you think I killed him?" The question was not only for me but for herself. She was not sure of its answer.

Of course not, don't be ridiculous, I wanted to lie: a big sister to be counted on. "I don't know," I said quietly. "But I do know this: If you did kill him, I don't want you to—"

"Get caught?" Bart's voice cut like a snapping whip. "What kind of nonsense are you suggesting? That she go 'on the lam'? Glamorous idea. I think you've been involved in too many movies." He turned to Clea, his face sending out blame waves. "John Heaney is going to be all over you, and—"

"Who's John Heaney?" I cut in.

"Major. Head of the state police, top of Westchester to Albany," Bart reeled off, each word a dart of resentment. "He knows us quite well," he added in a tone heavy with meaning.

"I think we're getting ahead of ourselves," Dev cut in dryly. "It wouldn't be exactly off the wall for Major Heaney to wonder whether *you* might have done the man in, Bart."

I watched the idea drop its way down into him like a quarter in a phone slot. "Yes, I see what you mean," he said, not moving an inch, not even glancing in Clea's direction. "But only a fool would get that carried away. A fool or a child," he added, his voice tight.

"What the fuck is the matter with you?" I shot back at

him. "That is your *daughter* over there, for Christ's sake! Why are you sitting across the room blaming her, like some stranger, when you don't even know what the hell's happened? You're supposed to be her father, remember? Help her! Hug her!" My eyes swam with sudden tears.

Bart stayed put, his face stony, desolate. "My daughter and I have not had a hugging relationship for some time, Emily," he said, "and blame in this house cuts two ways." Then he stood, as though his joints needed oiling. "Clea, in the circumstances, I believe we must talk to a lawyer, and you should probably have a session with Dr. Nicholas." And he strode out of the room, his eyes fixed straight ahead.

"You ice-cold bastard!" Clea shrieked at his back, and as each word ripped its way out of her throat, I felt the pain in my own. After he was gone, she sat very still, rubbing her finger back and forth along her lips, as though puzzling something. Moments later, she looked up at me. "Emily," she whispered hoarsely, "I . . . I didn't do it. I don't see how I could have. You know?"

"You mean because you loved him too much?"

"No!" Her impatience at being misunderstood slashed through everything in its way. "Not because of that. I *did* love him, but . . . Well, I blurred out there in the garret, I told you that. I was so mad when Zach didn't come, and I—well, you saw—I trashed the place. And while I was doing it, I remember kind of slashing at the air, yelling, 'I could kill you.' I mean, if he'd walked in right then, I might have killed him, and made myself forget it. But then, he'd be there in the garret, wouldn't he? How would he have gotten to your basement?"

"I don't know," I said simply, and felt a ray of light warm inside me. Call it the look on her face; call it a ring in her voice; call it wishful thinking. I had no facts to back me up, but I believed her. I stole a glance at Dev, and saw that he was going through the same process I was, but not necessarily ending up in the same place.

"Clea. Clea, look at me. This is important." I waited until the honey eyes fully met mine. "I don't know whether the police will find your name when they search Zach's things, but if they do, when they come to question you, hang on to what you just said. Remember it, no matter what anyone else tries to push you to say. You went to meet Zach. When he did not show up, you got angry. You broke some crockery, tore up some papers, kicked over some furniture. You drank too much wine. You waited, but he never did show up. And you never saw him again. Got it?''

She looked away, down at her fingers, which had begun to braid themselves in her lap. ''Got it?'' I repeated. ''You never saw him again.''

''Zach is dead,'' she told her hands. ''And I don't feel anything. I loved him. I loved him so much, and when you told me, I didn't feel a thing, not even sorry. All I could think of was, *Not me. Not me. I didn't do it.* What's the matter with me, Emily? Something bad must be.''

I put my arms around her again, not clutching tight this time, and she seemed to like them there. ''Lots, little sister. Lots is the matter with you. You are a moody, fanciful, willful, sarcastic, temperamental pain in the ass—just like I am. But what's *not* the matter with you is how you feel about Zach right now. You are numb, and that's what the folks out there call normal. You'll feel something. Believe me, you will.''

''And what do *you* feel, Emily?'' she asked, like the small voice of conscience.

I answered her true. ''I feel mad. Mad at Zach for being asshole enough to get himself killed, and even madder at whoever stowed him in my freezer.''

Bart came back, dressed now in khakis and a neat striped shirt. ''You'd better go home, Emily,'' he said, a man of business taking charge of the situation. ''I thank you for . . . for coming here first, but you really do have to call the police.''

''Bart,'' I said, my ankle beginning to throb again, ''have you told anyone about Clea and Zach?''

''I told Ariane yesterday,'' he answered, looking away. ''She was . . . distraught.'' Suddenly, he turned and rounded on Clea. ''Understand, I am glad that Zach Terman is dead, and whatever your defender Emily thinks, I am not accusing you of killing him. But do you know the damage you've done? Do you have any idea how many lives you've trampled on?!'' Her chin raised in defiance; she wouldn't have answered to save her life.

"Clea," he said in another voice, one of forced calm. "I'm leaving for a little while. Henry Talley is coming here to talk with us at nine. Can I trust you to stay put until then?" She made a face of disgust. "I know you don't like him, but he's a damned good lawyer, and we will listen to what he has to say, and you will do as he tells you. I've left a message with Dr. Nicholas's service."

She shot up her hand in a Nazi salute. "Don't *do* that," she said when he didn't respond. "Don't treat me like some naughty kid." Her face blushed that furious pink.

And his went white. "You have never stopped behaving like one. Everything your way. You complain about treatment? Do you have any conception of what it might be like to have your child try to kill herself? What a Damoclean sword that is? How terrified I am most of the time? I am not your Hitler; you are *mine!*" He ended in a scream of pain, his voice shaking as though racked with a sudden chill.

Nobody spoke for what felt like a long time; then Bart cleared his throat. "I am going to go over to Ariane's now. I don't want her to have to learn about her husband's murder from a state trooper."

I gave Clea's arm a small squeeze. "I'm okay, Emily," she said absently. She was staring at Bart, with a look I couldn't completely read. But I thought I saw an edge of satisfaction in it. "My father and I understand each other perfectly."

"D̶ev." L̶iam rose, teacup still in hand, an un-
settled smile on his face, and looked at his son. "I've been
expecting you, you know."

"You look ready for the country club, you old bastard,"
Dev said. "Sandals? And a tan? Maybe I should have stayed
away longer. You'll be taking up cricket next." But neither
moved in closer, and Dev's face didn't match the banter.
Their past together would never allow that kind of freedom.

"What's happened to you, Emily?" Liam did move now,
the smile gone from his face, and stopped himself just short
of touching me. Stopped because of my inadvertent flinch.

"Dev'll tell you," I said quickly, not sure whether the
sadness I suddenly felt was over Zach, or Clea, or Liam.

The trooper on phone duty made me repeat everything
twice. He was a slow writer. Then he asked my name a third
time. "Silver? You said Orchards, didn't you? The Otis
place. You a guest there?"

"I own it," I snapped, a quick flash of imperiousness
straight from the Tucker gene pool. Unwarranted. "I'm
sorry. Mrs. Otis was my grandmother. I'm an actress; Silver's my working name."

"You discovered the body, Miss Otis?"

"I did, yes. You coming over here, or what?"

"Oh, not me, but they'll be over. You can count on that—
no more'n ten minutes or so." I had the wild idea he was
going to tell me to have a good day.

"You want some tea?" Liam asked, not waiting for an
answer before he poured. "So, who knocked him off?" He
lobbed the question with little apparent interest.

"I don't know, Liam. You seem to be taking it in stride."

"Didn't really know the man, did I? Everything I've
heard, the world's better off without him. Surely Clea is."

"The police are going to give Clea a hard time, Liam.

They're going to think maybe she did it.''

"Balls." He said it fast enough and flat out enough to surprise me.

"How do you know?" Dev asked.

"That little girl wouldn't kill anybody." He looked at me over the rim of his cup as he sipped. "Emily might; Clea wouldn't."

Dev and I traded looks. We both knew how certain I'd once been that I could kill—and how uncertain he'd been that I wouldn't.

"Yes," I said, "I might. But Clea might too. She did try to kill herself once."

His face didn't react. "So she did. She'll not try it again."

"Now, how can you possibly know that?"

"Because her mother's dead."

"I don't think I understand."

"No, I don't think you do. Remember what I said about Clea getting lost in people? Well, that mother of hers had the hooks into that girl; played around with her like she was some personal doll. And who was the mother? A selfish drunk who read a lot of books, fooked a lot of men, and managed to kill herself in the end." He registered the twist of Dev's mouth. "I know what you're thinking, Dev. Who am I to talk? Another selfish drunk. Well, maybe I'm just the one to talk."

"And what about you?" Dev asked quietly. "Are you going to try it?"

"What? Oh, suicide, you mean. No, not just now, I think." I had to smile. He sounded like a polite guest refusing an hors d'oeuvre. He smiled back at me, with grave eyes. "Will you keep me a while longer, Emily?"

"Yes, I will." It felt odd to say that, and mean it. Something had just changed between Liam and me—and I wasn't at all sure what. The doorbell sounded. "Here we go," I said. I hoisted myself up onto Dev's arm, and we went to open it.

Two of them stood in the doorway, both in plain clothes, while four others in uniform piled out of police cars. The older one was three or four inches over six feet—sixty or so, slim and fit: the kind of guy you could imagine holding his own in backyard football with his kids and grandkids. He wore a slightly baggy gray suit, a little too short in the sleeves. The other, in a tan suit that almost could have been a uniform, was about my age and chunky, sprouting a mound of fast-food belly.

I saw them take in my bruised face, but neither commented.

The younger one moved into the doorway and spoke first. "Miss Otis?" I nodded. In the damp heat, I caught the freshly laundered smell of his shirt. "I'm Darrell Weems—Special Investigator. This is Major Heaney, our commander."

So this was the John Heaney Bart Held feared. "How do you do, Miss Otis?" He stuck out a rawboned hand. As I took it, I thought I saw a flicker of impatience cross his face. He couldn't know anything dangerous to Clea yet, so I figured that the presence of someone of his rank must be ceremonial—a tribute matching my grandmother's rank in Millbrook society. I remembered that the point man on Mike's murder had been an LAPD sergeant.

"I don't do all that well this morning," I said, too sharply. "This is Paul Hannagan. He and his father are my houseguests." The three men nodded at one another, manlike. "Do you want me to show you where it is?"

"Yup," Darrell Weems said. "Medical examiner'll be here in a few—and our crime-scene fellas. Let's go take a look."

Dev and I escorted them down without further comment. On the way, I saw them glance at Liam's back at the stove putting a fresh kettle on to boil. I offered no introduction.

"Well, there he is," I said. Zach lay just as I'd left him, except for the beginnings of a dampness on the floor around him and beads of moisture on his blue face. Seeing him again was no shock at all. In the moment, it seemed to me that he had been lying right there for as long as I could remember, and that he always would be.

"So you knew this man, Miss Otis? Zachary Terman. That the name you said on the phone?" Heaney asked. An answer wasn't really needed. I nodded. "Did you know him well?"

"No. Not well. He was married to an old school friend of mine. She and I hadn't seen each other for years until a couple of weeks ago." Weems asked for Ariane's name, address, and phone, and jotted the information down on a small pad he'd fished out of his back pocket—with a bit of difficulty, because of the tightness of his pants in the seat.

"What happened to your face, Miss Otis?" Weems asked, sounding sneakily casual, as though baiting a trap.

"His body dropped out and fell on me. I was down here groping around for a flashlight last night during the blackout. My match died and I tripped and released the freezer handle."

"You don't see these tall old verticals much anymore," Heaney observed. "My mother had one. Got rid of it years ago."

"My grandmother didn't much care about appliances, Major Heaney. Comes of having other people do your housework." I heard the snotty edge on my voice, and wished I could stop it.

"I guess so," he agreed, choosing not to be offended.

"The body just where it fell?" Weems this time.

"Yes."

"The blackout, you said, Miss Otis," Heaney began, and I knew where he was going. "That was over about three, three-thirty where I live, middle of Millbrook. What about here?"

"About the same time," I said. It would have been stupid to lie.

He made a point of checking his watch—a bit of overkill, I thought. "Seven thirty-five. What took you so long to call us?"

"I don't know," I said, as blank-faced as I'd been the whole time. The L.A. cops who'd handled Mike's murder had found me unnatural—sullen and uncooperative, when I ought to have been grief-stricken and compliant. I didn't expect it would be any different with these.

"The body knocked her cold for a while, and when she came to, that ankle kept her from getting up the stairs," Dev said smoothly. "I drove up here unexpectedly late. Fortunately I heard her hollering. It took some time to get her calmed down, get her bruises attended to."

"I see," Heaney said, his eyes on me. "I had the idea that maybe you wanted to go break it to his wife, before you called us? Understandable, old friend of yours. But you didn't do that?"

"No." I felt the roots of my hair start to sweat.

Heaney's eyebrows went up. He had a nicely used face, mouth with the potential for humor; good joke-teller, I'd bet—affectionate with his wife. I could have liked him, but he was the leader of the other team.

"So you pulled yourself together for a coupla, three hours before you called us."

I made a point of looking at his narrow gray eyes. "I was upset. My face hurt, and my ankle, and my shoulder." Heaney's return look said nothing.

Footsteps on the stairs, at just the right time. "Morning, fellas." The man was short and round, with half-glasses, a red bow tie, and a face with a default expression of cheerfulness. He looked me over with moderate curiosity. "You Emily?" At my nod, he put out his hand to shake. "Walter de Jaan. I knew your grandmother. From the hospital board."

"New York Hospital?" I asked as I took it. Of all her causes, that had been her favorite. She'd co-chaired a benefit luncheon for some new wing or other the day she died.

"No, no. I don't have much truck with the city. Vassar Brothers. We're small, comparatively, but she found some time for us." He put his doctor's bag down next to Zach's body, and turned to the two troopers. "Got something to tell me about what we've got here?"

"Darrell'll fill you in, Walt," Heaney said. "Miss Otis and I are going to go upstairs for a little more talk. If Mr. Hannagan will excuse us."

Dev left us at the library door. I settled myself quickly behind the big desk, as though it were a barricade. Heaney began, affable as he'd been since he'd arrived. "When was the last time you saw Mr. Terman? Alive, I mean."

"Almost two weeks ago. He's been away—at least I thought he was." They'd find out before the day was over that Zach had left Ariane, but they weren't going to find it out from me. Mindlessly stubborn, I supposed, or a superstitious bargain with the gods that if I didn't tell about Ariane, she wouldn't tell about Clea. Well, perhaps for Bart's sake she wouldn't.

"Away since when?"

"A week ago last Monday," I answered. Too quickly. "That's what his wife said." He saw my effort at repair; he didn't miss much.

"Where'd you think he was?"

"I had no idea."

I leaned in across the desk, my face disarmingly sincere, I hoped. "Look, Major Heaney, you suggested that I'd contacted Ariane before I called you. The fact is, I *didn't* call her—and I feel bad about that; she's a very old friend. I'd like to go see her now. She shouldn't have to hear about Zach from troopers." Somehow, those words had sounded more convincing in Bart's mouth.

"Who has access to your house, Miss Otis?" Heaney asked, as though I hadn't spoken.

"All of Millbrook. It's never locked, except at night, and I'm having some renovations done, so people are in and out all the time."

"Name the ones you know of. We won't worry for the moment about the rest of Millbrook."

I ticked off Chris and Jane, and the cleaning crew, whose last names I found I didn't know, much less anything else about them. "Chris and his helpers ought to be here any minute, if they're not already. You can talk to them yourself."

"What about friends? You do a lot of entertaining?"

"No, hardly at all. I don't really know anyone here anymore."

"You know Terman's wife. Who else?"

"Bart Held and his daughter, Clea." I concentrated on sounding neutral.

"Clea," Heaney said almost under his breath, and shook his head slowly. His face took on a wouldn't-you-know-it? look, which worried the hell out of me. "Darrell'll drive you over to Mrs. Terman's soon as he's done with the M.E. and the crime-scene boys. I don't have any more questions for you at the moment.''

Even I knew that it would be unwise to pull anything on him, like slipping out without waiting for Darrell Weems.

"Send in your friend Mr. Hannagan, if you would. I'd like to have a word with him, and after that, with his father."

As I limped my way down the hall, I almost collided head-on with Chris, who reached out a steadying hand and gave my face the same speculative scan everyone else had.

"I guess you've heard," I said.

"Sure have. Some guy got killed and stored in your freezer. Do they know who he was?"

I never got to answer. Weems's arm draped itself across Chris's shoulder, hand clapping him a firm thunk on the bicep. "Yo, buddy. This one of your gigs?"

"Right, Darrell. And I guess you're here on one of yours." Weems dropped his hands to his sides and shifted his weight awkwardly—one leg to the other, and back again, embarrassed at being observed fraternizing with a suspect, I supposed. The word, even unspoken, jolted me. But of course it was the right one. We were all suspects, weren't we?

"How's Lorrie?" Chris asked. "And the baby?"

"Sharon'll be four months next week. And Lorrie'll be great soon as her waistline comes back and she can get some sleep. What she is now is grouchy." He made a face and switched himself into professional mode. "You been doing maintenance here from when Mrs. Otis was still alive, right Chris?"

"Right. And I'm doing some painting, wallpapering for Emily here. Just installed central A.C."

"Ever have occasion to open that freezer while you were working down there in the basement?"

"Nope."

"Ever meet this fella?"

"Don't know who the fella is."

"Zachary Terman's the name."

"Nope."

"I saw Lisa Pontecorvo out there in the kitchen. She helping you out here?"

"Yeah. Smart kid. Starting her third year at Marist in the fall."

So Lisa was a Pontecorvo, a name as well known locally as Held: Pontecorvo Pharmacy; Pontecorvo Liquors. Pretty, round, juicy Lisa, rubbing arms with Chris, laughing, flirting. Maybe she'd met Zach Terman, too, somewhere in town. Had he wooed her with picnics and poems? Had they screwed each other in my bedroom?

"Well, I'm, uh, gonna want to talk to you later, Chris. Take your 'official statement.' " His self-mocking formality kidded the starchy words.

"Just give a shout when you want me," Chris said, and started to walk toward the front stairs. "I'll be upstairs. Hard to think of Lorrie grouchy," he added. Darrell Weems couldn't see Chris's face, but I could. His smile had a tinge of nostalgia to it.

21

....

WEEMS AND I LEFT HALF AN HOUR LATER FOR ARI-
ane's. Dev was still closeted in the library with Heaney. I
wondered uneasily what they might be talking about that
long. To get to Weems's unmarked car, we had to cross lines
of yellow tape, wound like streamers around the front of the
house, and as we left the grounds, I saw a gathering group
of press cars and T.V. vans, stopped from entering the private
road by a pair of resolute troopers. That scene and Weems's
portly body next to me in the driver's seat kept me edgily
aware of the charade: we were going to Ariane with news
that was not news at all; Bart Held had already broken it to
her.

And maybe it hadn't been a surprise.

The thought had been circling in my mind for the last
hour or so. Despite the protestations of devotion I'd heard
from her freshly bruised mouth, I knew damned well that,
love or no love, husbands killed wives, wives killed husbands.

"Take the next right," I said to Weems. "Did you and
Chris go to school together?" I asked, just to ease the silence. My guess was that any questioning of me was to be
left to Heaney.

"Yeah, Lorrie was in his class at Millbrook High. I was
a year ahead of them. He's some guy," he added admiringly.

*And do you know about him and Lorrie? Or do you
choose not to?* "How do you mean?" I asked.

"You shoulda seen him—basketball, football, baseball.
Never seen a guy with moves like that. I played too, you
know. I wasn't always porky like this. But Chris had the
stuff—coulda gone pro, I bet. At least in baseball."

"I wonder why he didn't."

"Well, you know how it goes; he had responsibilities.
Hey, he's grown himself a damned good little business right

here in Millbrook. And you should see the house he built. Well, I say built, but I guess I mean *re*built. Burnt-out old shell to start with, out in Stanfordville. He picked it up for nothing, four acres, besides, and . . . well, put it this way, Lorrie and me, we'd give our eyeteeth.'' He paused for a moment. I saw his tongue make a sweep under his upper lip, checking maybe to see that his eyeteeth were still in place. ''I suppose Chris might've left and gone and done something else, 'cept for his mother. Dolores never was well, and she didn't have anyone but Chris.''

''She died, didn't she?''

''Little over three years ago. But hey, Chris is doing great, and he'd've been a little old for a baseball rookie anyway.''

''That's the driveway, right there,'' I said, talk of Chris and the Helds banished to the back of my mind.

''I've heard about this place,'' he said as the car curved upward around the hill and the house became visible. ''So Terman was the guy put up the castle.''

Winona, the housekeeper, answered the door. Her face gave no sign she'd ever seen me before, and she barely looked at Weems as she said that Mrs. Terman was not home.

''When did she go out, ma'am?'' Weems asked.

''Wouldn't know,'' the woman said. ''I got here no more than ten minutes ago. She wasn't here.''

''You don't live in?''

''No *sir.*'' She shook her head emphatically. ''Live in? Good Lord, I've got my own house to look after. No, with my husband's state pension, I don't need but two days' work, and I give those to Mrs. Terman. You want to leave her a note or something?''

''I'm Investigator Weems, ma'am. State police?'' He eased his I.D. folder from his pocket and handed it to her to study. Courtly, respectful to his elder. ''Any idea when she might be back?''

The woman's brows drew together like a pair of doors closing on intruders. ''What's wrong?'' were her words, but the tune was, ''What are you trying to pull? You won't get away with it.''

"Just answer my question, if you would, ma'am. Any idea when she'll be back?"

"Could be anytime. Sometimes she plays her tennis first thing in the morning; sometimes she . . . Is this about the mister?"

Ariane's car appeared around the bend in the winding road, and the housekeeper's question hung unanswered in the warm, still air.

Ariane pulled up and slid quickly out of the car. She was not dressed for tennis; I hadn't expected she would be. But neither had I expected the utter happiness I saw in her face. It pinked her cheeks, glowed deep in her eyes. And I knew at once how wrong I'd been. We would be telling her something she did not know.

"Emily. What a nice surprise." She took a closer look. "What's happened to your face? Did you fall?" I nodded as I watched her, slightly puzzled, notice the stranger.

"I'm Special Investigator Weems, Mrs. Terman." He offered his I.D. as he had to Winona, but Ariane ignored it, and he put it away. "I've got some bad news for you. Could we maybe go inside?"

"Jamie?" The fear in her face was naked. Her lips remained parted, as though unable to shut themselves around her brother's name.

I stepped forward, my hands wanting to reach out to her, but unable somehow to do it. "No Ariane," I said woodenly, "not Jamie. It's Zach. He's dead. I found him last night in my basement."

At first she just stared—her eyes straight into mine, not comprehending what she'd heard. And then it hit, like something touching bottom finally in a deep well. Her mouth twitched. It seemed to be trying to speak, but there was no sound. I moved fast to take her arm, to steady her. But at the touch of my hand, she jerked ferociously away, and the look in her eyes hardened into something remarkably like fury.

A split second later, she went lifeless, appeared to be on the point of fainting. Again I reached out, short of touching this time, to break her fall if she went down. But she didn't. I stood there dumb, inches from her—breathing the spicy citrus perfume she wore, watching her torment, remembering the moment I learned about Mike's murder. I saw the same shock, the same anger burn their way into Ariane. She was not acting this. I would swear to it.

"I need to be alone now," she said, as though reciting in a foreign language, and walked between Weems and me—not looking at either of us—into the house.

Winona, hands on hips, stood in the doorway, blocking Weems's move to follow.

"Give her some time, can't you," she said, tears pumping themselves to the surface of her dark eyes.

I pictured Major Heaney efficiently moving Winona aside, like an upholstered easy chair in his path, but Weems's style was different; he backed off.

"No problem, ma'am. I'll just wait out here for a bit, let Mrs. Terman get herself settled."

"I am going inside, Winona," I said with a trumped-up tone of authority borrowed from Cordelia Tucker Otis. "I want to make sure that Ariane hasn't passed out. Then, if she wants me to leave, I will." I began to walk as though expecting Winona to move aside. Grudgingly, she did.

"That woman's a saint, you know. All she is to everybody is good. Only good," she said as I passed her. "She took such care of him, and he didn't appreciate nothing."

"You worked for them a long time, Mrs. . . . ?" Weems asked mildly. I stopped to listen.

"Mrs. Stringer. Ever since they moved in here—two years, two months, it's been."

"Sounds like they had their problems." She didn't respond right away. "I'm a policeman, Mrs. Stringer," he added mildly. "You're gonna have to answer me."

"They got along. I don't know how long you been married, Mr. Policeman, but getting along's not exactly what you call even steven. Oh, he could be sweet sometimes, especially after he was mean. A coupla times, I saw him walk in and give her a present, all wrapped up—and he'd kneel down, right in front of her, never even mind that I was in the room. And she'd smile, lean down and kiss his head.

"One time, he hollered at me for moving something in that little office room of his, and next time I showed up, he give me this silk scarf, butterflies all over it. You could tell it was expensive. Bow on the box and everything. Well, I thanked him, of course, but I said—just the way I'd say to my son, my Kyle—I said, 'Mr. Terman, I appreciate the scarf, and I appreciate the thought. But don't you ever holler at me again. I do something not the way you want it around here, you tell me, like a civilized person—or, scarf or no scarf, what you can tell me is goodbye.' ''

"You said that sometimes he was mean. Could you tell me a little more about that?" Weems asked.

"I don't really know anything, except he'd holler sometimes," she said in the cold, clipped way of someone who's decided she'd talked too much already. "Not my business, is it?"

"Ever see him hit her?"

"No." She turned angrily on me. "Didn't you say you was going to see to her? What're you standing there for?"

She had me nailed, and I marched myself quickly up the curved stone staircase. I had no idea where to find Ariane, but figured her bedroom would be the logical place. I guessed wrong; she was in Zach's dark-paneled study, sitting behind his desk, her face staring lifelessly at his computer.

I didn't quite enter the room. "Ariane, I'm sorry. I know that may be hard to believe, considering the things I've said about Zach. I can't tell you I didn't mean them, but I'm sorry he's dead." It was true: not entirely true, but mainly true. If he'd turned up with a nice, clean fatal heart attack, I suspect I'd have felt enormous relief.

"I don't care," she said absently, her eyes fixed now somewhere above my head. "I don't care what you feel or don't feel. It doesn't make any difference."

It was honest, and missing even a drop of her normal social lubricant. I had the sense that the woman sitting there was someone I didn't know at all. "Bart came over here very early this morning to tell you. He didn't want you to hear it from the police—or, I suppose, from me either. I guess you weren't home."

"No."

And where, I wondered, were you before seven in the morning? But even I wasn't clumsy enough to ask. "That trooper, Weems, is waiting outside. He won't go away. You will have to talk with him soon, and I'll bet his boss will be coming to see you too." I felt my mouth bend into a bitter smile. "We're VIP's, you and me and the Helds, they send out the big guns." All at once tact, even rudimentary decency, stopped mattering. If I didn't say it then, it would be too late. "Look Ariane, Clea had nothing at all to do with his death. Unless you mention her name, she won't be dragged into it."

Her face didn't react—not with outrage; not with anything else. To all appearances, she hadn't heard me. "It doesn't matter," she said softly. Then, suddenly, the blaze of fury returned to her eyes and ignited her face. Her voice was choked as it said, "It's all over." I watched her fight for control, and felt like queen of the rats. "Tell them I'll be down in fifteen minutes," she said, coldly calm. "And Emily, I would like you to leave. I don't want you here just now."

22

....

I WALKED SLOWLY DOWNSTAIRS. HEANEY HAD ARRIVED,
I saw, and surprisingly, so had Dev. They sat, along with
Darrell Weems, waiting in the living room. Winona was no-
where in sight.

"She'll be down in fifteen minutes," I said.

Heaney stood and nodded. "We'll want to speak to Mrs.
Terman in private. I asked your friend Paul here to come on
over so he could drive you home. You can come back later,
if you care to."

Even though, in nervous formality, I'd introduced him by
his proper first name, it was always strange for me to hear
him called Paul. The one time in her life Mim actually did
insist on something, she'd prevailed. She'd named her son
for his French Canadian grandfather, and Liam's commem-
orative Eamon De Valera tag had taken second place. But
Dev he'd been until he was ten. That's how Mike had known
him, and how I'd met him. Now, his father and I were the
only ones who called him that.

"Very thoughtful of you, Major Heaney," I said formally.

"I'm starved," I said to Dev the second we were out the
door. "Let's go get something to eat—and let's get it somewhere that isn't home, okay?"

"Just tell me where to point the car." He opened the
passenger door of his Mazda and took my arm, as though I
were a dowager. "How's the ankle doing? Looks like you're
getting around efficiently—limping almost as well as I do."

"From lack of thinking about it, I guess." I slid myself
into the seat. "You and Heaney seem to have gotten buddy-
buddy pretty fast," I said, unable to strain a note of wariness
from my voice. He shut the door with more energy than was
necessary.

We headed toward Poughkeepsie, and found some anonymous cavern of a diner. Somehow, the idea of the one in

Millbrook did not appeal to me at the moment. We took the drive in silence.

The place was beginning to fill with lunchers, but since it was about the size of the Hollywood Bowl, getting a table was no problem. What I craved was dorm food. I ordered a chicken salad and bacon on white toast, and my first chocolate milk shake in possibly ten years. Dev asked for soft scrambles and coffee.

"Ariane didn't do it." A dull ache between my eyes started up as I spoke. "I thought she must have; I wanted it to be her," I admitted, feeling more than slightly ashamed of myself. "But Dev, you should have seen her. She was . . . She was the way I was when the police called to tell me about Mike. I watched the life go out of her. I couldn't mistake that."

"The field is narrowing quickly, then. Somebody did it. Clea? Bart? Don't discount our Bart. He had a prime pair of reasons for doing Zach."

Clea's father a killer: it would destroy them both. "Does it have to be one of them?"

"No, it could be two of them. Or three—teamwork." The thunder in my face stopped him. "Okay, maybe not any of them, but it does have to be someone familiar enough with Orchards to know its basement pretty damned well." His eyes challenged me across the table. "Stop playing patty-cake with yourself, Emily. That man was almost certainly murdered by someone you know. If not one of those three, then who? Handyman? Decorator? One of the cleaning people?"

I didn't snap back. The widening range of possibilities gave me heart. In the unexpected moment of calm, I savored the satisfying crunch of toast and bacon swathed in smooth luncheonette-style chicken salad, and let a question that had been hovering around my edges move front and center. "Was Zach actually killed in my basement, or did someone bring him there?"

"Hard to know. If somebody dumped him, I'd guess he came through that old coal chute, same way I did. Car backs right up to it, killer drops the body in, slides down after it, drags it to the freezer, hoists it inside, and then walks up the cellar steps and leaves—or doesn't leave: goes about business, maybe, or has some coffee. Maybe the safest time to do it would have been late at night; you fast asleep in one of those thick-walled old rooms, Liam in the other. You have no alarm on the place, do you?"

"No." I screened the action he'd just laid out, and felt queasy as my head cast and recast the killer role. I couldn't make it play any way I liked. "Pretty strenuous activity, isn't it, carting around a dead man?"

"Sure it would take some strength," he admitted, "but no major lifting required. And Terman wasn't a big man. Hundred forty, would you say?"

Clea didn't weigh a hundred ten, and Ariane was no taller than five four. But Clea lifted weights, did gymnastics, rode horses, and Ariane played daily killer tennis.

"You would have been able to do it, Emily, and so would those women. If that's how it happened, some evidence would likely be stuck to the seat of my jeans. Heaney and I became buddies, by the way, when I told him about the chute, and offered to drop my pants for him. Maybe that will help mend fences, when he learns about our early-morning visit to the Helds."

"Mend fences? Well, I don't give a flying—"

"I'm going to yell cut right there, actress. You *need* to give a flying fuck about Heaney. He is a very smart cop. If he isn't onto Clea, one way or another, within a day, I will be amazed, yea verily speechless. It took him a second and a half to spot something off-key about your delay in phoning it in, and dunce that I am, I backed you up. When he finds out we went tripping off to warn the Helds, he is not going to be happy with either of us."

"I don't need him to be happy with me."

"If you could see for a moment beyond the confines of your own skin, you'd realize that all you've done is hurt Clea's credibility. You might as well've sent Heaney a letter saying that you're afraid she did it. And I'm worse for going along with it, because I'm no amateur. I should have grabbed you by your bad ankle and knocked you cold."

The freshly eaten sandwich dropped in a sodden lump to

the pit of my stomach. What he'd said had a painful ring of truth.

"Tell me about the rest of it. What was he, strangled?"

"No. Crushed windpipe—some kind of quick chop. No sign of struggle. Looks like the man was either drugged or dozing, and we'll know about drugged in a day or two, as soon as they can defrost him and do the autopsy."

"I wonder how long Zach's been dead," I said.

"I wouldn't be too surprised if the M.E.'s wondering also. Freezing's a bitch, especially if it's done promptly."

"What I really mean is, did he come back sometime during the week and get killed, or did he never leave?"

"The night before he supposedly took off, he paid you an impromptu visit, right?"

"Yes. And left intact—though if he'd hung around one minute longer, I damned well might have killed him myself." I had my first sickening flashback of Zach's bug-eyed, blue face, and knew it wouldn't be my last.

"So, you saw him Saturday night. His wife claims he left her Sunday night. And Clea took off for the city more than a week later—Monday—to keep a date you'd overheard them make on the phone two days before he disappeared."

"That's right."

He leaned across at me and fired. "Did Clea know he was going to leave Ariane? Were they in any contact during that intervening week? If not, didn't she find his silence at all strange in this hot and heavy romance of theirs? Where did she think he was?" The questions hit me like stinging pellets of birdshot—only a preview of the way Heaney would come at Clea. That was Dev's point, and he'd made it. But he wouldn't let me up. "Here's another one for you: Where's Zach Terman's car?"

I let my head fall into my hands, and for the first time, missed the curtaining fall of my old, wild hair. "You want me to just holler uncle? Is that it?" I raised my head and I looked straight at him. He was not going to mow me down with footwork. "I know you think I'm off the wall. A wild card, isn't that what you called me once? Well, you're right, but I love Clea, and I fucking well won't let her go down the tube. You say I'm playing patty-cake? Well, Professional

Investigator, what can I do to help her that *isn't* patty-cake?''

"Fair question." His face dropped its attack mask. "I don't want you to holler uncle, and I'm by no means convinced that your little sister killed him. In fact, if he was killed after she went to the city, I'd say she's clear. As she pointed out herself, no way she could've killed him in his studio, gotten him down four flights of stairs, and transported him back to Orchards, especially without a car."

"And she didn't kill him before she left, either," I said, decisive now. "I cannot see Clea strangling Zach, stowing him in my freezer, going on to spend a blitheful week adoring your father, and then running off to Zach's studio to work herself into a hysterical stupor pretending to wait for him. This morning, I told you I didn't know whether she'd killed him, and that was true this morning. But it isn't now. I know she can lie, and I know she likes to play games, but she is not a psychopath. She did not kill him."

"Let's suppose I agree with you," he said offhandedly. "Is Clea as sure she didn't kill him as you are?"

I bit my lower lip while I tried to find a version of yes that I could believe. But I kept hearing echoed snatches of her talk about broken mirrors and visions blurred—not quite real. The taste of blood let me know I was biting harder than I'd realized. I reached into my pocket and pulled out a twenty. "Let's get out of here," I said. He got up. Surprisingly, he took hold of my hand, and we rushed out of the huge diner together like a pair of battered runaway kids.

I watched Dev's profile as he drove, nose straight, jaw and chin sharp, almost jagged. He'd lost weight; under the gold of his skin he looked tired, and not merely from the lack of one night's sleep. I wanted to touch him, but sensed that if I did, it might be beyond me to stop. The time was wrong, the place was wrong. At the moment, everything I could think of was wrong.

To the left on 44, I spotted a big, cityish Radisson Hotel— new to me—and stopped thinking. "Why don't you pull into that parking lot?" I asked, barely loud enough to be heard. He glanced quickly at me, and at the last possible second, swerved into a turn.

• • •

"Hello."

"Hello."

We spoke the word—each of us—with the almost shy civility of acquaintances on the steps of a library or church, not lovers at the door of a hastily booked hotel room.

Dev walked past me inside, then stopped, turned back and reached out a hand. His magnetic draw, the exact opposite of Chris Held's, was so intensely personal that it left me breathless with its danger. I saw, as I had in my dream, the two of us alone in a universe that was nothing more than a sheet of clean, white paper.

He took a few steps closer. The purple eyes shone, as improbably vivid in his tired face as fresh-cut flowers in a sandstorm.

My own eyes blinked. I felt a sharp pain pierce my throat, and the words hurled themselves out of me with the destructive swing of a wrecking ball. "You should know that Liam walked in on me. I was in bed with someone."

"Oh." Almost soundless. Dev's face moved not a muscle.

"Well, you were too, weren't you?" I couldn't stop.

Quickly, his hands took hold of my shoulders, firm but not hard, no attempt to pull me to him. "Now, does your soul feel improved with confession and blame?" The eyes darkened: polished glass, the light behind them switched off. "One Our Father? Two Hail Marys? A purging walk through hellfire, perhaps? How did a lunatic WASP-Jew like you get to be such a Catholic?"

His hands dropped to his sides. "I was on an island off Vancouver most of the last two weeks. I took it into my head that you might be here, and called one night right after I got there, but you weren't home." I knew somehow that had been the night I'd come back after dinner at the Termans', raced to catch the ringing phone. No way I could blame Dev for that. But I did.

"Win some, lose some," I said bitterly. He didn't reply, except for the tensing of his mouth in something far from a smile. Then he turned away.

In an urgent flash of clarity, I knew that the danger of

destroying what I most wanted scared me far more than the risks of trying to have it and failing. And in that same moment, I pitied my mother as I never had before. Starved, grabbing Celia, aching to keep what she loved, every desperate move driving it farther away.

I dove at him with the spring-compressed force of longing and fear and something I called love, all coiled up too long together, reimagined too many ways. I almost knocked both of us over, my tears boiling out onto his neck, arms wrapping him tight, every atom of me aroused—nothing held back in self-defense.

His arms broke free and he became the captor. After minutes like that, he reached up and held my face in two hands, tensed fingers hurting my bruised cheek. "You may live to regret this," he said.

"You, too."

"I know."

No further words. We undressed each other with unsteady hands. As we began to make love, my body seemed stripped of its skin, every sense hyperalive and entirely unguarded. When the hardness of his cock brushed my thigh on its blind way home, we spun out together into territory completely new.

23

THE RUMBLE OF DEV'S VOICE ON THE PHONE ASSURED someone at Troop K that we hadn't left the country and would be there within the hour to give official statements. We'd fallen dead asleep in the Radisson bed, my ear to his chest, and even my worst bruises feeling no pain.

I mumbled some indecipherable sounds into his skin, mostly just for the feel of it against my mouth. He began to stroke the back of my neck, but not, my fuzzed-up mind belatedly realized, until after he'd dialed another number.

"Paul Hannagan, Marty. Ronnie there?" He must have felt my body jolt and stiffen, but the strokes against my neck continued rhythmically steady.

"Bellissima," he said into the phone, "I need a favor. Late-model red Jag, registered to a Zachary Terman, either in the city or in Dutchess County. State police—Troop K—will be looking for it too. I'm not asking you to bump heads with them, but if it turns up anywhere in the city, I want to know immediately, okay?" Pause. "No, no one I know—friend of Emily's. He turned up strangled in her basement." My head rolled under a wave of his laughter. "Right, I'll watch it." He reeled off my phone number, as though he'd known it for years. "How're you managing? . . . Good. It'll get easier, I promise. *Mille grazie.*"

I shook off the stroking hand, and sat up on my haunches. "Was she the one you went with, Sergeant Ronnie?" I asked sharply. "I tried calling her when I was looking for you. She was nowhere to be found."

"Was Chris Held the one?" He lobbed it at me. Point, counterpoint. Our eyes met in a silent standoff. "Emily, don't do this," he said slowly. "I'm not going to answer your question, and I don't want you to answer mine. Ronnie's a longtime friend, who's coming off a rotten divorce, and Chris is . . . whoever he is. Neither of these people has fuck-all to do with why we haven't seen each other for over a month, or with why we're here together now.''

While my gut divided itself in civil war, I clamped my teeth together tight enough to ache, just to be sure they stayed shut. *I am not Celia*, I told myself. *I am not Celia.* ''Where do you think they'll find Zach's car?'' I asked, after what either was, or simply felt like, a long time.

''Just a guess, but I don't think it will be up here,'' he said, and planted a kiss on my forehead.

Half an hour later, Dev grabbed my arm and ran interference past the determined band of mikes and minicams waiting, ready to pounce, in front of the police barracks. Their presence was predictable, and everything it brought back to me was predictable also. I lowered my head as though it were a battering ram and charged through, trying not to scream obscenities, succeeding only partially.

The trooper at the front desk summoned an exhausted Darrell Weems from his office.

''Probably just as well for you that you spent the day out,'' he said genially, giving me a nod and Dev's hand a shake. ''The older guy—your father, I guess—had a run-in with some T.V. vans, got past our guard and close to the house.'' He chuckled. ''He went ballistic, busted a windshield. Not that I blame him. I drove back there myself and read them the riot act about private property. I told them anyone sneaked in would be out of our information loop. Should be clear for you now, but the Major said you might want to lay on some private security next few days. It *is* a big piece of land.''

I goddamned well did, and asked him if he could arrange it for me.

He took me back to his office for the statement. A cooling meatball hero, barely bitten into, and a large coffee, its cream skinning over, sat on the corner of a loaded desk. A long day was about to become a long night.

Rehashing for the stenographer what I'd said that morning didn't take me more than ten minutes or so, but Dev seemed to be spending a great deal more time at it. While I sat waiting none too patiently for him, I spotted the back of Clea's red head going quickly by at the opposite end of the corridor, with Major Heaney striding alongside. I squashed the impulse to run to her.

"Official from the M.E.: he could be dead weeks; he could be dead a day," Dev said as he started the car. "So, either he had the bad judgment to come back sometime after he went away, or—as you suggested—he never did leave."

"Darrell told you that? Pretty chatty."

"Professional courtesy." His tone was only a trifle smug.

"I saw Clea there," I said. "It looks like Heaney's handling her personally. That scares hell out of me, Dev. I didn't like his face one bit when Clea's name came up this morning. He sort of shook his head as though she were some incorrigible case."

He grunted an "umm," and went off into his own thoughts.

It was almost nine before we turned into the private road to Orchards. The yellow police tape remained, but the vehicles all appeared to be gone, and a sense of relief washed through me as I realized that Zach's body would be gone too.

As I slid my way out of the car, a flash of searing light exploded in my face. My mouth opened in a scream that never moved into sound, as I froze for a second, arm thrown up to shield my eyes. Then, through the circling red and black, it took form in my brain, and I dove, hands clawing to destroy anything in their reach: camera and photographer.

Dev was there ahead of me. When my vision cleared, I saw, trapped from behind in his wrestler's hold, a terrified and guilty-faced kid, camera clutched in a desperate one-handed grip. The thing was, I recognized him: Vince, from Chris's At Home cleaning crew.

"What the fuck do you think you're doing?" I asked, with the sense of ridiculous anticlimax Dorothy must have felt when she finally got a look at the Wizard.

"Please," he almost whimpered, "my camera. Emily,

could you make him stop? It's gonna drop if he doesn't let me go.''

"What do you say, Emily? You know this asshole?'' Dev's voice was as unrelenting as his grip, but he rolled his eyes at me over Vince's head.

"Yeah, he works for Chris,'' I answered deadpan. "Hold on to his camera for him till we get this sorted out.'' Dev turned him loose and commandeered the camera. "I'm waiting, Vince,'' I said.

"I'm a photographer.'' Hard sell rushed to replace fear in his voice. "That's what I do, but it's not that easy to find the work. One shot of you. Just one shot. What do you say?''

"I say no. That's what I say.''

"I wouldn't even bother with the *Poughkeepsie Journal*. Right straight to the *New York Post*. I mean, what would it matter to you? You're an actress; you have your picture taken all the time.''

Dev didn't consult this time. He snapped the back of the camera open, removed the film and stowed it in his pocket. "We're going to play a game,'' he said. "It's called, you get your ass off these grounds in two minutes or less, or I get the fun of kicking it off. You have a car parked somewhere?''

"Over that way.'' He pointed toward the far west boundary. "On the *public* road. Can I have my camera?'' Vince asked, resentment controlled with some effort.

"Only if you're going to be a good boy,'' Dev answered cheerfully.

In sullen, silent defeat, Vince's hand reached out. Dev handed the camera over, and Vince took off at a pretty good clip—but not so fast that I didn't get the words he shouted over his shoulder. "Bitch! You think all I can do is clean rich people's houses?'' If distilled hate could kill, I'd have dropped on the spot.

"You okay?'' Dev asked, his face sour.

"I suppose. But that little fucker had a point. He's a first name to me, no more. Someone who cleans rich people's houses.''

"Want to say cheese and give him his shot?''

"No way in hell.''

Liam was pacing the house like a zoo critter. "Fooking phone doesn't stop its racket for three running seconds," he barked.

"I heard about your bashing the T.V. van," I said. "Thanks."

"Well, my friend Jane won't thank me. I used one of her doodads to smash it."

A man after my own heart, I caught myself thinking, before I realized it was Liam Hannagan I was thinking that about. "Which doodad?"

"One of those big candle things from the dining room. It got a little bent."

"If I know Jane Benzinger, she'll be far more upset about her candlestick than some stranger's murder." But I didn't know Jane Benzinger at all, I realized, so I had no real idea whether Zach Terman was a stranger to her or not.

As Liam had warned, the phone began to ring. Thinking it could be Clea, I ran to the library to answer.

"At least you could've given a sincere face to the camera, Silver. You looked like a snarling bitch."

"I wasn't trying for reviews, Bernie," I said, oddly comforted to hear my agent's hoarse rasp, saying the kinds of things he always said.

"Christ, you're just the one who found the guy. You ought to be taking lessons in how to behave from the widow."

"What?"

"Snap on your set—CNN or whatever."

"They have it this soon?!"

"What planet you been living on?" A planet where people work on television, but don't watch it. "The story hit hours ago. Made a ripple out here; Terman had a pretty fat deal at Disney. But I was going to call you anyway. That *farkakte* script I sent you? *Arden!*?" Bernie Clegg was as proud as any midwestern Baptist of his Hollywood Yiddish. "Well, she's going to be in New York. Wants to meet you Monday."

"Oh no," I moaned. All my fancy plans about getting in

shape to play Rozzie, and Claudine Augier, filmmaker *extraordinaire*, would shake hands with someone who looked like a mugging survivor.

"Look, don't get your hopes up, but she claims to have cash from De Niro, from Miramax, from Santa Claus, for Chrissake—and some small change from the Canadian film board. Personally, I think she's full of shit, but she's going to meet you at the Miramax offices, over in Tribeca. You know where?"

"Uh huh."

"Eleven A.M. Hey, maybe she knows the janitor."

I gave it a gracious-lady reading: "Goodnight, Bernie."

As soon as I'd hung up, I snapped on the small television set, semi-hiding in a bookshelf, and dialed around until I caught a newscast smack in the middle of sports. While I was waiting, I returned to the phone and tried Clea's number. Bart Held answered, sounding shell-shocked.

"Hasn't she gotten there yet?" he asked.

"Here? I saw her with Heaney about an hour ago when I was over at the barracks."

"Heaney? Oh Jesus," he said miserably. "We met with my lawyer this morning, and I thought Clea understood what he told her about talking to the police: 'Cooperate, but do not volunteer.' Then, an hour and a half ago, she hollered that she was going to Orchards. I was up in my study, and before I could get downstairs even to answer, she was in her car and gone. I don't seem to be of much use to anyone."

"Why do you think she went to see Heaney?" I cut in sharply, knowing as the words came out that they were just so much sound. Her father was more clueless than anyone about why Clea did anything. "How is Ariane managing?" I asked more gently.

"I wouldn't know." The pain in his voice made me feel like an eavesdropper. "She doesn't want to see me. I assume Clea will want to stay the night with you. Tell her I'll speak with her in the morning. I must go now." He hung up.

As if summoned, Ariane appeared then on the T.V. screen, chin high, unfazed as a plaster Madonna by the thrusting mikes and milling reporters littering the entrance to her house. I rushed to turn up the sound.

"I have allowed you to come to my door because I respect that you have jobs to do," she said with an unearthly calm. "I have nothing to tell you except that I am devastated by my husband's death. I know that each of you, as well as anybody watching, will understand that. I will now, with your cooperation, insist on my privacy." She turned and walked slowly up the steps and inside. Close-up of door closing. Not one reporter attempted to follow her.

It was a stellar performance, one I wished I were capable of—and knew I never would be. Yet her face, as she spoke, reminded me . . . Reminded me of what? These past weeks, occasional glimpses of Ariane had stirred the faint, not-quite click of insubstantial memory. The girl who wouldn't sweat in hell. But she was other girls, too: compassionate Nursey who took care of those who needed it; achieving student; brilliant tennis competitor; loving sister of a round-faced blond boy with a dog; secretive daughter of a scandalous mother. Secretive. Still, I couldn't pin down the expression I'd just seen in the fleeting close-up of her eyes. It looked as dead as burnt-out coals.

When I came back out of the library, I saw that Clea, newly arrived, was standing in the entrance foyer with Liam, her hand in his. She was wearing a long denim skirt—the first time I'd seen her in one—and a high-necked sleeveless blouse. From my vantage point, she looked like a painfully shy schoolgirl.

I kept myself from rushing to envelop her. "Hi Clea," I said, forcing tension from my voice into the clenched fist at my side.

"Hi Emily." Her face was more than usually pale, even for her, with that pink-eyed white-rabbit look she'd had the first time I sat with her in the early hours of morning, drinking tea in the kitchen I'd just claimed as mine.

"Clea love," Liam said, "I bet you skipped dinner. I'm going to make you a cuppa tea and a sandwich." Liam Hannagan as caretaker—that was novel.

"I'd love the tea, but I'm not hungry," she protested.

"Just like you're always telling me, you must eat a little." He smiled at her. "Come on then, I'll tell you a story," he teased. It should have been sticky-sweet sick, but instead I felt the sharp stick of impending tears at the back of my nose.

"I saw you at the barracks," I said finally, once the four of us were sipping tea at the kitchen table, and Liam had coaxed a toasted cheese sandwich into Clea. "How come?"

"I needed to tell Major something," she said, glancing at me, expecting an argument. "I needed him to know that my father had no idea at all about Zach and me."

"Of course he didn't," I said, relaxing in relief, "not until I brought you back from the city and I told him." And he'd said that Zach deserved to die.

"But that was the same day you found Zach," Clea said with some energy—the first I'd seen in her tonight. "Don't you see? If my father had somehow hunted him up and killed him, he couldn't have gotten that frozen in just an hour or two, could he?" This last directed to Dev, who'd been letting his tea grow cold and who had not said a word besides hello, since she arrived.

Dev did not answer. Instead, he leveled neutral eyes at her. "There's something more, isn't there?" he asked.

She looked back at him, chewing her lip like an undecided kid. "I'm not lying," she said. "I *did* go to see Major to tell him what I just told you. My father didn't kill Zach; I can't stand him, and he doesn't understand anything about anything, but he's not a murderer! And besides, he didn't have a motive." Sure he did: Ariane. But I didn't say it. "This morning that dorky lawyer was sitting there next to me, and every time I tried to answer a question, he'd butt in to say how I didn't remember this, or I couldn't possibly know that. And then he'd point out in this mortician voice that I was a 'delicate person, under psychiatric care.' I just wanted to coldcock him!"

Liam and I broke into the same laugh of spontaneous approval; bottom line, we were both people who shared impulses like that, and had on occasion indulged them. And we both loved this girl. Dev did not laugh.

"Come on, Clea." I'd heard that note from him before; usually right before he called me "actress." "That isn't all. Now let's have it. Don't make me pull it out of you; it's been a long day."

She looked vaguely startled. "You sound like Major. Both of you, like you just knew. How?"

"Come on," Dev repeated, this time with the supportive, coaxing tone of a swimming coach.

She said it flat and fast. "I saw Zach that Saturday night—the day before he . . . left."

"*What?!*" An astonished yelp escaped me, cut off by Dev's sharp "sshhh."

Clea continued into the silence. "It was late—well, not that late, I guess, about ten. I was up in my room watching an old movie. *Breakfast at Tiffany's*—my mother always loved that one, but this time it kind of bored me. Then I started to hear these sounds at my window, like gravel kicking up against it. And I went to look, and it *was* gravel. Zach was standing down there tossing it." Jesus, was there any romantic cliché he'd missed? "I ran down the back stairs, and we walked out to the stables so my father wouldn't hear. Zach had parked his car back there anyway."

"Your father was home, then?" Dev asked.

"In his study. That's where he always hangs out. But once he's locked up in there, you could explode a bomb and he wouldn't notice. That's what my mother always said." I saw her face turn sad and uncertain, and knew that whatever came next was going to be very bad news. I glanced quickly at Liam, who looked as worried as I was. He kept himself quiet, but I saw his hand move to Clea's forearm.

"Go on, Clea." This time Dev's tone was gentle.

"He wanted to break our date," she said, the surprise of betrayal still fresh and sore.

"The date you went into the city to keep?" Dev asked.

Clea just nodded, her lips bitten back from behind to form a thin, down-turned line. It was between the two of them now: Dev and Clea. He pitched his questions softly, and she wanted to answer them.

"That date was made a week and a half in advance," he said. "Was that usual with him?"

"Sometimes," she mumbled.

"But then he disappeared, Clea. Did that surprise you?"

"No." Her voice rang stronger. "The thing about Zach

was . . . everything was a surprise. That's what was so *wonderful*.''

''Did you hear from him at all during that week?''

''No.''

''So, even though he was gone, out of contact, you went into the city to keep a date he'd already broken.''

''That's not how it was.''

''Then tell me how it was. What else happened the last time you saw him?''

She spoke with her eyes fixed on Liam's hand covering hers, as though staring at a good-luck charm. ''He said he'd stopped loving me . . . in that way, but he always would love the memory of what we had, that he'd keep it locked up safe in his heart for the rest of his life—and that I should too.'' One of her hectic pink flushes, but she did not cry.

''And then?'' Dev prodded softly, as though he knew what might be coming.

''And then it . . .'' Her eyes shifted down into her lap. ''It broke down. I was all split apart. I screamed at him—awful things, like I wished he would die. I . . . I said if he didn't meet me next Monday night, I'd ki—kill myself for real this time. And then he put his arms around me very gently, and he told me he *would* come. Emily, he promised!'' The tears that had eluded her this morning came now in racking sobs. *''Zach! Oh God! I wished he'd die—and he did!''*

24

· · · · · · · · · · · · · · · · · · · ·

SHE DID NOT KILL HIM, I TOLD MYSELF, MY EYES ON
her lowered head, bright curls shaking as she wept. Somehow, all three of us knew to let her alone while the keg of
anguish inside her drained itself out.

"I want to go to sleep," she said after what seemed like
a long time, her voice muffled and hoarse with crying. "Can
I stay here?"

"You've been spending half your nights here for the last
two weeks," I said tartly, needing to cut through the syrup
of emotions bubbling in my own blood. "Why so formal?"

I was rewarded by a faint, watery smile. "I packed some
things, just in case I didn't want to go home for . . . a while.
They're in the car."

While she was out getting them, I asked Dev, "Do you
think Heaney's out to nail her? Is he going to try and arrest
her?"

"Answer one: I told you I thought Heaney was a good
cop. He's out to nail his perp, whoever that really is. Answer two: If Clea's finally leveling with us, I'd say he
doesn't have the goods to make an arrest. If she's not, I'd
add, 'yet.' "

The phone bleeped just before five A.M. I'd spent some of
the past six hours watching Dev sleep, and most of the rest
trying to get back into *Arden!*—anything to keep my mind
off Clea. I had drifted off finally less than an hour ago. I
grunted into the mouthpiece, and a second later, gave Dev a
not entirely gentle awakening nip on his ear. "It's *Bellissima*," I said as I handed him the receiver.

"Ummm. Uh huh. *Uh huh.* I owe you one. . . . Okay,
two." He reached across me and hung up the phone.

He half propped himself against the headboard, black

brows drawing together in a puzzled frown. Return to sleep was not in the cards for either of us. "Well?" I prompted.

"Terman's Jag was in the long-term parking at Kennedy. It's been there since three thirty-seven P.M. the Sunday he disappeared."

Now the two of us sat side by side in the bed, like a pair of competing quiz show contestants, lathering our wits to come up with something to ring the buzzer about.

It made no sense at all—or rather, it made perfect sense, until you factored in Zach's body. Without that, man leaves his wife, provides a note, drives his car to the airport, and takes off with his new lady for Paris—or anywhere at all. In fact, if he buys the tickets for cash, takes enough with him, and stays in the U.S., even a pro like Dev would have an extremely hard time finding him.

But somebody crushed his windpipe, and the scenario I'd just spun out would have been a perfect cover for that person. So why blow the whole thing and stow Zach in my freezer, where he'd certainly be found—if not one day, then another?

Back to the starting gate: it made no sense.

"This may not be good news for Clea," Dev said, his hand playing absently with my shoulder, while his eyes studied the wall opposite him. Then, in an abrupt change of pace, he sprang out of bed and headed for the shower.

I stayed put, and thought some more. Two possibilities: Either Zach drove his own car to the airport and was killed and brought back here, or somebody drove the car there after he was dead. If I just kept resolute in knowing that Clea didn't do it, then this development had to be useful—just *because* it made so little sense.

What kind of person, under what circumstances, would set up a good, workable cover-up for murder, and then shoot it in the foot by stowing the body where it was sure to be found?

I got myself out of bed and walked stiffly into the bathroom. The ankle felt much improved, but the rest of my body creaked worse than it had after that first day of riding with Clea—which, as I thought of it now, seemed as long past as a sepia photo out of an old album.

After I used the john, I glanced over at the steamed-up

glass of the shower, and felt a surge of pure lust for the blurred, tawny shadow of Dev's body soaping its chest. I opened the shower door without knocking, and stepped inside . . .

Chris arrived at eight-thirty to get started painting the living room, which, with the glaze effect that Jane had mandated, would take a good few days. Miraculously—despite beatings, disappearances, death—decorating continued without a hitch. Dev looked up from a half-filled coffee cup and greeted him with an unexceptionable, if curt, smile.

Chris smiled back. "Morning, Emily. Morning, Dev? Is that the name? I didn't quite catch it."

"It'll do," Dev said.

"Look, I heard about the thing with Vince and his camera. I'd apologize if that would do any good, but I guess the best I can say is, he's off your crew. You won't see him here again. By the way, I notice you got a coupla, three guys out there making sure of that."

"Hardly just for Vince," I said, nettled by something in his tone I couldn't quite identify. The phone rang: third press call of the morning, which I disposed of less gracefully than Ariane would have. "What he did was rotten, though," I said, just because I needed to. "He broke trust."

Chris's eyes narrowed. "Let's say he was just a guy trying to skip a few squares to get ahead."

Liam chose that moment to appear. He nodded at Dev and me, and muttered something out of the side of his mouth that sounded like, "Twerps are up early," to which Chris replied with a scornful snort, and left the room.

"I'm going shopping," Dev announced, rising from the table.

"For what?" I asked. "I've got food enough in this place for a restaurant convention."

"For an answering machine. I'm tired of hearing you abuse those hardworking, dues-paying motherfuckers. Besides, all the underwear in my bag needs washing."

"Washer and dryer are in the basement."

''Basement's a sealed crime scene. Besides, buying shorts helps me think. See you in a couple of hours.''

After Dev had gone, and Liam's tea was in its cup, he said, ''I looked in on Clea. Fast asleep. Do her good, my little pet.''

''Maybe Chris is not all wrong,'' I said, less for Liam's benefit than my own. ''Maybe too many people think of Clea as just a pet.''

''Balls! Nobody ever took care of that little girl, except for what could be bought with money. Don't bother to tell me I'm a piss-poor one to talk about fathering. I did worse than poor Bart Held with my own child, and I know it. Can't even trade two words with him now—as you can see—much less touch him with my hand. It was easier boozed up.'' He gave a short laugh. ''What wasn't? But, worthless as I am, I have something to give that girl. And if she likes being my pet, let her for Christ's sake have it. God knows it ain't much.''

I heard the front doorbell, and wondered whether some wily reporter or photographer had managed to slip through the security net. I stayed put, and heard Chris open the door, then the rumbling of male voices. A few minutes later, Major Heaney's long frame loped into the kitchen.

''Morning, Miss Otis, Mr. Hannagan.''

Liam did one of his nods and I rose. ''Good morning, Major,'' I recited crisply. ''What can I do for you?''

''I hoped we could have a little talk. Your ankle any better?''

''Yes, thank you, and so's the rest of me.''

Liam stuffed a few lumps of sugar in his pants pocket, grabbed his pot and his cup, and walked toward the corridor. ''I'll make myself scarce.''

''That coffee smells good,'' Heaney said. ''Mind if I pour myself a cup?''

''Not at all. Cups are in that cupboard just above your head.'' He wore a dark blue summer suit, crisp white shirt, and skinny yellow-and-blue-striped tie. I could see the damp comb marks that emphasized the remaining strands of chestnut in his mostly white hair. He looked ready to attend a summer funeral—or to spring a trap. There were questions I ached to ask him, but didn't, fearing that I'd reveal more in the asking than he would in the reply.

He settled into a chair, the bend on his long legs forming acute angles. "Only way I can drink this stuff now," he said, pouring lots of milk into the cup. "Ulcer."

"You don't look like the ulcer type."

The twist of his smile told me that I knew nothing about him or his "type"—but the point was scored without obvious malice. "Emily . . . Do you mind if I call you Emily?"

"You can call me anything you want," I said, irritated at him for being there and at myself for being suckered into banal chat with him. "What is it you came to talk about? In particular?"

"Emily, some things you should know about me: I'm a transplant, see, from the Bronx, but I've been up here forty years, since right after the Korean War. Joining Troop K was really like re-upping in the Marines, and lots of us loved the hell out of that idea. We even lived over there in the barracks. But that was a long time ago. I've been commander of this troop eight years. Come September, I'm a retired man; state of New York says so—sixty and out. And I don't mind that a bit. Marilyn and I might do a little traveling, then I got a good security job lined up over at Vassar. Life is good, long as my number two daughter stays out of trouble and I handle the ulcer with kid gloves.

"Now, this is Darrell Weems's case, and he's a damned good investigator—should be: I trained him, and I'm a damned good teacher. I got no reason to be anywhere right now but in my office okaying his reports and keeping my colonel up in Albany in the loop. The reason I showed up here yesterday was out of respect for your grandmother, but the reason I'm keeping my nose in is because of the Helds.

"The old man and I used to hunt together when I first got up here. He was pretty important in town even then with two papers; what's it now? Eight? I don't really know why he fastened on me, except I think he liked the idea of hanging with cops, and I was a pretty fair shot. He paid me to teach Bart. The kid was eleven, nervous as hell—stuttered when he put more than two words together. But I tell you, that rifle worked like a charm for him, once he got the feel of it. Master of the Millbrook Hunt. Maybe his daddy finally would've been proud of him.

"Some piece of work, old Chris Held. I'm glad he wasn't my father; I'd probably have been as scared to death of him as Bart was." I looked at the set of his soldier's face, the leather of his skin, and doubted that. "He never cared much for Bart, of course. Christy was his boy—that is, until he screwed up and ran away with some of the old man's money. But that wasn't the worst. I tell you, Emily, when the old man found out that Dolores Rance, who carried his drinks at the Millbrook Towne House, was also carrying his grandchild, and that she was gonna call it Christopher Maddock Held the Third, it burned him like acid.

"He was one tough man, and he could be a damned mean one. Only thing after that that could make him smile was starting up a new paper or watching Clea toddle around. He did like that baby, even if she was a girl."

I waited, eyes fixed on his, for him to get where he was going. He took a long sip of milky coffee. "What I'm trying to tell you here, Emily, is that with Clea and Bart tangled up the way they are in this thing, I'm gonna be working for my paycheck on this case. And I want to tell you another thing. I believe that you took yourself over to see the Helds before you phoned us about the body."

I suppose I shouldn't have been surprised, but my face said I was. "No, Paul Hannagan didn't tell on you, nobody did. It's just that I've known Bart since he was eleven, and he's not much of an actor—and maybe you're better at it up on the T.V. screen. But the point is that your buddy Clea doesn't need to be protected against me, unless she's done something she shouldn't. And if she has," he said with a face both Old Man Held and the Marines would have approved, "I'm gonna know it."

Then suddenly, he shifted gears. "Zach Terman was a pretty romantic kind of guy, right?"

"I guess it's fair to say he thought of himself that way."

"Favored picnics—bread and wine, poems, that kinda thing?"

Pop goes the weasel! Score one for Heaney. "Zach Terman was an asshole," I said flatly. "He started to make a move on me the first night I met him, at a dinner party at his house, in fact. First thing the next morning, he dropped that idiot basket on my doorstep and drove off so I'd find it—and be charmed, I suppose. I tore up his cute note, but the damned basket was too big to fit in the trash can, so I dumped it in the basement."

"That would be two weeks ago. Saturday, day before he supposedly disappeared. So you never saw him alive again?"

"I did, actually." *Go for it, Heaney! How about me as suspect.* "That same evening, he appeared in my garden ready to begin our grand affair. I threatened to kick his balls in if he didn't get the hell off my property."

Heaney's head cocked slightly to one side, his listening mode. "Looks like he did get off your property alive. At least that time. Went to pay a call on Clea, I hear, and then home to rough up his wife. Nice fella.

"Maybe he went out again after that," he suggested casually. "You got a pretty fast temper, Emily, don't you? Always did."

Now it was my turn to give him a how-the-hell-would-you-know? look. "No reason you'd remember me," he said, "but I met you a long time ago, back when your folks died, and Mrs. Otis brought you up here to get you away from the vultures. I was a lieutenant then, and I paid her a visit to offer to lay on some security. A trooper drove me over, waited outside in the car. You fired a rock at that car, missed the windshield, but you dented the fender pretty good. I tried to talk your grandma out of spanking you for it. I don't know if it worked."

"Neither do I. Probably it shouldn't have."

"Just a quick karate chop could've crushed his windpipe that way. Ever do any karate?"

I stared at him, hoping not to blink. "Couple of kicks here and there, but I told Zach Terman I was a black belt."

"Well, Emily, I'll tell you, it sounds extreme to me to kill a stranger for making a dumb pass with a picnic basket. Unless, of course, there was more to it." He leaned back in his chair. "Maybe he wasn't such a stranger."

"He was a stranger. What about the seat of Dev's jeans?"

"Dev? Ah, yeah, Hannagan. Well, that's the other thing of course. The lab says Mr. Terman likely did come down your coal chute wrapped in a tarp of some kind; fibers stuck to the body hair match the ones on your friend's rear. Maybe you tossed him down there—figured he belonged with his basket."

Wouldn't it be easy to confess and solve everyone's problem! Then I felt my face harden into the kind of anger he'd recalled from my childhood. He didn't think I did it. This man was doing a damned good job of manipulating me. And I was too old to throw rocks.

"I understand that you and Mrs. Terman go way back," he said blandly.

"We were at school together. We were never close friends then. When I bumped into her at the diner a few weeks ago, we hadn't been in touch for years." He waited expectantly, but I stopped right there.

"Oh," he said, sounding mildly surprised, "I got the impression you were closer—maybe because you were so hot to go over there, be the one to break the news to her." *Stupid, Emily.* "I figured you might be able to help me understand how a classy woman like that came to marry Terman. You called him an asshole. I don't disagree. She seems more the type of woman I'd pick out for, say, Bart Held."

"Don't play with me, Heaney. Yes, it's fairly obvious that Bart Held is in love with Ariane. That doesn't mean he murdered her husband."

"It surely doesn't. But what about your friend Ariane? Her father left her more millions than Terman got around to making, so she didn't do it for cash, but maybe she was fed up with getting hit."

"If she wasn't, she should've been."

"Darrell tells me she just about passed out with the news."

"Yes."

"Folks over at the tennis club say she has a wicked serve." He pantomimed it. "Question is, does she have your temper?"

"Probably not, or she would've killed him years ago." I

stood. "If you're looking for sharp insights on Ariane Warburton from me, you're wasting time. I didn't understand her when we were fourteen, and I don't now. She must have other friends you could talk to more profitably."

He nodded. "You'd think so, wouldn't you? I guess she spends a lot of time with this retarded brother."

"Autistic, not retarded."

"Sorry."

"He lives in a group home. Union Vale, I think she said." I thought of the way she'd exploded at Zach across the dinner table when he'd called her brother crazy. Maybe she didn't have my temper, but she had her own. "Ariane adores Jamie. That's one thing about her I can tell you for sure."

"Umhm." He unfolded his body from the chair. "Well, have Clea give me a call, would you? What is she, still sleeping?"

"How did you know she was here?"

"No fancy detective work. I saw her car out front. By the way, that yellow dress—you know, the one you found her wearing at Terman's place in the city? Pretty messed up, I understand. You know what became of it?"

"Why?" My barbed wire sprang back up. He was good: lob a few; soften you up; then barrel in with the hard stuff.

"Just wanted to have a look at it."

"I threw it in the trash."

"Funny, we went through your trash yesterday. Didn't find it." Suddenly, I didn't trust his intentions toward Clea one bit. The phone began to ring.

"You'll have to excuse me now, it's probably another reporter wanting a keyhole peek." It was, and I hung up on her with a slam. Then went out the French doors, determined to jog myself into some kind of copable shape, or into oblivion.

25
....

Wʜᴇɴ I ɢᴏᴛ ʙᴀᴄᴋ, ᴀɴ ʜᴏᴜʀ ᴀɴᴅ ᴀ ʜᴀʟꜰ ʟᴀᴛᴇʀ, ᴍʏ ankle actually did feel stronger, and my aches and I had become friends of a sort, rather than hostile roommates fighting for possession of the same space. If I could only throw a veil over my face, maybe I'd actually survive the power meeting at Miramax with a shot at playing Rozzie. But the run hadn't been much of an antidote to my session with Heaney: I was less confident than ever about protecting Clea.

Dev was sitting on the side porch staring off into space.

"Portrait of the thinker," I panted, out of breath as well as soaked with sweat.

"Part of what I do for a living," he said. "Bart Held just called. Whatever his sins, between his daughter and your friend the Widow Terman, the poor sod sounds ready to fall apart."

"Clea come down yet?" I asked.

"I think she's inside with Liam or Chris."

"Heaney was here while you were gone. He gave me a pretty expert going-over."

"I know. We talked on his way out." Dev grinned. "He said you looked ready to grab hold of a skillet and brain him."

"Why am I feeling surrounded by some brotherhood of lawmen?" I felt my face flame up. "I don't care what you say, I think he's got Clea earmarked."

"Go have yourself a shower. I think I'd like to meet your friend Ariane." The gleam of pure concentration in his eyes sent me into the house without another word. I knew he was chewing on something, and I knew equally well that he wasn't ready to talk about it.

I debated with myself about calling Ariane first, and decided not to take the chance of a no from her. As I started up the back stairs to shower and change, I heard Clea's voice up at the front of the house, and followed it to the living room, where I lurked beside the doorway and frankly eavesdropped.

"I'll do it," she was saying. "I know how. It's not exactly rocket science."

"It may not be rocket science." Chris's voice. "But I need someone reliable. This is how I make my living, remember?"

"Oh Chris, I didn't mean it that way. I sound like such a condescending brat. How can you stand me? I just meant . . . well, you're short a cleaning person, and I'm here." Her voice speeded up with urgency. "And I need to have something to do right now, besides *think*."

"Clee, what about you and that guy?" The question rolled out of him easily, but there was an undertone I didn't care for.

"What do you mean?"

"Well, Emily brought you back that day, you were not just a mess, you were out of it. Kind of reminded me of the way you were when . . . you know when I'm talking about."

"When I tried to check myself out, and I didn't exactly remember." She said it slowly. That son of a bitch! Was this the kind of kick he thought Clea's behind needed?

"It looked to me like there was blood and guck on that dress you were wearing. What I'm asking you is, you sure you didn't kill him?"

"I didn't kill him," she said, sounding not angry, but rather, thoughtful. "Chris, I know why you're worried about me, but I'd remember if I killed Zach." Beat. "I *think* I would." It took my entire store of restraint—always scantily stocked—to keep from bursting in and making him stop. But I knew that Clea would hate me for it.

"Okay, that's good enough for me," Chris said quickly, in an almost embarrassed rush to change the subject. "Now, if I put you on my crew, you promise you're not gonna fuck up on me?"

"Promise."

"Okay. Five bucks an hour. I pay the others seven, but they've got more experience."

"I love you, cousin."

I tiptoed back down the hall and up the stairs, wanting to cry.

Twenty minutes later, we were on our way to the house that Zach built. As Dev turned into the twisty road that led to the castle, I was a bit surprised to see no evidence of either security guards or persistent reporters, and wondered whether the power of regal will in her dignified statement last night was truly enough to have held the jackals at bay.

It turned out that regal will had marshaled some assistance. When we drew close to the house, we heard a furor of heavy-duty barking, and a pair of large, very fit Dobermans bounded to meet our car, stopping about three feet from the passenger-side door.

Dev and I exchanged a stare, and stayed where we were. A moment later, the front door opened and a chunky, blond teenager with a choirboy's pure face stepped out.

"Pal! Friend! Down!" The command, in a ringing high tenor, had a toneless quality, like something recorded. The dogs subsided into sudden stillness. "Sit! Stay!"

"Now, who are you?" he asked. "Tell me your names." His voice modulated some, but the toneless precision of it didn't change.

I rolled down my window and took a closer look at him. I saw that he was older than I'd thought, early twenties perhaps, with the face of a coarsened cherub. "Are you Jamie?"

"Yes, I am Jamie. Tell me your names. We don't want any reporters here."

"We're not reporters," I said. "I'm a friend of your sister's. I'm Emily. We—"

"You and Ariane went to school with each other. That was from 1976 until—" Ariane appeared beside him, squeezing his shoulder affectionately. He didn't respond; nor did he pull away.

"That's all right, darling," she said with a warm smile, "Emily remembers the dates as well as we do. It's safe for you to get out of the car, Emily. Jamie's dogs make a great deal of noise, but they are really very sweet." Jamie snapped his fingers at the dogs. They had sat obediently, as commanded. Now they stood and went to him. He pulled a pair of biscuits out of his pocket and doled them out.

"I'm impressed," Dev said, walking over to brother and sister. "It must have taken a lot of work to get them into that kind of shape."

"And you're Dev, of course," Ariane said, the smile still on her lips. It occurred to me that she had the look of someone recently waked from a troubled sleep, to find herself in a strange place. But even in her sleep she had taken the trouble to dress herself in smooth white pants and shirt, a white silk scarf tying back her well-brushed hair.

"I've met your father at Orchards," she continued, mindful as always of people's families. "He told me you'd be coming up to Millbrook one day or another." The smile gave itself up to blankness. "He told me that you'd be able to find Zach for me, if anyone could."

"I'm sorry," Dev said simply.

"Won't you come in?"

"Yes, it did take a lot of work," Jamie said, his attention still on the dogs. "I started when they were three months old, and it took two months for the basic obedience training. That was in September of 1993. Ariane bought them for my birthday, but I had to leave them at the kennel to live." For the first time, I saw his face look something like animated. "Now we can all live together."

"Yes, love. Yes we can. As of last night, Jamie lives here," she said, a note of quiet satisfaction in her voice. "And Pal and Friend, too," she added quickly. I remembered her dinner table skirmish with Zach about her brother. The blond young man standing shoulder to shoulder with Ariane had moved into this castle over Zach's dead body, which was the only way it ever could have happened.

"Jamie's always been amazing with dogs."

"I work for Heartland Breeding Kennels, right near where I used to live in Union Vale. It won't be such a long drive from here. I'm a good driver."

"Me, too," I said. "Some people just are. I'm glad to meet you, Jamie. You know, when we were at Fletcher, Ariane always had your picture standing on her dresser. There was a dog in that picture, too, but not a Doberman."

"That was Pal. He was a King Charles spaniel. He died when I was thirteen, on June nineteenth, 1986."

"You named this one after him?" I asked.

"After?" He didn't seem to follow. "Pal is a good name for a dog. I would always name a dog Pal. Ariane says there can only be one Pal at a time, so I named the other one Friend. That's good too." Until now, my only exposure to autism had been Dustin Hoffman playing Rain Man. As I listened to Jamie Warburton doggedly communicating with a distanced world from the isolation of his own vault, I awarded Hoffman his Oscar all over again.

"Would you take the dogs out back, Jamie dear?" Ariane said as she turned back into the house. "I'm sure they'd like a chance to get used to their new stamping grounds. If you and Dev will settle yourselves—in the living room, I think; it's awfully warm out on the terrace—I'll get us something to drink. What would you like? Coffee? Iced tea?"

"I'll do it. The last thing you need is to wait on people," I said quickly, guilty at hearing myself sound more impatient than compassionate.

"I want to." Ariane's voice was soft, but her tone insisted.

Dev gave my arm a small nudge. "Iced tea would be wonderful," he said.

We sat in dentist's-waiting-room silence—me in the same spot where I'd sat that first evening, Dev separating himself in a tapestry easy chair. Ariane joined us with a tray of tea and cookies: the perfect hostess. Odd, though: no friends; no relatives. Not even her devoted housekeeper was anywhere in evidence.

"Where's Winona?" I asked.

"I hope I didn't hurt her feelings too much, but it's easier for me to be alone right now," she said, sitting herself, back straight as a wand, on a large velvet hassock. "Except for Jamie, of course. Emily, I know you understand how much it means having him with me."

"Had he ever lived with you before?" Dev asked. "Before you were married, I mean."

"No. No, he hadn't." She studied Dev's face as she spoke, as though trying to select some part of it to talk to.

"My father was alive then. I would have loved to have Jamie live with me up at Cornell, but my father wouldn't hear of it. He was . . . a difficult man." The last few words did not come out with her usual ease. She shifted her glance to me. "I know what you must be thinking, Emily: that I married a difficult man as well, and that's true enough. But Zach was nothing like my father. Nothing at all."

"But neither of them would let you live with your brother," Dev commented, as quietly unobtrusive as a sub-title spelling out her own thoughts.

"No, neither of them would, but there was a difference. My father was a cruel person, and Zach was such a frightened . . ." She pressed her open hand firmly against her lips.

Suddenly, I could see myself sitting on that hassock, Mike one day dead, a pair of intruders who didn't give a fraction of a damn planted in my living room, picking the flesh off my bones. I shot up from my seat fast enough to lose balance on my bad ankle. "Ariane," I blurted as I steadied myself against a table, "I apologize for breaking in on you like this. We'll leave. We . . ."

Dev didn't move, and for what seemed ludicrously long, the three of us held our positions. "You needn't go," Ariane said. "I can't, you see, be with people easily just now. But I'll have to learn, won't I? But I find I'm so unreliable about even completing a sentence properly."

"What was it Zach was so frightened of?" Dev asked, as though no disruption had happened. I reseated myself; and bit my lips shut.

"Everything," she said with a small, sad laugh. "He tried to be such a swashbuckler: a grown-up version of the boys in his books, only so many things frightened him terribly. But what I started to say, Dev, was that Zach was frightened that if Jamie moved in with us, he'd take up all my attention. I've told you, Emily, Zach was such a child. He was child enough to be jealous of me, even while he acted the great lover with one new girl after another." Her lips parted slightly, beginning a word, but no word came.

"And you thought he'd left you for one of those women," Dev said. "Was Clea Held the one you had in mind?"

"No. Good Lord, no. I had no idea in the world about

Clea. That probably makes both Bart and me extremely stupid. I thought at first it might be Emily." I bit down harder to keep from talking; I'd said what I had to say on that score.

Dev gave me a quick glance, probably to ensure my silence, and then turned back to Ariane. "He printed out a goodbye note for you, and he took his laptop with him? Isn't that what you told Emily?"

"Yes. I knew if he packed his rod, he was serious; he never traveled without it. That's what he always said, 'I'm packing my rod.' " She smiled. "Zach was a great fan of hard-boiled detective stories." She turned to me with a look that almost pled. "You never got to see the good side of him, Emily. The side that was fun."

"No," was all I could manage to say.

Her eyes shut, as though in pain. "Oh God, I wish he were somewhere wonderful, surrounded by a hundred girls, all crazy about him!"

"So you were completely surprised when Emily found his body?" Dev asked very quietly.

For an instant, Ariane's face set into the cement-hard mask of furious shock I remembered from yesterday—and then, with visible effort, returned to its almost unreal serenity. "Yes," she said almost to herself, "I was completely surprised."

Dev waited a beat. "Ariane, not only have you given us tea and cookies, and not thrown us out, but you haven't asked me who the hell I think I am to be sitting here grilling you." With a wave in my direction he added, "As your friend over there surely would have done in your place." That got a wan smile from Ariane, and put a crack in the mounting tension, just as it was meant to.

"I'm going to tell you anyway," Dev went on, utterly low-key charming, "because you have every right to know. Your husband's body was stowed in Emily's freezer, which, along with the fact that he put a move on her, makes her a suspect. Now, I damned well know that she didn't kill him, but the police are not ready to give her an automatic exemption, for which I can't blame them. I know I'm right; I just need facts to prove it." He drained the tall glass in his hand and placed it, in a precise motion, on the table beside him.

"Delicious tea." His body didn't lean over to her, but his voice did. "I'm good at what I do, Ariane. I can find out who killed Zach."

"You may not understand this," she said, looking for the first time almost like herself, "but I don't think I care about that. Zach is dead, and I will miss him for the rest of my life. Nothing can change those two facts. Not for him; not for me."

It was Jamie who broke the silence. "Ariane? Ariane?" His heavy running steps followed the slam of the back door. A moment later he appeared, face flushed, an excited smile on his face. "I've found the perfect place to build a dog run! Can I start it tomorrow?"

Ariane rose gracefully from the hassock. "Of course you can. Why don't we go over to the lumberyard right now and buy whatever you need?" She turned to Dev with her Mona Lisa look in place. "I'll cooperate with you, because you care so much. Jamie and I are going shopping now, but if you want to stay and go over the things in Zach's office or . . . our bedroom, you have my permission." She walked over to me and placed a surprisingly cold hand on my arm. "It's the least I can do."

Zach's office had been picked clean by the police. There was no desk calendar, no appointment book, no files. All that seemed to be left were boxes of computer supplies, blank yellow pads, and scores and scores of sharpened pencils.

The bedroom, as far as I could see, contained nothing unusual, except apparent confirmation that Zach and Ariane had shared it, and were both bed-readers. A new biography of Dickens sat closed on what must have been Ariane's night table, a bookmark indicating that she hadn't gotten very far into it. On the table at the other side of the huge bed, a Tom Clancy paperback was splayed out facedown, marking the reader's place smack in the middle of it. It lay on top of a leather-bound volume of Kahlil Gibran.

Dev poked around in clothes closets and armoires, but looked like his heart wasn't in it.

"What do you think you'll find in there?" I asked.

"Not a damned thing, probably. Did Ariane tell you he'd taken many clothes?"

"I never asked her. All she mentioned was the laptop computer. I was just a little distracted at the time. Your father had just collapsed, so what the hell did I care about how many undershorts Zach Terman might have packed?"

"It was a question, not an indictment."

I sighed—a sound I hardly ever make, even onstage. "Sorry, I . . . I'm so damned jumpy. Ariane does that to me. She always did, even when we were kids. I seem to remember feeling naive with her, and unworthy."

"Unfortunate mixture," he said thoughtfully. "You left out angry."

"That, too. As long as we're laying it out, right now I feel guilty because, hard as she took the news when she first heard it, I had started to hope again that she was the one who killed him. I also hoped that somehow my friend, the great detective, would take a look at her, ask a magic question, and prove it. And Clea would be off the hook."

"Not to mention Bart. And you, of course."

"Oh come on! If I thought I could sidetrack Heaney onto me for a while, and get him off Clea, I'd do it in a second. Okay, let's say I went ballistic and chopped Zach's windpipe. Why would I be crazy enough to slide him into my own basement and put him in my freezer?"

"To divert the police by getting them to ask just that question. I don't think you read enough thrillers, Emily."

"And why did I drive his car to the airport? And what did I do with his computer?"

"Why and what, indeed?"

"But Dev, my point is that Ariane didn't do it either. I watched her reactions very carefully while you were grilling her. She was as shocked about Zach's turning up dead as I was."

He nodded. "I'd say so." He looked ready to say something else, but I saw him change his mind. "I'm going to check out the bathrooms. You have a look through her dresser drawers."

"For what?"

"A portable computer, perhaps?"

I didn't find the computer, or anything else notable. The only thing at all out of the ordinary was a crumpled pair of lacy, flesh-colored underpants—fragrant of citrus and obviously worn—which had gotten mixed in among a stack of freshly laundered white nightgowns. The guilt I'd spoken of to Dev surged through me in a wave of self-disgust. I stuffed the pants back where I'd found them and closed the drawer with a slam of finality.

I stood there, eyes scanning this strange bedroom of a strange woman. Every pulse in my body began to hammer. Ariane: people kept coming to me to ask who she was. What made her tick? Why might she have chosen a Zach? My single answer: *I don't know.* Suddenly, I saw that I needed to know, needed to understand. Otherwise, what was I doing here but—as Dev put it—playing patty-cake?

Without allowing time to talk myself out of it, I picked up her bedside phone, punched in Connecticut information, and asked for the only number that occurred to me. I only hoped someone would be there.

I got an answer on the fourth ring. From a machine. "You've reached the Fletcher School during its summer holiday. No one is in right now to speak with you, but if you'll leave your name, number, and a convenient time to reach you, one of us will return your call. Thank you."

"My name is Emily Si—Otis. I'm an alumna, class of '82. I'm trying urgently to reach a former assistant headmistress, Bailey Hutchison. Please call me at 914 677-8215, if you have any idea where I might contact her." Beat, beat. "As I said, it's urgent."

Just as I got the phone back in its cradle, Dev reappeared. "Anything?" I asked, tensed by an unreasoning desire to keep the call a secret.

"No."

"Then can we get the fuck out of here?"

"We can." He stood in the doorway, giving me and the room a searching sweep of his eyes. "Poor bastard didn't get to finish reading his Clancy," he said.

26

WE ROLLED DOWN THE TACONIC TOWARD THE CITY IN silence. I was at the wheel of my Lincoln trying every concentration exercise I'd picked up in twelve years of acting classes to focus myself. I was an adventurous reporter named Rozzie, who comes disguised as a man to infiltrate a band of defeated senators in retreat to a forest called Arden, somewhere south of Virginia, and stays to fall in love. Of course, the way I'd been treating adventurous reporters lately, they'd probably picket the film if it ever got made—if it ever got made with me in it.

But my mind would not behave. Rozzie kept getting blocked out by Clea, Arden by Millbrook, and the crucial eleven o'clock meeting at Miramax by a rocky evening, and a sequence of dreams that had made last night worse than sleepless.

Dev and I had spent an oddly restful Sunday, easily together yet quite separate in our thoughts. No contact from the police—a relief, whatever its reason. We returned from a late-afternoon walk to find Jane and Chris were both in the living room, seemingly oblivious of each other. He was on a ladder rubbing pale orange glaze onto the front wall, while she stood staring trancelike at a cobalt-blue vase—new to me—on top of the mantel. In her hand, brandished like a sword, was the candlestick Liam had bent out of shape bashing the T.V. van. I was still mad enough at Chris for the goading insinuations I'd overheard him laying on Clea the previous morning to feel like grabbing it from her and braining him with it.

Instead, I said a general hi, which broke Jane's concentration and turned her around. She was not wearing her tinted glasses and, perhaps by a trick of the western light, her eyes looked huge and mournful against a face more sallow than I'd remembered. I realized that this was the first time I'd seen Jane and Chris together—or Jane at all—since I'd spotted them screwing in his truck, a very long four evenings ago.

I introduced her to Dev, who volunteered a favorable comment on the vase. They chatted briefly like a pair of museumgoers at an exhibit, with Dev dropping names like Fragonard and Hitchcock, as though he knew what he was talking about. And maybe he did. His collection of unexpected pieces of knowledge surprised and delighted me. Even now, it lifted my mood—for about thirty seconds.

"Where's Clea?" I asked Chris.

"I think she went home to ride," he answered without turning around, his rag massaging away rhythmically at the wall. "She's going to be the fourth person on your crew here tomorrow. If she's any good, I may keep her on."

Go fuck yourself, Chris. That would be a novel experience for you.

"Have the police gotten around to you yet, Jane?" I asked.

"Yes, of course," she said, studying the bent candlestick. "I may be able to get this stick straightened out. It isn't bent too badly, and not in a place where the design will be damaged." I nodded, certain that Jane would step calmly over Zach Terman's body—or mine—in her quest for a perfect repair to the perfect candlestick. "I'll let you know tomorrow," she added.

"No rush. I'll be in the city all day tomorrow. I've got some fairly urgent business." It was her turn to nod—curtly, I thought.

Liam was in a snappish mood. We found him in the library, dealing out hands of double solitaire. "You were gone long enough," he growled.

"You've got some problem with that?" Dev snapped back, sounding not unlike a surly teenager.

It was a different exchange from any I'd heard between them. During Liam's late-night, drunken visits, Dev had listened to the blather and watched the tears, his own pain tethered tight behind his closed mouth. Now, by sobering up, his father had suddenly leveled the playing field: it was man to man, both with their wits about them, one with a lot to answer for.

Liam stood and in a single, fluid motion swept the cards to the floor. His face reddened. ''You watch your mouth, boy!''

Dev covered the ground between them on the run and closed his fist around a handful of Liam's shirt. They stood that way for a good fifteen seconds. I could not see Dev's face, but I saw Liam's fade from angry red to stricken white. I walked slowly to Dev's side and put my hand on his shoulder, wondering as I did it, if he'd turn on me.

He released his father, and reached the same hand up to cover mine. ''Forget it,'' he said quietly, his eyes looking not at Liam but at the wrinkled shirtfront.

''I wish we both could, you know,'' Liam said just as quietly, and bent to pick up the fallen cards.

''What were you so pissed off about when we came in, Liam?'' I asked.

''Just that Clea was not right all day. I couldn't cheer her up, no matter what I tried. And she wouldn't hardly talk. I thought that she might to you, but of course you weren't here, were you?''

Dev's hand dropped to his side, and he left the room.

''Well, I've fooked that up,'' Liam said. He stood, tapping the cards against the table back into a smoothly uniform deck. ''I don't think I ever loved his mother, but I loved him all the while, even in the worst times; even when I knocked him down and broke him. He's a better son to me than I deserve. He doesn't love me of course, but why would he?''

The child beater was saying things that only days ago had made me want to scream in outrage against his right even to feel them. Now I was disturbingly unsure. Righteous blame is so rounded, so full, so satisfying. Once you get used to the feel of it inside you, you miss it when it's gone.

''I guess it depends what you call love,'' I said, flat and weary. ''I'll see you later.''

By the time Clea arrived less than an hour later, the three residents had separated themselves, each from the others. Liam was stationed in the kitchen with a cup of tea, while

Dev rocked on the side porch sipping an Irish whiskey, and I sat on a drop-clothed sofa in the living room inhaling fresh paint.

I was grateful that Chris and Jane had both gone.

Clea's face was strained and tired, despite the fact that her cheeks were pink from riding. I ran to let her in, hoping for a private word. "Where's Liam?" she asked before she was even fully inside the door. "I think I hurt his feelings."

"He's had them hurt before," I said. And since. "But he was worried about you." I folded her into a hug, and her body hugged back tight. "Are you okay?" I asked carefully.

"Uh huh." Her old mischievous smile flickered. "I'm cleaning this place tomorrow." I saw the smile die as she ran back toward the kitchen.

I fixed some basic, salad-type food; the four of us picked at it. Nobody felt much like talking, and what talking there was was of the pass-the-salt, did-you-have-a-good-ride? variety. The murder, by mutual unspoken agreement, was not mentioned. Liam took a fresh can of Coke and left for the music room. Clea pushed away from the table, ready to follow him, but Dev raised his hand in a stop motion. "Did Zach Terman ever hit you?" he asked.

"No," she said, standing despite him.

"Was he able to have normal sex with you?" Hesitation, and then no answer. "This isn't prurient curiosity, Clea. Was he?"

She sat back down. "Depends what you mean by normal." The answer had a teasing edge, half an inch away from snotty—and I damned well couldn't blame her.

"Score one for you, Clea." Dev would give her no break. "Does that please you? I'll be more explicit. Could Zach Terman get it up with you."

My fist banged the table, sending coffee cups into a startled little jump. "Do you have to do this *now?*" I snapped.

"Yes," he returned in kind. "Could he, Clea?"

"Sometimes," she said. "I didn't care. We did other things. He kissed me." No trace of snottiness now. "Boys my age don't bother kissing—at least the ones I know. Zach was a man.'' She leaned over toward Dev in the chair next to hers and spoke urgently. ''Do you understand what I'm saying? There's better parts of making love than just '*getting it up*.' ''

''I do understand,'' Dev said, his voice thoughtful, and gentle as I've ever heard it.

He and I lay together that night, uneasily separate now. At one point, my hand reached out to his chest, right above the slow thump of his heart. If he hadn't turned away, we might have talked, but he flipped over onto his side, back to me, so we went to sleep in silence. And I had my bad dreams— of a place that looked like a fiery hell, but froze the bones of all who entered; of slaughtered, gutted deer; of Clea in a padded white satin coffin on the floor of my old bedroom, and Chris standing over her, a sexy smile on his face. Perhaps Dev had bad dreams too. Neither of us said.

''You're driving too fast,'' he said now. ''If you stay out of the clutches of the law for murder, you don't want to get nailed for speeding.''

''Not funny.''

''I agree. Forced. I'm off my stride.''

For about ten minutes more, I kept up the pace for no really defensible reason but the tensions that jumped like fleas around my senses, and the lingering feeling that he'd been unnecessarily hard on Clea last night.

The cab made its way down the West Side Highway. I'd parked the car in the East Sixties. The plan was to meet there at three. Dev had made himself an appointment with Zach's business manager and, with Ariane's permission, was going to have a look around the Park Avenue apartment. I had no idea how long my audience with Claudine Augier might last, but afterward, I intended to check out Zach's garret—just in case the police and the super, between them, had left anything worth finding.

The cab's windows were rolled open. The slightly humid air was warm today, rather than stifling, and the river smell coming gently off the Hudson not at all unpleasant, evocative of something I couldn't quite grasp, but which felt vaguely hopeful.

Tribeca, jauntily named for its shape and location—the triangle below Canal Street—is tucked in right above the city's financial district, which forms the southern point of Manhattan Island. Even twelve years ago, when I'd left for California, Tribeca was fast joining SoHo, north of it, as a center of what they call "downtown chic," and while I was gone, the transformation had barreled along. Chic notwithstanding, I loved the area's vast old warehouses, each with an awning, a portico, a set of dented steps, a bit different from the one next to it. The buildings used to house crates of butter and eggs and hats, but now they house the people who prefer, and can afford, to live and work in sprawling lofts.

I'd fantasized about becoming one of them. A few rosy daydreams: Dev and me, sipping drinks on a roof garden, gazing at the Hudson; munching a sandwich on a sofa facing the same water view through huge windows; making love on a soft rug under a peaked skylight.

These visions, which came close to matching Zach Terman's for romantic clichés, had not lasted very long. Not only was Dev perfectly content in his Brooklyn Heights aerie with a view of the other river, but he and I had far bigger problems between us than whether to look at the East River or the Hudson. And the high, wide, light loft in my head turned surpassingly sad when I thought of occupying it alone.

Miramax money is instrumental in maybe half of what appears on movie screens. The Miramax building, on lower Hudson Street, is, like a good many others in the neighborhood, owned by Robert De Niro, who has cleverly substituted real estate for a rich grandmother. I'd been here once before to meet with a De Niro cohort on what had turned out to be a big nothing.

As the driver pulled over to the curb, I gave my hair one last finger run-through and pulled a mirror out of my bag to check the thin film of makeup I'd applied to my normally naked face in an attempt to hide the scrapes and bumps of my tussle with Zach's body. I walked into the building with a blip of stage fright in my gut, a suspicion that I might've been better off skipping the makeup, and the certain knowledge that my white linen pants and shirt were sloppily wrinkled.

The receptionist on the twelfth floor did not immediately recognize Claudine Augier's name. After a few backs and forths, a bell went off somewhere under her slicked black hair. "Oh, wait a minute. That must be Peggy's friend. Okay, what did you say your name was?"

Claudine Augier was tiny. Since she was sitting I couldn't say for sure, but four ten would have been a guess. Behind a large black glass table of a desk, she looked doll-small: a doll of about my own age, with olive skin and a white-blond punk crew cut; a doll who wore a crisply tailored black silk man's (or boy's) suit, complete with tie; a doll who puffed a small, spiffy white pipe.

She did not stand up—just scanned my long, tall body in its wrinkled linen and unaccustomed street makeup. Up and down went her sharp black eyes, up and down like some sort of diagnostic X-ray machine.

Since I had worked as an actress for twelve years, none of this was a surprise, so I stood there silent. One of the lessons Bernie Clegg had drummed into me was, let them talk first.

"So," she said in a voice deep enough for a much larger container. "So, you're Emily Silver." The trace of a Montreal French accent. A trace of disappointment, too? "Sit, sit." She motioned at a plump black leather chair opposite her, and watched me lower myself into it with some care.

"I had kind of a fall the other night," I said. "I'm not usually this creaky."

"Are you serious?" she asked, her brow rising at the point eyebrows would have been if she'd had them.

"Yes." I caught myself running my tongue around my lips. Great! I was rattled already.

"No, no," she said quickly, "what I mean to say, Emily, is I do read the papers and the friend I'm staying with owns a television set. Three, in fact."

My laugh was a beat or two delayed, but it was real. Of course, the whole damned juicy story was all over the place. Ostrich Emily: head in the sand, butt in the air. A position all too familiar to me.

"The *Daily News* had a close-up of you, long lens—not very flattering."

"To set the record straight, Claudine, I should be in good operating order within a week, and in shape to start fencing, dancing, and all that a couple of weeks later, if—"

"I liked the way you worked in *Running Fast*—the energy, the edginess." She spoke slowly. "I like it very much for Rozzie."

My heart sat up and panted at the praise. It takes very little encouragement to elate an actor. "Thank you."

"Your mother was an actress, correct?"

Now she'd astonished me. My mother had never made a movie or worked in a Broadway theater. Even her T.V. parts hadn't been large. "Yes."

She nodded at me for a while, in a way that suggested a spring-necked Chinese doll. "How do you feel about my concept for *Arden!*?" she asked.

I didn't think I could manage a quite convincing reading of "I love it." Something essential in me shared Dev's distaste for modern knockoffs of Shakespeare. "The screenplay reads quirky and exciting. I did *As You Like It* at the Seattle Rep; I'd love to play Rozzie for you."

"Bobby adores my movie. And Marty."

I nodded recognition of the De Niro and Scorcese references. "Great. How's your financing package coming along?"

"Fabulous. Almost closed." She narrowed her eyes and puffed at the pipe. "We see a big international market, in addition to here. We'll shoot in Quebec. Cheap, but beautiful. I see it in the way Branagh saw *Much Ado*. But completely different, of course."

Bet your ass, different. He kept Shakespeare!

For the next two hours, all that could be heard in that smart office was the sound of names dropping. I played the game; I did my share. We talked more about the movie, in what initially seemed a common language, but which veered off into obscurity whenever the word "dollars" came up.

When—after a sent-in lunch of artistically arranged vegetables washed down with mineral water—we performed our goodbye handshake, I knew as much concrete information about the likelihood of this project going forward as I had when I came in.

It was just after two o'clock when I reached Eighty-second Street. I let myself into the building with Clea's keys, and despite all my talk to Claudine about how speedily I was getting back into shape, my ankle throbbed by the time I reached the fifth floor.

The key turned easily, and the door swung open on a room pin-neat, fresh-smelling, and bare almost to the point of emptiness. I entered and went through the motions of looking around, but there was nothing much to look at, certainly no papers, diaries, photos. I looked inside the single closet, and saw a matched pair of scarlet kimonos, golden dragons embroidered on their backs, hanging side by side. Oh Zach, you pathetic creep! I locked the door behind me and trudged slowly downstairs.

Just as I walked out the front door, there she was on the street in front of the brownstone next door, a large plastic garbage bag in each hand.

"Kolonsky!"

"Ah, lady with the sister."

"You did a good job cleaning the apartment."

"I clean it up right after you leave. I figure, what the hell, I'm up, might as well work. The police were not happy, but they are never happy. It is not their nature," she said with a mournful Russian irony. "I told you Terman was not good man. I am not surprised somebody kill him. Not you or your sister, I hope." Her small bear-eyes glinted at me.

"I suppose the police questioned you pretty thoroughly about who came and went here," I said, fishing.

"Of course. But I tell them nothing. Girls come, girls go; is not my business, I say, so I never look at them. But I tell you, is four month now, the only girl is your sister—who is not your sister after all, Miss Otis. I see on the television, you have no sister. She is Miss Clea Held.''

"Thank you, Kolonsky," I said. "Can I . . . ?" I made a move toward my purse.

"No. Of this, I make you a present—for free." She waved her arm over toward Park Avenue. "You know that lady watching you?"

I spun, just as the lady was speedily rounding the corner onto the avenue. With my bum ankle I didn't have a prayer of catching her, and I couldn't have quite sworn to it, but the almost subliminal impression I got was of someone wispy and beige, with large sunglasses.

27
....

"WELL, DID YOU GET THE PART?" DEV HAD BAILED the Lincoln out of the lot and was in the driver's seat, parked in front of a fire hydrant when I arrived.

"Don't know." My glimpse of Jane Benzinger had swept that question into the wings of my mind. I expected to tell Dev about it first thing, but for some reason, I asked instead, "Are you planning on driving?" An edge of sarcasm to the question.

"It's your car." He held out the keys. "And you can't neglect your training or you'll never make the Indy Five Hundred."

"Oh, go ahead and drive," I snapped, annoyed at myself for initiating a trivial bicker while real troubles mounted faster than either of us could cope with. I slid into the passenger seat. "Why don't we not do this?" I asked, miserable in a way that was far too familiar.

He started the car, then abruptly turned the engine off. "I've had a lot of practice hacking it with Liam drunk," he said. "I got so I could do it with my eyes closed—and pretty much did. I don't know if I can stand him sober." Both his hands lay tensed on the dashboard, the long fingers ready to strike a violent chord on an imaginary piano.

One of the stories in Dev's book was a kind of fable about a boy and his father who walked arm in arm into a tunnel through a mountain. Each was humming to himself a different private song. Somewhere inside the long, dark tube, a confounding exchange happened: the father's song began coming out the son's mouth, and vice versa. When the two of them reached daylight on the other side, their eyes met in a long, silent moment of perfect understanding—and profound dislike. The *Times* reviewer had called that particular story "both searing and chilling." Dev and I had never discussed it; any mention of his lone, long-ago book was certain to provoke a battle.

" 'Changing Tunes,' " I said—the story's name.

" 'Changing Tunes,' " he agreed, sounding desolate. His hands raised themselves from the dash, the tension of a moment ago spent. One hand started on its way to touch me, but midway changed its mind and went instead to the ignition key. But when I put my hand on his thigh, he did not brush it away. "You need someone to cosset you, my love," he said. "I'm not sniping now; I mean it. But I don't cosset well. You know I'm talking true; that's why Mike's watch is still bobbing around on your wrist."

My eyes went automatically to it. "Maybe by now I just wear it out of habit. I don't know what's true. Mike used to say I'd leave him sometime, and that he'd push me out of the nest right on my ass if I stayed too long."

"Unmistakably Mike," he said, voice furred with emotion, as he pulled out into the late-afternoon traffic. "You're better than I deserve, Emily."

"What a Catholic thing to say. I thought Hannagan's philosophy didn't truck with concepts like deserve."

He grinned. "Hannagan's philosophy is not plagued with the hobgoblin of little minds. In fact, maybe I *do* deserve you." And immediately changed the topic. "So, come up with anything?"

"Maybe. Zach's garret was whistle-clean. But Dev, I think I saw Jane Benzinger."

He gave me a quick, sharp glance that told me he was as unprepared for that as I had been. "What do you mean think?"

I told him what had happened, and that when I questioned Kolonsky, who'd gotten a closer look, her description was of Jane.

"Or at least a million other thin, dun-colored women with sunglasses who might be tempted to stare at you. You have been all over the tube, my friend."

The wind left my sails. "But suppose it was Jane. Could she have been having an affair with Zach too?"

"Stranger things have happened—but not much stranger. I had a long talk with his business manager today. He knew our boy pretty well, or thinks he did. They went to high school together.''

"*De*Witt Clinton.'' In my head, the orange-brown frozen carcass gave way to a sixteen-year-old with a flashy smile, and a yen to get out of the Bronx.

"According to Harvey, Zach was a cocksman's cocksman. However, Harvey Ortwasser married at twenty and calls himself 'a family man,' so I suspect he was a prime audience for some very tall locker-room tales. The thing is, even in those tales, Zach was strictly a one-romance-at-a-time man, and though he never treated Harvey to names, he called him on a certain Saturday afternoon about two weeks ago to say he'd just met a gorgeous actress—'I'm talking Audrey Hepburn, but picture Audrey as a baaad girl.' He mentioned something about the two of you striking sparks.''

"Oh Jesus.''

"I thought you'd like that. But bad Audrey aside, the most recent girlfriend Harvey describes is unmistakably Clea Held. There's a predictable pattern: each of Zach's liaisons lasted about four or five months, and all of them had the schmaltz of a fifties movie.''

"What about the romance with Ariane?''

"Ah, interesting. Ariane was different. When Zach first met her, he was even more lovesick than usual; a goddess, cool and pale as alabaster, was the way he described her. She went almost double the five-month mark, and he pulled out all the stops to make her marry him. Harvey mentioned a skywriting plane flying over the Cornell campus. Looks like it worked.''

"Had he ever been married before?''

"No. He was forty-two when he met Ariane and, Harvey says, lived with his parents in the Bronx until he was thirty-eight and published his third book. That's when he rented the studio on Eighty-second Street. The parents were Orthodox Jews and declared him dead when he married the *shiksa*. They live in Florida now. Poor Harvey got to be the one to break it to them. Ariane called him before the police released the news of Zach's identity, because she knew how broken up he'd be, and she made him promise to call the Termans right away, because they wouldn't want to hear such news from her, and she was terribly worried they'd learn it from their T.V. set.''

"Nursey," I murmured. "She's always been that way, ministering to patients and their families. And she does it so damned well you have to think she means it.''

"Harvey agrees with you. He calls her the most considerate woman he's ever met—not that he saw her all that much; the Termans kept mostly to themselves socially. What shocked him was that a few months after the marriage, Zach was back to packing picnic baskets, sending long-stemmed roses, and asking girls if they'd ever before been kissed on the George Washington Bridge. He says he told Zach more than once that he was crazy to play around on a paragon like Ariane: beautiful, smart, good, and—of course—rich.''

"So was Zach. That was his whole thing, what a big success he was as a writer.''

"Yes, but the really good money came only on the last three books, and Harvey claims he spent most of it. That crazy castle up there cost him over a million, and he insisted on paying cash, which brought our poor friend Harvey pretty close to a heart attack. No, in the money department Ariane is definitely the one with the loot. Compared to her daddy, your grandma was strictly middle-income.''

"Harvey's a fund of information. Is he Ariane's business manager too?''

"No, her money's tied up in a fairly complicated trust. I had a look at James Lewis Warburton's will. It's helpful occasionally to work for a law firm. One of the partners called Chicago for me. Warburton was roundly considered a son of a bitch, but it seems he owned half the real estate in Winnetka, and that was only for starters. Bottom line, Ariane's income is over four million a year. Brother Jamie has his own trust fund to support him in a 'suitable facility, and attend to all his needs.' But here's the wrinkle: if Ariane ever takes her brother to live under her roof, her trust is dissolved and so is his. It all goes to the Chicago Zoo and a few other institutions.''

"She said he was cruel," I said, "and now she's essentially told him to take his money and shove it. Good for her.''

"Ummm. But even the cruel have thought processes of

some kind. I'd love to know what James Warburton's were. I'd also be interested to know whether Ariane told her husband about Daddy's little strings on the loot."

"I bet not," I said, sure I was right.

"Now why do you think that?" The question seemed important to him.

Why did I? "Because she thought of Zach as a child, and she handled him that way. From what you heard today, he had very little sense about money, except he liked to spend it a lot. I doubt he knew squat about her father's will. He was already against Jamie living with them for his own set of reasons, but I'll bet she thought she'd wheedle him around one day. This would've killed any possibility."

"Maybe it killed Zach," Dev offered.

"You're saying that he found out about the will? Look, if she wanted her brother to live with her, and she was prepared to give up the millions, why didn't she just leave Zach? He was a rotten husband, they had nothing intellectual in common the way she does with Bart, and their sex life was no good."

"The lady claims love, which, as you know, does not divide up sensibly into a set of components. Think of it as a prime number. But let me propose something to you. Zach was killed with a chop to the throat, which could be delivered in a split second—planned or unplanned—by anyone with good arm strength: Ariane, Clea, you."

"Or Jane, who was lurking around his block today."

"May have been lurking."

"All right," I conceded, "may have been. What about Bart? Why are you giving us females preferential treatment?"

"Because, although Zach Terman wasn't big, he was reportedly quite fit. The blow was delivered from the front, straight at him, while he was lying down. No other signs of force on the body; no alcohol to speak of, no drugs."

"Does your buddy Heaney tell you everything?"

"Far from everything. Weems told me about the stomach contents, and I did see the body, as you may remember. Someone killed our guy while he was sleeping or having sex."

"Sleep or sex: Ariane or Clea. That's what you're saying, isn't it?" The momentary high of fitting one puzzle piece into another evaporated instantly. I felt trapped now, painted by his logic into a corner I couldn't bear to occupy. "You think it's Clea, after all." Despair seeped into me, because any perception of Dev's could not easily be brushed away.

"Do *you?*" he asked, an irony in the tone.

"No, I don't," I said. We'd been over this ground. "It's just that Ariane was so unmistakably surprised."

"Now we're getting to it," he said. I could hear an excitement enter his voice. "What do you think it was that surprised her?" he asked.

"Zach's body turning up. Why the hell are you playing games with me about this?"

With no warning, he took the car off the highway at the Pleasantville exit. "Let's find a place to get a cup of coffee. I don't feel like driving while we talk about this."

In the center of town, we found a cool, dark, nondescript bar. Dev ordered vodka and tonic, which suddenly sounded a lot more appealing than coffee.

"We've got a sequence here," Dev said. His eyes gleamed an almost neon purple I'd seen in them before. For all his talk about tracking down small-time crooks, he got the occasional big professional kick. It was a fresh surprise every time I saw it. To me, Dev was a writer working at a temporary substitute job, like an actor waiting tables. I admitted to myself now that it was not that simple.

"One"—he raised a tall, blunt-tipped finger—"Ariane suggests that Zach might leave her. Two"—a second finger—"he *does* leave her: note lying on his keyboard, laptop computer gone, car gone. Three." The next finger went up. The waitress reached around it to set down the drinks and a bowl of goldfish crackers. "Clea disappears, telling Liam she's off for a romantic interlude, and you come and ferret her out, only because of the coincidence of her car being vandalized at the train station. Four"—pinky up—"that night Zach's body falls out of your freezer, because there happens to be a blackout: another coincidence. Five"—his thumb shot out from behind his palm—"the car is parked at JFK the day he disappears, but no record at all of any plane tickets, and in the time he's thought to be missing, no credit card charges, not even a phone call.'' He stopped, his face asking me to see what he saw. ''Take a sip of your drink and think about it.'' I did. Then I took another sip.

''Okay,'' I said, knowing that I was about to make no triumphant *jeté en l'air,* but a series of baby steps. ''Let's eliminate the two coincidences. If Clea's car hadn't gotten trashed, she still would have come home sometime—one way or another. If I hadn't stumbled into the freezer that night, the door would certainly have been opened another time, when I might have needed extra storage space or more ice. I still don't get it.''

But by the time those words were out of my mouth, they were no longer true.

Suddenly, I was as stimulated as Dev. ''Why didn't he just disappear? He never left at all; the whole disappearance was faked. And if he had just been dumped in the river, it probably would have worked. He'd just be . . . gone. But he was put in my freezer because he was sure to be found there, sooner or later.''

Dev raised his glass and clinked it against mine. ''Congratulations. Now comes the hard part. Ariane could have killed him. So could Clea.'' His palm went up to preempt my interruption. ''All we're talking about here is typing and printing out a note on his desk computer, ditching his laptop, and driving his car to the airport. I admit that Ariane had more opportunity, but you cannot rule Clea out. Much as she may have adored Zach, she also loved the cute little intrigue of getting it on with the husband of her father's beloved. And I will bet you anything you want that, at least a few times, she managed to get it on with him in Ariane's house. In fact, she could have killed him there while Ariane was at your place showing you her black eye.''

''And done what with his body, smartass?'' I thought I had him nailed.

''What would Ariane have done with his body, smartass?'' he fired back.

''Arranged for it to disappear,'' I said slowly.

''And that is just what I think she did,'' he said just as slowly.

"You mean you don't think it was Clea?" Sweat broke out along the edge of my forehead and chilled instantly in the cooled air.

"No, I don't, but I went through the exercise to show you how easily Heaney might."

My teeth massaged my middle fingernail. "Someone helped Ariane out," I said, my whole body tingling like a banged funny bone. "Someone took the body to get rid of it—and then decided instead that Zach had to be found."

"Umhm." His sound of approval resembled my acting teacher's when I'd finally gotten a scene right. "While I was poking around the Terman apartment, finding fuck-all, it occurred to me that once you separated the feeble evidence of Zach's disappearance from the discovery of his body, the whole thing began to make better sense."

"So the surprise I saw was perfectly real. Ariane was shocked to distraction, not by the death but by the body. And finding out that she'd been double-crossed by her partner." I stopped then, the discovery losing its buoyancy, sinking fast. "You think it was Bart Held, don't you?"

"Maybe."

28

·····················

WHEN WE GOT BACK, A LITTLE AFTER SEVEN, A T.V. van and a couple of unfamiliar cars were parked as close to the foot of the private road as the guards would let them. A minor whirring and popping of cameras and a volley of questions greeted us. As he turned the car through the arch, Dev opened his window and waved. I looked resolutely at my lap. The tan Honda parked in front of the house was more disturbing than the other vehicles. I recognized it by now; it belonged to Major Heaney.

When Dev opened the door, piano music echoed down the hall at us—not the collection of Irish tunes that made up Liam's usual repertoire, but a noodling set of notes with a randomly sad sound. Neither of us spoke or even looked at the other, but I knew our fears were the same: though Dev was having a tough time with a sober Liam, the slide back to the more familiar problem might be even tougher.

Liam sat alone at the piano, his mouth compressed into a lipless line. He damned well noticed us coming into the room, but chose to stare at the keyboard and ignore our presence. Then suddenly, he turned sharply, showing the flattened face of an agitated bulldog.

"Look at the pair of you, now. 'Is he drunk?' you're asking. 'Poor old villain, couldn't make it after all.' " His left hand shot out to his far side, then swept around quickly, raised high in a flourish. It held an open can of Coke. "Cheers, then," he said bitterly, and threw his head back for a long swig.

Dev clapped his hands slowly three times. "Nice performance, Liam." His voice was harsh with anger and relief in some proportion or another. "Maybe you ought to talk to Emily's agent."

"What's going on?" For once, I asked, a chill of fear in my back, because I sensed that his alarming mood had to do with Heaney's presence in the house.

"She called him. There wasn't a fookin' thing I could do about it, short of knocking her down." Almost exactly Clea's own words, blaming herself for her mother's death. "She's back there in your library talking to him, telling him all kinds of things that aren't true." His eyes brimmed with the first tears I'd seen in them unprimed by alcohol. "Not true at all, no good reason to say them."

"How do you know what she's saying?" Dev asked.

"Because I got down on all fours like a fookin' dog and listened at the door," Liam shouted. But by the time he'd finished, I was out of the room, headed for the library on the dead run.

I flung the door open with enough force to bounce it off the side wall. Heaney was seated behind the desk, the chair pushed back by his long legs. "What the hell are you trying to do to her?" The question boiled out of me like the hiss of an old radiator.

From Heaney's reaction, I might have been a buzzing gnat.

"Not a thing," he said, taking an ostentatious amount of time about it. "Clea asked me to come; I came."

"And if I ask you to go?" My eyes jumped to Clea, who looked unusually white, even for her, against the dark leather of the armchair facing him. "This *is* my house," I added nastily.

He smiled and shook his head. "Your grandmother wouldn't approve of the way you're talking. She didn't care for silliness one bit."

"If that was meant to be charming," I said, "it isn't. I'm sick of all your phony nostalgic crap about my grandmother, your devotion to the Helds. It looks to me like you're manipulating Clea right into—"

"Stop talking about me like I wasn't here!" Clea cried out. "I did ask him to come, and he's not manipulating me. I can't remember what happened, Emily. *I can't remember!* So how do I know what I did or didn't do?"

I lashed out the way a mother does at a toddler about to run in front of a car. *"That's what you told him?!"* If I'd been closer, I think I'd have slapped her.

She sat straighter in her chair, her neck long and stiff. "I am nineteen years old, and I have known Major all my life. I trust him."

"Oh, you trust everybody for ten minutes apiece! You know damned well you didn't kill Zach. Why are you hinting that you might have? We talked about it; you *know* it. Think! Are you just parroting back that stuff Chris was feeding you yesterday?"

Their responses came in chorus. Heaney's military snap, "Chris?" Clea's indignant yelp, "You were spying on me."

"Yes!" My throat opened in a runaway bellow now. "Right, you moron, I was spying, huddling against the wall, thrilled by the shit I was hearing. I love to eavesdrop, especially on people too dumb to—"

"Whoa!" Heaney outshouted me, and gave my head a chance to shut my mouth. Then he dropped the volume a bit below normal and asked, "What was it Chris said, exactly?"

"For starters," I said, speaking to him, but keeping my eyes on Clea, "you should know that Chris resents Clea, because she had it too easy, grew up too pampered. He thinks a good kick in the behind wouldn't do her any harm. I am quoting here." Her eyes flickered the quick pain of an unexpected needle jab. I raced ahead, not sorry. "Yesterday, I overheard him trying to convince her that her memory had blurred out, the way it did three years ago when she tried to kill herself. Perhaps that was the sort of kick he had in mind," I added, my fury iced now.

"Chris is right; I *have* grown up too pampered," Clea said. "And maybe I did blur out. How can I be sure?" She turned to Heaney. "What I told you was true, Major. I don't always tell the truth, but I wouldn't lie to you."

He nodded. Then he rose and scratched the back of his neck. "Funny. One of my daughters is in law school down in Washington—Georgetown. Other one's been in and out of drug rehab three different times. Go figure." He looked down at Clea opposite him in the chair. His shadow on the wall was huge: a looming God, a full nine feet tall. His creased face did not contradict the impression, just added the information that God was tired.

"You and Terman have a meal together that last time you

saw him, Clea?'' he asked with a weary offhandedness. ''Think you might remember that? What did you have to eat?''

''I . . .'' She blinked like a creature unused to the light. ''I don't know.''

''Oh yeah. You'd lie to me, Clea,'' he said, ''if you took it into your head there was some good reason, you'd lie in a minute. Now, you know that as well as I do.''

He turned crisply about face, still the United States Marine, and left.

Clea and I did not have an air-clearing conversation. She would not speak, and I found myself in the idiot position of a ventriloquist doing unscripted dialogue with a dummy. Finally, in exasperation, I marched out of the room and into the kitchen. There was Liam, head down, a knife in his hand, chopping an unlikely assortment of leftovers into a single mass on a large cutting board.

''What are you doing?'' I asked carefully. ''And where's Dev?'' When he looked up from his task, I was relieved to see his face at peace.

''Dev's outside chatting up Major Heaney, and I'm following directions,'' he said.

Clea walked in and stood behind him, avoiding eye contact with me. She wrapped her arms around his waist in a hug. ''Don't be mad at me, Liam. Please?''

''Put some water on to boil, pet, I'm not mad at you,'' he said matter-of-factly, after helping himself to more Coke. ''My son is threatening to cook this cut-up slop and kill a pot of perfectly good noodles with it.''

My son. I smiled to myself, but didn't comment. It wasn't much that Dev had asked of him, just to chop some scraps of ham and chicken and vegetables. But it was enough. Liam sounded as close to happy as I've ever heard him.

29
. . . .

MY ACROBATIC GUT WAS SOMERSAULTING WITH AN-
gry confusion. Clea would barely speak to me and Dev returned from his confab with Heaney tense and inscrutable. I
didn't stay around to watch him wreak havoc on noodles.
Instead, I took myself upstairs, where after a couple of aspirin and a steamy shower, some divine force decided to give
me a break and let me fall dreamlessly asleep.

I rose to the surface slowly from a cool, bottomless uncon-
sciousness, felt myself floating up through warm, jelled water. I sensed Dev's bare body next to me in the bed, though
we weren't touching, and when my eyes blinked open and I
raised my head, I saw in the bluish moonlight that his eyes
were open too.

"Things seemed to be looking up with you and Liam,"
I said tentatively, no way of knowing how they might have
deteriorated after I'd left the scene.

His eyes stayed fixed on the ceiling, and he waited a beat
before he spoke, haltingly as an unwilling witness. "I was
out of town while he was coming off the booze; he did it on
his own. Last time I saw him, before here, was the night he
smashed up his bar with his hands. He called me from the
emergency room at Presbyterian, and I jackassed up there,
wishing the whole time I'd been someplace he couldn't reach
me. They hadn't gotten around even to cleaning him up yet
when I arrived. He was lying on a gurney covered in blood
and vomit, and cursing what was left of his guts out. I hated
him so much it took my breath away.

"Tonight I got to watch him not take a drink when he
was dying for one, and I felt proud of him—the first time in
my life. It made me think some more about Liam sober."

"That it's worth trying to hack? Worth it for you, I mean."

"I'm not talking about magic moments or movie fade-outs. But worth it for me? Yes, I think it has to be."

He didn't shift his eyes toward me as he switched gears and tossed his question, so it caught me even farther off base than it might have. "Who's Bailey Hutchison?"

"*Yes!*" The mattress bounced as my fist punched up in victory. "She called me back that fast. I can't believe it. Why didn't you wake me?"

"She left a message on the machine this afternoon."

"Shit! I never remember to check that thing. Well, what did she say?"

"Are you going to go on this way? Or am I going to hear something informative?"

"Bailey Hutchison used to be assistant headmistress at Fletcher. She was the only person I remember as being really close with Ariane. Strange that her best friend should be faculty, not another girl, but Ariane *was* strange. Is strange."

"Lesbian, you think?"

"No, I don't think. But I don't *know*. And that's the trouble. You keep asking me about Ariane, and all I can come up with are tiny pieces of her, pieces that don't fit together. I was standing in Ariane's bedroom, snooping pointlessly through her underwear, and I just had this impulse to track down Old Bailey, ask her . . . I don't even quite know, but I wanted to talk to her. So I left a message on the Fletcher machine. I'm amazed she got it so fast. What did she say? Where can I reach her?"

"She left a pair of Connecticut numbers, home and office."

"That's odd. She left Fletcher at the end of our junior year, when Ariane did. I heard at the time she'd gone back to England. She's British, and she got to mete out punishments at school. Old Bailey seemed to us a screamingly sophisticated nickname for her."

"She also said that yours was—quote unquote—a fortuitous call, and that she would find it useful to talk with you."

"Really?" A thrill of anticipation buzzed my fingertips. "What time is it?"

"Little after four."

"I guess it's too early."

"I'd say so."

"How was your little private chat with Heaney?" I asked.

"Less cozy than you make it sound. He took me on a brisk verbal trip to the woodshed. The substance was that while nothing you'd do could surprise him, he'd expected better sense from me—a pro—than to go blundering off into police territory. I suppose he has a point."

"Does that mean you're going to stop?"

"No," he said, as though speaking to someone unfluent in the language, "it means only that I suppose he has a point."

Dev had a point too, and I supposed I deserved to feel the stick of it. "Did you get any clue to how he's feeling about Clea?" I asked.

"I inquired. He said that when they got ready to roll out and make an arrest, I'd know about it. Translation: 'We are no longer buddies, Sam Spade, so you can go fuck yourself.' I'll tell you my own feeling, though. Clea's got him confused. I wonder whether it has occurred to you yet that confusion is precisely what she's trying to pull off."

"No, what's occurred to me is that you don't like her." I pounded the headboard behind me hard enough to hurt my knuckles. "I wish the damned time would pass, I'm ravenous to get to Old Bailey!"

"Me, too." Beneath the quilt, I felt a warm hand trace a wide circle on my belly, and begin to make its way south. I ducked all my hungers down under the covers into the dark tent, where all I could touch and smell and taste was Dev.

I called Bailey Hutchison's home number at eight sharp. She answered with her name, after two rings. Her voice did not sound freshly awakened, nor did it sound as though it was talking to someone it hadn't talked to in fourteen years.

"Emily, yes. I expected you might call last evening." *Emily, your English teacher would like to know what excuse you care to offer for this term paper. Well, what excuse shall it be?*

"I didn't get your message till about four in the morning, Mrs. Hutchison." Old ways die hard; it would have been next to impossible to address her as Ms. "I thought about calling you then," I said with an edge of teenaged sarcasm, and was tempted to add that I might have, except that I was getting laid. Old ways.

"Well, I'd have been awake," she said dryly. Hutchison's deep contralto had deepened a note or two. I remembered a Camel fixed between her fingers. "Emily, it's rather a co-incidence that you called me."

"And a coincidence that you're back in Connecticut. The work number you left was Fletcher."

"Yes, I'm head there now."

"Look, I can get in my car and be there in less than two hours."

"Good. I take it then you haven't forgotten where we are. I'll expect you in my office by ten."

30

·······················

I SPED ALONG ROUTE 84, NO DEV AT MY SIDE TO TELL me to slow down. Before I left, I asked him if he'd keep an eye on Clea. "You read my mind," was his response, but with a twist of face and voice I wasn't crazy about. "I might even have a few words with the much maligned Bart."

The Fletcher Academy for Young Women, in Southbury, a suburb of New Haven. The more precocious Fletchies and the male Yalies too shy or unpopular to cope with females their own age found the proximity convenient. At the time, I'd found it the school's single redeeming feature.

Fletcher was established in 1863. My great-grandmother attended, my grandmother did, and so did I. My mother, whose mother sewed wedding dresses in New York's garment district, did not. Celia Silver had never—birth to death—been one of the privileged.

The school's campus, favored today by perfect blue skies and civilized sun gracing white clapboard and bleached red brick, is a picture-book fantasy of an elite boarding school. Or maybe the version is accurate. Its students go on to top colleges and universities; many of my classmates, even while they were bitching about the place, spun out misty-eyed daydreams of someday packing their daughters off to Fletcher. I assume some of them will. The school has character, history, reputation.

Should I ever have a daughter, I doubt I'd take a crack at sending her here. I'd hated it too much. Anything but a fairminded evaluation—during my four years, I'd hated Fletcher the way I'd hated anything my grandmother favored, and a lot she didn't.

The place was mid-July dead quiet, its students off summering in the various places rich people summered. As far as I knew, a dozen of them might have been at that moment eating their breakfasts within a five-mile radius of Millbrook.

A lone car—a tanklike Saab, dulled with age to a winy brown—was parked in front of the main building. I glanced at Mike's Seiko and saw that I was ten minutes early, but I missed the inner hum of comfort at seeing the chunky thing there on my wrist. It had been, I realized, a fair while since last I'd felt it.

Bailey Hutchison sat behind a large, completely simple teak table, most of its top covered with a cityscape of paper: neatly stacked towers of varying heights. At her right hand was a large ashtray, a few butts already in it. She was just finishing one—Camel, I presumed. For some idiot reason, I liked that she still smoked. She stood and moved out from behind the desk, with an athlete's spring.

When I knew her, Old Bailey had been perhaps forty. To my eye, she looked very much the same as she had then. Fourteen years ago, she'd been an angular, sharp-faced woman who didn't favor makeup and wore her hair brushed back in a twisted bun from which a rebellious lock or two kept escaping. She was in no conventional way pretty, but she had presence. She'd been an adversary then, and her smart, brown, lie-catching eyes had troubled me. Now, I was glad to see them.

She put out her hand for a quick, firm shake with no pumping, and thanked me for being prompt. She offered me coffee from the drip machine behind her, which I accepted, and a cigarette, which I declined. "Please permit me; I'm one of the last of a dying breed," she said, that British accent of hers carrying its own irony, as it always had—just enough to force an unwilling laugh out of you as you were being grounded or assigned punitive amounts of extra homework in punishment of some infraction.

"You look good, Emily." She indicated a spot on the green leather sofa where she meant me to sit. "My congratulations on getting rid of all that hair. You're over thirty now; time to face the world squarely. Condolences on your grandmother's death. I do hope you managed to recover from your sulks and get to know her a bit before—"

"Excuse me, *Ms.* Hutchison," I cut in, irritation clipping

the tail of each word, "could we skip my hair and, for that matter, my grandmother?"

"Quite right," she said briskly. "Headmistress's complaint, I suppose: the inability not to govern. Or perhaps I'm merely avoiding what we do need to discuss. Curious, I did have rather a hard time getting used to 'Ms.' At some level it will always mean manuscript to me. Yet, I must confess I like it. Clean and straightforward."

She'd remained standing while I sat, as directed. Now she fetched her cigarettes and ashtray from her desk and placed herself in a square tweed chair at right angles to me.

"I want to talk to you about Ariane."

"Yes, of course." She was not smoking at the moment; no stage business to distract from the disciplined distress in her eyes.

"Have the two of you stayed in contact?" I asked awkwardly.

"Hardly," she said, narrowing her eyes in irony. "I have not seen nor spoken to her since we both left Fletcher. Ariane Warburton came rather close to decimating my life."

I took a deep breath, said a silent "What the hell?" and put the question out there. "Were you and Ariane lovers?"

She laughed, the rolling, throaty, world-weary laugh of a Jeanne Moreau. "Is that what you thought? What an idea— or rather, what a delicious joke."

"I'm glad I've brought some mirth to your morning," I said starchily, aware, somewhere behind my impatience, that the actress in me was playing back to her in her own style.

Her face turned suddenly grave and, in the set of it, I saw the pain of someone accustomed to living with pain. "How well do you know Ariane, Emily?" she asked, an oddly urgent note surfacing in her voice.

"I don't know her at all," I said, my eyes trying to see what might be behind hers, and failing. "We roomed together, but she was close to being a stranger."

"And you, as I remember, were such a self-absorbed girl that other people didn't quite register."

I couldn't protest that one; I remembered the same thing. I was about to learn, apparently, I'd been Rosencrantz or Guildenstern, submerged up to the eyes in the utterly absorbing drama of my own life, and completely out of the loop about the real goings-on with Prince Hamlet at Elsinore.

"Tell me about her, then," I said, feeling a touch of excited queasiness. "That's why I'm here, after all. Her husband's body landed in my basement. I keep thinking there are things I should have . . ." I groped for precise language to offer her. ". . . would have realized, except that—as you say—my eyes were on my own navel."

"I will tell you, only because it's necessary. I've debated with myself whether it was or not, and come to the conclusion that it is, if only to keep some innocent person from blame. I hope you'll be able to do something to prevent that. But understand that I am not willing, under any circumstances, to become involved." Now she lit a Camel—not, I thought, for effect, but to get her through the next sentence. "Ariane killed that man, or else she drove someone else to do it."

The back of my neck dampened with a fresh sweat. This was what I'd come to hear, wasn't it? Clea would be safe, out of danger, protected from her own reckless instincts. But even to my receptive ears, it seemed too large a bite to swallow whole. "You haven't seen her since she was seventeen; you didn't know Zach Terman. Do you have some facts to back up what you just said?"

"Your assignment now is to listen," she said sharply. *Yes, Mrs. Hutchison.* The hands in my lap balled into fists. I shut up. "As you know, Ariane came from a difficult family background. You do too, of course, and both you girls arrived at Fletcher with warnings attached to you." From my record at Chapin I knew damned well that my warning must have read "Explosive, uncooperative, defiant," but what sort of warning might have come with the model girl?

"Ariane's came from her father," she continued. "I'd just moved from the classroom into the assistant head's job, and the head was ill the day Mr. Warburton came to see us, so I met with him. He told me that his wife had recently left him and the children to run off with someone ridiculous—a golf club bartender, I believe—and that he was deeply concerned that his daughter, shall we say, tended to take after her mother."

My vow of silence was short-lived. "For Christ's sake, she was fourteen, and from the impression I get, her mother was smart to leave her father—for anyone."

"That was my impression, too, at the time. James Warburton was not a nice man, and it wasn't difficult to see how dented his pride was by his wife's rather public rejection. I put it down to that. But it did bring Ariane to my attention—happily. She was a totally rewarding student from our standpoint: bright, eager, cooperative, friendly, good at sports. And there was something more. She had a certain sweetness about her, an empathy for anyone who was troubled."

Nursey: that facet of Ariane, it seemed, everyone had noticed.

"What ever became of her brother, young Jamie?" she asked. "The papers didn't mention him as part of the household. I know the father was determined to keep them apart, but still, I'm surprised that Ariane didn't find some way to get around that. She is . . . quite resourceful."

"Jamie, in fact, has just moved in with her. She'd wanted it for a long time, and Zach was no happier than Mr. Warburton about the idea. But Zach was a jealous, childish man, so I understand about him. What was her father's reason?"

"We'll get to that," she said briskly. "For Ariane's first year here, you may remember that she was quite close to Regina Barth, the athletic coach." I did. I could even picture them, weekends and spring evenings slamming a tennis ball back and forth, though Barth's face didn't jump to mind.

"Barth was here only the one year, right?" I asked.

"Wrong. Barth had been at Fletcher for seven years. It was after that year that she left."

Her face put it to me, so I said the words. "Barth left, you left. You laughed when I mentioned lesbianism. What was Ariane's magic touch?"

"Barth's husband taught at Yale. They had a son of twelve, an extremely handsome boy. He attended the country day school; no reason you'd ever have met him. But Ariane did. She spent a great deal of time at the Barths', including part of the summer holiday; her father was not eager to have her at home." She looked at me pointedly. But with a point I didn't get.

"Where is this going? The Barths caught golden boy and Ariane in the hayloft together, and blamed her? Is that it?"

"You really always were the most impatient girl," she said with a grim smile. "No, unfortunately nobody caught them. That August, just after Ariane had returned to Chicago, Matthew Barth killed himself. And then his parents did blame Ariane."

"Why?" The word came out almost soundless.

"They claimed she molested Matthew. There was a note, apparently. I never saw it. It was kept private, but Regina Barth felt it her duty to speak to someone in administration, and I was elected. If his note was true, Ariane was mistress of sexual sophistications—perversions, if you choose to regard them that way—quite unbelievable in a fourteen-year-old from a rather sheltered background."

Ariane? I didn't know what I had expected to hear, but this seemed . . .

Old Bailey's voice sliced through my surprise. "Though Barth was far from an hysterical type, I chose to believe that an oversensitive, fantasy-filled boy couldn't manage to cope with galloping puberty."

"And what happened to change your mind?"

She stubbed out her cigarette and lit another. "I'd always been—or thought I was—a good judge of character. What's a school administrator doing in her job if she isn't? I spoke with Ariane candidly, not about Matthew Barth but about her father's accusations. He'd told me, you see, that Ariane had molested her little brother."

I stared. "That isn't possible," I said, with a certainty firmly rooted in the sands of my ignorance.

"I believed," she continued over my interruption, "that was the fairer way. I reckoned that if she could persuade me that her father was misguided or lying, then Barth must be mistaken too, and it would be cruel even to raise the possibility of blame in Matthew's suicide to a girl who must be feeling quite ghastly about it already." Some faultily inhaled smoke or maybe bad memories sent her into a paroxysm of coughing.

After a few moments, she wiped her tearing eyes with the back of her hand. "Serves me right," she said with a sniff.

"I see you've quit, though. Good for you." She smiled. "Surprised I knew? My dear Emily, I knew many things. My nickname: Old Bailey—a bit obvious, but not bad. More to the point, I could probably reel off the names of girls in your class who were sexually active. You, I believe, began shortly before you were sixteen; there was a boy at Yale, then another."

"Emily Otis: this is your life," I said curtly. "But my life isn't the subject here."

"I'm not showing off to no purpose. When I tell you that Ariane persuaded me that her love for her brother had not the slightest sexual overtone, I'd like it to *mean* something to you."

"And how exactly did she persuade you?"

"I listened to her and I looked at her. At that time, I was forty-one. I'd handled almost two decades' worth of students—I'd dealt with manipulation and emotional disturbance; with truth and lies. I was certain I could recognize the difference."

"And something happened to make you less certain?"

"Yes, something did. That was the real reason I needed to leave Fletcher when I did. It took me better than ten years to regain some modicum of confidence in my judgment—in other parts of my life, as well."

"Ariane decimated your life, you said. That's what you really want to tell me about, isn't it?"

"Yes Emily, that's what I must tell you about. Do you happen to remember my husband?"

"Only that you had one," I said.

"Tom was a sculptor. Very few sculptors make much money, even the good ones, and he was never all that good— just good enough to sell the odd piece, teach some classes. Our living was mine to earn, which was one of the reasons I stopped teaching English literature and became an administrator.

"We never had children, Tom and I. A deliberate decision. We wanted none; needed none. We were complete. And I'd never cared to bring students into my private life. Oh, the odd end-of-term party for Honors English, but I preferred a certain distance. I did not examine my motives; I'm afraid that the American taste for self-analysis is one part of my transplantation here that never quite took root.

"Then Ariane walked into my home. It was my own doing. She never pushed herself on me; her manners were always impeccable. But the child was despondent about Matthew's death, bereft of Barth's companionship, and she seemed utterly devastated by the things her father had said about her—things I'd told her. I felt . . . responsible. I invited her to tea; teas led to dinners; dinners led to weekends. For three months, life was full in a way I'd never expected. We played tennis together, we talked novels; we talked and talked. Tom . . . Well, artists are often not great talkers. I'd got used to that, but here suddenly was the daughter I'd never imagined I wanted: a joyous gift. Gifts come with their strings. In case you're ever tempted to forget that, don't."

As she spoke, part of my mind imagined thick layers of protective skin, long weathered, peeling off down to the sensitive pink. I sat stone still, afraid somehow that if I moved, she'd rethink the wisdom of baring her soul to such as Emily Otis, and stop.

"I didn't know," she said softly. "I didn't catch a clue, a nuance. During these past few days, I've unavoidably looked back. Even now, I see no footprints, no markers. Tom spent a great deal of time in the barn he used as a studio. He often worked all night, perhaps they began then. But I knew nothing at all. Tom and I had planned a holiday in England. A cousin of mine was lending us a cottage in the Lake District—Wordsworth country, splendid for walking. We'd been before; Tom especially loved it. He'd sketch; we would drink good scotch, eat local lamb."

Her face seemed to freshen with the memory of the walks. More locks of hair had escaped the pins of their bun to frame her thin cheeks like soft parentheses. "Our life together was good—in every way. Including sex. Tom loved me."

The nostalgic glow abandoned her face abruptly, leaving it dull. "Just at term-end, he told me that he had to leave me. I have never been quite that furious in my life," she said starkly. "Tom did not give up Ariane's name voluntarily, nor easily. I beat it out of him with my fists." She stared

into my face looking for shock, and didn't find it. "I bloodied his nose," she said. "He stood there, the red dripping
down on the kitchen floor while he told me about ecstasy.
Told me about it, wanted so desperately for me to understand. He meant to run away with her; he said it was the
only possible thing. My husband and a sixteen-year-old girl.
I almost did begin to understand. But not quite.

"I telephoned James Warburton. I did not need to say
much. Ariane was gone very quickly."

"And you were, too," I said.

"Yes, I was gone too."

"Tom?"

"He followed me to England. We spent four years apart,
seeing each other occasionally." She spoke now with re-
move. "We're together again. I think he regards it as having
caught some sort of flu bug, and recovered. I can't be certain
of that; we don't speak of it."

"Mrs.—"

"Oh, I believe you may call me Bailey," she cut in, irony
back in place, "all things considered. The 'Old' I'll leave to
your discretion. You appear to have grown up, Emily, despite
your best efforts."

We tried pallid smiles on each other; they worked like
half an aspirin after major surgery. "Bailey, what do you
think—about the murder?"

"I know nothing specific to that, how could I? But, one
way or another, I do know that Ariane is responsible, and
that another man must be involved. The rest I shall leave to
you."

The phone on her desk rang. "Hello? . . . Yes, darling.
Swordfish will be fine." The throaty Jeanne Moreau laugh.
"Perfect, I'm just in the mood. I'd say six or so . . . Have
the gin nice and cold, will you? . . . Me, too," she whispered,
and hung up.

"I won't talk to the police, Emily, if that question is in
your mind. Neither Tom nor I could stand it, and of course,
I've no facts to reel off to them." She reached out for my
hand and held it firmly. "This is your responsibility now.
Unfair of me to place it on you, perhaps, but life is seldom

fair—and you did, in a manner of speaking, volunteer. I trust you to handle it well.''

Our hands parted. ''I'm afraid you'll have to excuse me now. This chaos on my desk won't sort itself out. Few things do.''

31
. . . .

WHEN I GOT BACK, THE HOUSE WAS EMPTY; EVEN
Liam was nowhere in sight. Inside my skull a pinball machine sent small, silver spheres dinging their way down to
nowhere, then popping back up ready to begin the process
again.

Had Ariane driven Bart Held to murder? Or her brother?
That was a new idea, and the one Bailey Hutchison might
bet on. But no. Both those pinballs fell with a pair of dull
clanks. Dev reasoned that the chop to Zach's throat had been
delivered while he was asleep or during sex—no struggle,
no other bruises on his body. Made sense. So, let's say Ariane killed him herself . . .

"Emily, just the person I wanted to see." The flat, quiet
sound of Jane Benzinger behind me brought the thought to
a grating halt. "Jane comes on little cat feet," Clea had commented once, more than a little maliciously, on just such an
occasion.

"Looks like you were able to fix the candlestick," I said
coolly, pointing at the object she held. My eyes strained to
find any sign in her face of sheepishness about yesterday's
missed encounter on East Eighty-second Street, and came up
empty.

"Yes, luckily." She ran a professional hand along its
shaft, now ruler-straight, and handed it to me. "The man I
use does a perfect job."

"The man you use, where is he?" Somewhere near
Eighty-second and Madison: good cover story coming, I
thought, and waited for it.

"Up in Amenia," she said blandly.

I made myself take a full beat. "Would you like a cold
drink or a cup of tea?"

"Anything cold," she said, sitting herself at the table, her
large tan bag of wonders at her feet. She sits like a cat too,

I thought: still, precise, erect—perhaps just the slightest twitch to indicate she's nervous?

I took my time getting ice into glasses, pouring Sprite on top of it. I wanted the right words. Not that finding right words has ever been a specialty of mine, but Jane was such an enigma that the challenge was tougher than usual. My head bent over the soda bottle and I stole a peek at her. Goddamn it, my skin knew she was involved in this some way, but . . . It made no sense at all.

As I handed her the drink, I said it, casually as commenting on the weather. "You know I saw you yesterday."

"Did you?" A quiet challenge. The show of resentment on her face was quiet too, but unmistakable.

"On Eighty-second near Madison. You took off like a thief when I turned around. You knew Zach Terman, didn't you?"

She eyed my face silently. It was like being gazed back at by a painting on a wall, but I didn't turn eyes away. The painting talked in a voice tighter and flatter than usual. "It wasn't me you saw." I heard the tension and pressed my advantage.

"I think it was."

"You think wrong. I don't go into the city. And I never met Zach Terman in my life." The partly opened book snapped quietly shut in my face.

At that moment, Liam appeared at the French doors, dripping wet, a towel around his bare shoulders. "I've been for a swim," he said, chin jutting a bit, just in case anyone planned to make a joke about the extraordinary occurrence. "Hello, Janie. Not seen much of you lately."

"We're just about done here, Liam. Chris and me both."

"Glad to see the last of him, but I'll miss you. We've had some good talk, haven't we?"

"We have," she said. One more thing under my nose and beyond my notice: as far as I knew, Jane and Liam's conversations were at the level of "good morning."

"I was going to mention to you that the work's almost finished, Emily," she said, "but we got off talking about other things." Bland, entirely bland. I knew that the moment of possibility for nailing her had passed. Nothing to prove it had been Jane I'd seen—but now I was sure of it. "Chris's last touch-ups here are Thursday," she said, "and the living room sofa will be back early next week. Then I think the house will be just the way you wanted it to be."

And right she was. Through all the weeks, despite death and heartbreak the work had proceeded. The rooms flashed through my head like a series of slides. "Yes," I agreed, "just the way I wanted it to be."

After placing the rehabilitated brass candlestick on the dining room mantel in the precise position she had in mind, Jane left.

I asked Liam about the "good talks" with her, and how he'd managed to have much talk at all with a person that skittishly reticent. "The two of you don't seem like natural soul mates."

"I wouldn't say soul mates." He scowled down at the Coke he'd just taken from the fridge. "Filthy stuff; I don't even like the taste of it." He pulled the tab from the can and drank. "You never did meet my Ethne, did you?"

"No." I'd never been to his bar, and she'd never joined him on his boozy late-night drop-ins at Dev's apartment.

"She'd remind you of Janie. Shy little wisps by the look of them, but that's just the outside. I used to tell Ethne that the stuff inside her was so hot she needed to keep it in a lead-lined box." His face warmed to the memory.

I didn't want to hear him. Was it prudish distaste at the frank sexuality of my lover's sixtyish father, or was it the knowledge, there between us, that he'd found me in bed with Chris Held? "Let's get back to Jane," I said unceremoniously.

"Jane. Well, a good long time ago, I sat at a desk—when I showed up at all—at St. Joan of Arc grammar school on the south side of Boston. Sister Mary Filomena was a great fan of old Joan, talked about her all the time. I can hear her now, that squeaky Southie sound of her talking about Joan's *paaassion,* how she'd ride her horse into the fiery mouth of the devil for what she believed in—and pull his teeth out while she was at it. Now, of course you might take that ride too. But you'd make such a fuss that the devil would see you coming and shut his jaws. But Janie's passion sneaks up on you. And I wouldn't want to get in the way of it.''

"How did you get her to talk to you, though?"

"No spilling her guts, if that's what you mean by talk—no secrets. She told me once over a cup of tea that people have a right to their secrets. I don't disagree. But I did try to warn her off that strutting, rutting goat.''

"You know about Chris and Jane?"

"Even old drunks whose bladders are bursting with Coca-Cola have eyes in their heads." *But excitable actresses bumble around stone blind.*

"Have your eyes caught sight of who killed Zach Terman?"

"I don't think they want to. No-win situation, isn't it? Any way you look at it.''

32
....

I SUPPOSE I COULD HAVE SIMPLY WAITED FOR DEV TO get back, but I was too restlessly eager to do that. Liam didn't know where he'd gone, but I thought I did, so I got back into the car and drove to the Held house. Dev's car was parked in front. When nobody answered my first ring, I opened the door and went in. I found Dev and Bart drinking together on the large, screened back porch, and had the immediate sense that I was about as welcome as a female cub reporter in the team's locker room.

"Hi," I said. "Where's Clea?"

"Ah, the most asked question in all of Dutchess County: Where is Clea!" It would have been difficult to imagine Bart Held drunk, but imagination wasn't required: here he was. All things considered, he had a right.

"Clea went out," Dev said, his irritation at my arrival plain. "I do not know whether she is traveling by car, horse, or on foot. She said she'd be back here before dinner. That gives her three or four hours to do whatever she damn pleases with no one gazing over her shoulder."

"I think I'll have a drink, if you don't mind, Bart," I said, giving it a nonchalant reading, and helped myself to the scotch bottle and ice bucket on the long bar table.

"Your friend here has been what I guess they call in his business grilling me," Bart said, a vague smile out of place on his tormented face. "Isn't that so, Dev? Paul? What do you prefer, by the way?"

"Dev will do for now," Dev said. "It's what Emily calls me, and her presence seems pervasive at the moment."

Bart laughed, a doleful bottom-of-the-well sound. "Don't give her a bad time. It doesn't matter that she's here. Not really. Maybe she can provide some feminine insight." He leaned forward, a bit unsteady in his chair. "All right, Emily. Now for the sixty-four-thousand-dollar . . . No, wait, inflation! The sixty-four-*million*-dollar question: Why do women loathe Barnet Held?'' I didn't speak, just waited. ''The clock's ticking here. Don't you have the answer?'' His face creased into folds of comic disappointment. ''Come on, here's a few hints. His wife found him a boring stick, preferred his sexy nephew; his daughter calls him a heartless tyrant; the woman he loves will no longer even talk to him. Now, what do you say, Emily?''

With no warning, his head bent and he began to cry, deep racking sobs that sounded grating and painful—the way a stick might weep, if it could.

''If you gave me the answer, it wouldn't do much good,'' he said, raising his head finally. ''I don't think change is in me. If it ever was, my father scared it to death a long time ago.'' His eyes were dry.

The screen door from the kitchen squeaked slightly as Clea walked through it, wearing riding clothes. Whether she'd just arrived, or had been inside listening to her father's agony was impossible to tell.

''Hi Emily,'' she said, ''you saved me a phone call. I wanted to talk to you. Could I come over tomorrow morning?'' I thought I caught something different in the look and sound of her. She seemed suddenly older—or perhaps stronger was more accurate. I saw her eyes meet Dev's and then bounce back to me. ''I think I'll stay home tonight, unless my father has to go back to the office, that is.''

''No,'' Bart said, his face flushing a color close to the deep pink I'd seen on Clea's face. ''I plan to be right here.''

By the time we got back to Orchards in our separate cars, Dev seemed ready to forgive me for intruding on his session with Bart. It was close to five, and a faint breeze was tickling at the leaves of the old trees. Birds were giving their all for anyone within earshot. In the late-afternoon light, the islands of flowers polka-dotting the green were brilliant.

''Let's go for a swim,'' I said. ''I have things to tell you. And things to hear.'' And then, because I couldn't wait, I asked, ''What's going on between you and Clea?''

''Privileged communication. I'm not the fatherly type, as

you well know, but I may have a real future as an Irish French Indian Dutch uncle. A swim's not a bad idea.''

We sat at the edge of the pond, dangling our feet in the luke-cool water, and I told him about my time with Bailey Hutchison. As usual, he did not interrupt. He also did not look astounded, as I'd imagined he would. ''Did you expect something like this?'' I asked, with an increasingly uneasy sense of being isolated in my ignorance.

''Let's just say I'm not overwhelmed with surprise.''

''Well, I guess you're just a lot smarter than I am,'' I said, not pleasantly, as I edged my butt off the grassy bank and into the water.

Dev stayed where he was and grinned. Then he called across to me, ''We're different genders, remember? You don't see what I see in Ariane; I don't see what you saw— it is saw, isn't it?—in Chris Held,'' and plunged in after me. I dove under and bit his thigh hard enough to make him yelp, then swam quickly away. He didn't follow.

We paddled back and forth for a while. ''Okay, I deserved that,'' he said.

I restrained a ''Damn right you did,'' because I knew he'd come back with something about graceless overkill. It occurred to me how very well we knew each other. But the warmth of the thought chilled instantly as my mind shifted, inevitably, to the girl I'd lived with and had never known.

I saw Ariane's face beaming healing kindness at me in my hospital bed. I saw that same face suffused with distilled love, talking about her little brother Jamie.

I saw her looking at me from the other end of the long hall that night after curfew, glowing, smiling in an entirely different way—and knew now that the radiance had come fresh from Tom Hutchison's bed. As I screened the scene this time, it reminded me of something else, but I couldn't quite capture what that was.

''What is it that you do see in Ariane?'' I asked Dev, still mystified.

''If I were a writer . . .'' he said—words I'd never heard him say before. I felt my jaw begin to move, but didn't let myself speak. His mouth turned downward, mocking itself. ''If Flaubert were writing Ariane, he'd get her right. A sexual appetite that shines like a lighthouse beacon—and all the more intriguing because the beacon is housed inside a kind, good-mannered, intellectual, not overtly sexy, nor especially beautiful woman.''

"And you see all that?'' I still could not quite believe it.

He flipped onto his back and stretched his arms out in floating position. "I see all that.'' His eyes were closed, visions behind them of a modern Circe, an Ariane invisible to me.

"And this beacon is what enthralled Bart Held, not their mutual taste for Victorian literature?''

"Maybe that, too,'' Dev said lazily, as though his mind were elsewhere.

"I can't believe the thing about her brother. I just don't. You've seen them together, how he trusts her. Back at school, she was always so . . . protective, so loving when she talked about him. Can *you* imagine that she was indulging her sexual appetite on a little damaged kid she adored?''

"My imagination is boundless. As the man said, nothing human is alien to me. But, that aside, maybe she wasn't doing anything but reading Dr. Seuss to her brother. The father was a mean son of a bitch, and over the top with rage when his wife left him. I gather from my Chicago sources that Ariane looked like her mother. It's not beyond the realm of possibility that he noticed both his daughter's sexual glow and her affection for her baby brother, and the poison in his own head drew the wrong conclusion.''

"Or not,'' I said, feeling a bleakness made worse by the Eden-like scene around us.

"Or not,'' he agreed.

I lay back and joined him floating, and remembered fleetingly that I'd had a dream about floating together in this pond. But not like this; not talking of incest and murder, graves and epitaphs.

33

I⊤ HAPPENED THE FOLLOWING MORNING—FOR ONCE, nothing I had any way to anticipate or prevent.

Clea arrived just before nine. I was alone in the house. Dev had gone to Millbrook for the papers, and had on the spur of the moment asked Liam to come along for the ride and a spot of breakfast at the diner. I figured that Dev knew precisely what Clea had to say to me, and was giving us a clear field alone together. Though he and I hadn't discussed her further, I suspected I knew what I was going to hear—at least some of it.

When she walked in the door, I noticed again that unaccustomed air of maturity, which seemed suddenly to have slightly remolded her face. She was wearing her "What part of NO didn't you understand?" tee-shirt, but somehow the message was only funny now, its pained stridency as absent as its wearer's.

"You told me once that Dev wasn't handsome," she said with a trace of her old, mischievous grin. "You were wrong. I think he's very handsome—like a brooding poet: that dark Byronic look, and then those beautiful purple eyes as a kind of surprise."

"Yeah, okay," I said, embarrassed faintly, as though the extravagant description were of me. "Look, little sister." The words were strange in my mouth; I hadn't used them for what seemed a long time. "I suppose part of me is sorry that I blasted you that way the other day in front of Heaney, but part of me isn't sorry at all, especially that I told you how Chris really feels about you. You needed to know that."

"Poor little rich girl: I've played that hand over and over, the way Liam does his solitaire. I've wallowed in it. Sure I've had a hard time, but in other ways I *have* been pampered. Maybe that kick in the butt was useful. Valuable."

I could hear Dev in what she was saying, and wondered

whether Clea truly believed the words, or whether she was losing herself one more time, in her new Dutch uncle.

"Is that what you and Dev talked about yesterday?" I asked.

"Part of. We talked about lots of things. You know," she said seriously, "you ought to marry him, if you have the chance."

I punched her arm lightly. "You sound like somebody in a novel with dried flowers between the pages. What's your next suggestion? That I tell him I'm in a family way?" We walked past the pond in companionable silence the way real sisters might, taking a stroll together after one of them had come back from a trip. But the trip was not over—no safe harbors yet.

"You once told me that Ariane was going to be your stepmother," I said. "Did your father ever say that to you?"

She stopped and looked at me, her face flushing too suddenly to blame on the sun. "No," she said, that bell-clear voice of hers muted. "I was playing. It was a story I told myself: Zach would leave Ariane, so the two of us could be together, and then my father and she . . . Well, everyone would be happy. It was a story—not a good one."

"Not a good one," I agreed. "And you enjoyed playing with me, too, didn't you?" I asked with a harshness I hated hearing. "You played with Heaney, too," I said more gently. "To lead him away from suspecting your father. You knew damned well that you didn't kill Zach."

Her chin raised in the manner of someone who had something to say, and was going to say it, no matter what response it met. "You know how I feel about my father: I don't like him much." She speeded up now. "But I guess I love him in a way, and no matter what all of you think, I know he didn't kill Zach either. This is my fau—"

It happened in the space of a second, and yet every detail within that no-time-at-all was separate—distinct as a particle of dust under a magnifier.

The shot cracked.

Clea rammed me sharply aside, elbow to the ribs, doubling me over.

She fell to the ground, graceful as a dancer, one arm wrapping around to the other shoulder.

I knelt at her side, staring into her white, motionless face and the spreading deep purple blot on her left shoulder. My circuits jammed, refused to process anything except the certainty that she was dead. I saw blurrily in double exposure two Cleas lying perfectly still, one on the blue rug of my old bedroom, the other here on the bright green grass. One passed out in drunken parody of death, the other . . .

My head jerked stupidly, as though waking from an instant nightmare. I held my hand under her nose and felt rapid puffs of warm breath. Then she groaned. She was alive! For an ecstatic moment, I almost burst into a whoop of thanks that had nowhere to go but out into the warm summer air.

Now my eyes surveyed, full circle: a perfect country landscape, every aspect of it, suddenly turned treacherous. We were smack in the middle of forty-two acres—clear targets in a wide-open field; fair game for anybody who cared to take another shot.

The fear was savage, punishing, but it was not blind panic. Panic, I learned in an instant, is a luxury unaffordable when someone you love is helpless, dependent on your protection. I covered Clea as well as I could with my own body—my hand pressed firmly against her shoulder in an amateur attempt to stanch the blood—and then launched as earsplitting a scream as a pretty good actress could manage.

Dev might be back and hear; one of the security guards at the edge of the property might hear. Then again, the shooter might be the only one to hear. I shut my eyes and screamed again. I didn't figure I had much choice.

A rustle in the bushes. My eyes flew open. I hadn't realized they were shut. A small, curvy black woman in sharply pressed chinos and a blindingly white man's shirt was running toward me, hunched over close to the ground.

"Who the hell are you?" I called at her.

"Arlena Watson, *New York Daily News*. Keep your head down. That's Clea Held there, isn't it? And you're Emily Silver."

"*Yes*," I bellowed. "Do you have a car phone?"

"What happened?"

"She's been shot! Please call nine-one-one. *Please.*"

"Did you see who—?"

"I'm not giving a fucking interview while she bleeds to death!"

Even lying there terrified for Clea and me, I marveled, as I watched the white shirt disappear into the trees, on the poetic justice of a reporter as my lifeline.

The Millbrook Rescue Squad was there with its ambulance less than ten minutes after Arlena Watson called 911 from her car. If she called her story in first, I'd prefer not to know about it. The medic checked out Clea's shoulder, and in a few quick motions, he had it wrapped in a neat tourniquet.

"What is it?" I asked, fearing the answer.

"Looks like a rifle shot clipped her. Happens a fair amount in hunting season. Not usually in the middle of summer." Clea opened her eyes and mumbled something unintelligible. He gave her a comforting wink from behind his thick glasses. "You're gonna be fine, honey." He turned to me. "They'll fix her up down at Vassar Brothers, don't you worry. Looks clean, like the bullet went straight through and out the back." He signaled to a pair of stretcher-bearers, and spoke again to Clea. "Now, I'm giving you a little shot here, for the pain, and then we're gonna lift you nice and easy. It'll hurt some, but try and relax and go with it, much as you can."

I took hold of the hand on her good side, and squeezed lightly. "Did you hear, little sister? He said you're going to be fine." I managed to keep my voice from shattering.

She opened her eyes again, wider this time, and a smile of pure delight bloomed amazingly in her ghastly face.

"I saved your life," she said. "I did it this time."

I rode with them, holding Clea's hand. Though she didn't open her eyes or speak, I believe she was awake, because her hand closed from time to time around mine in a private signal. I read it loud and clear.

Major Heaney was waiting at the hospital, looking grimmer and more worried than I'd seen him. Once Clea had been spirited off to an emergency room cubicle, he took me into some office he'd commandeered.

"I had security guards," I said, my tension breaking out into pointless accusation. "Where the hell were they? How could someone get onto the property to shoot at us?"

He blew out the long breath of an ex-smoker. "One guard. The other fella called in sick. Quiet morning, no new developments, not much press hanging around, manager figured what the hell. Says he left a message on your machine. Big, irregular piece of land like that, anybody who knew it well could've parked clear over the other end, done the rest on foot, and got away quick. Security guard's just a man in a car. Good enough to discipline a few reporters, but . . ." He held his large hands out in a what-can-you-do? gesture.

"Lucky that one was around," I said. "Arlena Watson, *New York Daily News.* Be extra nice to her—if you ever get hold of any information to give out, that is."

He managed a thin smile. "Of course, it could've been some jerk of a hunter getting in some out-of-season shooting on posted land."

"Is that what you believe, Major?" I asked, my hand tensing as though to grab at him.

"We're not talking about what I believe, Emily." His tone was stark, stripped of that fatherly, faintly indulgent quality I was used to hearing in it. "Tell me exactly what happened."

"There was a shot, Clea pushed me out of the way, and then she went down." It flashed again through my head. "Maybe she pushed me first, before I heard the shot. Now I'm not sure."

"From what direction?"

"West—no, slightly northwest. From out past the stables, I think, just about where the horse trails start. Could he have ridden over?"

"Not impossible. Who knew you were walking out there?"

"Nobody. No, that's not true: lots of people, in a general way. I walk or jog most days, usually in the morning."

"Where's Paul and Liam?"

"They went into town for the papers and breakfast. I

wanted some time alone with Clea.''

"Besides the two of them, who knew Clea would be there?''

"Just Bart. I think.'' I looked at him and decided quickly that this was not the time for evasion. "She's been manipulating you, you know, to protect her father.''

"No kidding,'' he said sourly. "Bart ought to be here any second. I called him from the car. Maybe Clea's instincts weren't so far off.'' His gray eyes, through narrowed lids, challenged me—in earnest or teasing, I couldn't tell. "He's pretty sweet on Mrs. Terman; he's got a horse; he's better than good with a rifle.''

"That's the stupidest thing I've ever heard, Heaney. You think he'd shoot his *daughter?*''

"Not on purpose. But he might've wanted to clip you. Now, if I try real hard, I can imagine how you could annoy someone that much.''

"A direct hit, Major,'' I said, smiling despite myself. Without warning, my eyes stung, and tears began their way down my face, as Clea smiled in my head. *I saved your life. I did it this time.*

34

···················

Dev, Liam, Bart Held, and me. The four of us sat in the front living room at Orchards, picking at quartered ham-and-turkey sandwiches from a Route 44 deli, and drinking cup after cup of the hot tea Liam kept refurbishing. Even those of us who hadn't given up alcohol, and who might have been expected to crave a drink, didn't seem to want one. The general atmosphere most reminded me of the dispirited get-together after the last AIDS funeral I'd attended in L.A. That, too, had been held at a newly done-up house, which had seemed on that particular evening to mock the notion of building anything.

We'd left Clea asleep and, according to her bristly gray woodchuck of a family doctor, perfectly fine. Luckily, the bullet had—as the medic said—exited her wound, only grazing the shoulder bone.

"Hell Bart, I probably could send her home tonight with a bottle of antibiotics and some painkillers, but I'm going to keep her, at least till tomorrow." He'd shooed us all out the door, saying that he and the nurses could take swell care of Clea, if we could do the same for her daddy.

Dev was, to my eye, restless as a circling boxer waiting for the strategic moment to throw his punch, not sure the moment would come. He kept leaving the room and returning, off in his own thoughts and largely silent.

Liam was talking jumpily about anything that sprang to his mind, as though if he stopped, he might disintegrate. We heard bar jokes, stories of his growing up in St. Filomena's parish (". . . and she's not even a saint anymore. They tossed her out on her ass. Renamed it St. Brigid's"), and of two fighting years spent in Korea, which until this minute I'd never heard mentioned. Curiously, as he went on, the bogus brogue receded like a spent wave, overtaken by newly strong, flat vowels straight out of south Boston.

Bart Held sat stunned, like a man immediately before he realizes he's just been thumped on the head with a mallet; in a second he would fall unconscious.

"I blame myself," he said, from time to time, to no one in particular.

"What is it exactly you blame yourself for, Bart?" I asked too sharply, after the fourth repetition.

He ran a palm over his face. "I didn't shoot her, but I may as well have," he said wearily.

Before anyone could question that, the front doorbell rang—a surprise to us all, except Dev, who sprang up as though he'd been waiting for it.

A moment later, Ariane, her eyes radiating concern, walked in and headed quickly for Bart. He stood just as she reached his chair, and looked back at her, mute. She took his face in both her hands, and seemed about to kiss him. Then didn't.

"Oh my dear," she said, "I am so sorry." Her voice sounded clogged with puzzled shock. "I know I'm no help, but I came as soon as—"

"Why don't we get you something to eat, Jamie?" Dev cut in. "How about a sandwich?" It was only then that I saw a disoriented Jamie standing in the archway, shifting his weight from one leg to the other, uncertain about whether to come into the room or wait in the hall.

"Yes, I would like a peanut butter sandwich and a glass of ginger ale," Jamie said precisely.

"Oh, here you are, darling." Ariane held out a paper shopping bag to him. "Jamie's fairly particular about food," she explained, directing herself to Dev, "so I thought I'd just bring along what he usually eats at this time of the evening."

"Fine," Dev replied. "Come on into the kitchen, Jamie, and help me get your sandwich on a plate?"

Jamie hesitated for a beat, looked to his sister—who gave him a small nod—and followed Dev down the hall. Ariane said her hellos to Liam and me, and accepted a cup of tea. I looked hard, tried to see the femme fatale, the child abuser—and couldn't spot a trace. "I understand Clea's going to be fine," she said, seating herself beside Bart on a sofa.

"So I'm told," Bart said quietly. "How about you, Ariane? Are you going to be fine too?"

"I'll have to be, won't I? There's Jamie to consider." She held her hands folded neatly as a schoolgirl's in her lap. "Bart." She covered his hand with hers—her left one. I noticed that the chunky gold wedding band was not on her finger, but whether it had been there the last time I'd seen her, I couldn't have said. She spoke to him slowly, and as though the two of them were alone in the room. Something in the air made even Liam shut up.

"It's not too late," she said. "You can make it up to Clea. You can. The two of you have something to build on; you must believe in that. It isn't the way it was with you and your father, or between me and mine," she added, only then a note of bitterness creeping in.

"Oh my God, Ariane, I've missed you." He turned finally and met her eyes. "Why didn't you let me try to help?" It was almost a cry.

"I just thought it would be . . . better."

The noble sweetness of it might have been unbearable, if it hadn't been so goddamned poignant. These two as the Macbeths? I'd have sooner cast Joan Fontaine and Leslie Howard.

Dev and Jamie returned with the sandwich properly plated, and Jamie looking somewhat more relaxed. Dev led him to a wing chair with a table beside it, but he himself continued to stand, avoiding my attempt to catch his eye.

"Why don't you make us some more tea, Liam?" he asked, his voice edged with some kind of impatience. Liam responded with a wordless nod, and trundled off to the kitchen to do it. Then Dev questioned Jamie about his dog run and we all listened to the lengthy, enthusiastic answer.

This time there was not even the warning of a doorbell ring. He appeared in the archway from the direction of the kitchen. But then, he would, wouldn't he? It was the entrance he always used.

Jamie jumped from his chair in delighted surprise, and went to him. "Chris! Hey Chris, what're you doing here?"

My eyes darted to Ariane, in time to see her face draw tight, masklike: an animal that knows it's been trapped.

And in that instant, I knew. I remembered exactly when I'd recently seen the radiant smile of sex on Ariane's lips—the morning I came to tell her about Zach's body. And I remembered something else: the spicy citrus perfume she'd worn. The smell of Chris.

Chris recovered first, or perhaps, being Chris, he needed no recovery. "Hi Jamie, how you doing, fella?"

"What a coincidence, you two knowing each other," Dev said casually.

"Chris comes and works where I used to live, Dev," Jamie explained to his new friend. "Chris can fix anything. Right, Ariane?"

"Right, darling," she said, her voice entirely steady.

35

· · · · · · · · · · · · · · · · · · ·

T HE DRAMA, BASED IN SEX, DID NOT REACH A TOWER-
ing climax. No one was clapped in irons, or even accused of
anything. The closest it came to that were the glares of loathing beamed at Chris by his uncle and by Liam, who returned
with fresh tea, which nobody ever did get around to drinking.

"The A.C.'s working good," Chris said. He gave Bart
and the rest of us his back as he turned to Dev. The move
was Chris's trademarked sign language for "fuck you."
"You called," he said, pro to pro. "Which john's acting
up?"

"Upstairs hall," Dev answered coolly.

I don't think I could have spoken, if I'd tried. My head—
balloon-light and filled with a twanging, like the vibrating of
a broken spring—was screening a jumpy movie, clumsily
cobbled together from clips it hadn't understood first time
around.

And, illogically, I hated Dev for grasping what I didn't;
for planning in the seclusion of his head the dreadful scene
that had just played out. For exonerating Clea and her father?
I wondered seriously, in a way I never had, if I might be
crazy.

Bart laid his hand lightly on Ariane's shoulder, and said
quietly, "I'd like to see you home."

"I can drive your car, Ariane," Jamie said. "I have my
driver's license. I always carry my driver's license and my
Social Security card and my blood type, which is A positive.
I'm a very good driver."

"Yes, you are," she agreed. "Thank you, Bart. I'd like
to drive home with you." Friend to friend.

Dev had baited his trap with that friendship, and counted
on her to walk into it. How would he have set it up, I wondered, if Clea hadn't gotten shot? I felt a sudden revulsion,

a gut quake, and was afraid that if I didn't get out of the room fast, I'd ruin Jane's perfect new rug.

I heard Dev open the bedroom door. The stiff-hipped roll of his walk looked to me more pronounced than usual; no handicap, an emblem of defiance. I sat on the bed, knees to chest, the crosspiece of the headboard hard against my back. I was still fully dressed, though hours must have passed since I'd made my running retreat upstairs. I wasn't sitting here this way waiting for Dev; I just had no capacity to move, or even to see past the snaking tangle of games and obessions, traps and betrayals.

"I suppose you're going to say you had to do it that way," I said.

"Don't suppose about what I'm going to say or do. It gets us into nothing but trouble," he said, ice-cold. His eyes were cold too, and from where I sat, shone as black as his straight—now overgrown—hair. Framed in the doorway, he might have been a rogue brave who'd just deposed the chief of a warlike tribe. The door shut behind him with a hollow bang.

"You bastard," I said, quietly as a sleepwalker. "You couldn't trust me, could you? I'll suppose again. I'll suppose that you've told Heaney."

"Yeah. And no, I couldn't trust you. Every one of your relationships in this thing was too damned loaded."

"Why don't you say what you mean? I fucked Chris."

"Okay, you fucked Chris."

"You fucked Ronnie. I thought you didn't care about all that."

"No, but *you* do. And I couldn't take the chance. You're a potentially lethal mix of outlaw and sheriff, Miss Emily: the reckless moralist." He pulled his shirt over his head, unfastened his jeans and let them drop.

"And you're professionally amoral. Bad bet for both of us."

"Maybe so." He stepped out of his underpants and stretched himself out flat on the bed, hands behind his neck, massaging it.

''How did you know?'' I couldn't not ask.

''I didn't know, it just figured: two sexual lighthouses in that kind of proximity, with that many connections in common; maybe they flashed each other. Even after I called Jamie's former residence and found out that Chris was their plumber and general maintenance man, I didn't *know*. Of course, you and I have different definitions for that verb.''

''For lots of things. What happens now?''

''I'm not sure. Maybe nothing happens. There's no proof of anything, except that they knew each other.''

''And lied about it.''

''And chose not to mention it. Bart was her great and good friend. She knew he hated Chris because of the carryings-on with the late Wendy. Ariane's a considerate lady. She didn't want to cause her friend Bart any discomfort. Next?'' he added nastily.

''Did Chris shoot Clea?''

''I don't think so.''

''Who did?''

''An out-of-season hunter?''

My arm swung back and then into a lashing whack across his face. I was crouched now on all fours, panting and horrified and sorry. And not sorry. He didn't change position or expression while his hand made a short arc that returned what I recognized, even as it landed, as a reined-in slap. Nevertheless, it hurt like hell. I wasn't sorry about that, either.

''Feel better now?'' he asked, his voice as tightly controlled as his hand, but just as rigid with anger.

''Yes, thank you,'' I answered, aping civility. ''And you?''

''I feel like shit,'' he said. ''I am going to sleep now.''

And incredibly, he did. Another of his capacities that I'd never grasped. The man I knew so well. What a joke.

I did not sleep. I didn't even turn off my bedside light and try. After some amount of time or another, I reached a zone where nothing matters and boundaries are made of fog. My body lay still as a corpse in the bed, knowing that at some moment well before morning, it would get up and leave the house.

I know where I'll be going, I thought languidly. *I have all night. No need to rush.*

36

· · · · · · · · · · · · · · · · · · · ·

It was four twenty-five when I turned the Lincoln's key, and ten past five by the time I'd wandered around Stanfordville, taken a few wrong turns, and found it. It wasn't so hard, even in the dark: networks of roads traveled as a kid, thrilled to be finally behind the wheel, remain engraved somewhere in the brain. And I'd heard enough about that house in the woods to know approximately where it was.

I found the mailbox called Held, and opposite it, a narrow graveled road cut through a husky forest. The feeling was of plunging into a one-way tunnel. As I entered it, the rustle and skitter of animals fleeing an intruder blended with the buzz of alarm trying hard to pierce the mist inside my head.

About two hundred yards in, I glimpsed the house. I stopped the car a good fifty yards before the clearing and stared at Chris's creation: the tall Victorian, cream and white and curlicued, stood on a flat-topped rise, like a wedding cake incongruous on a rough wooden platter.

I slipped out of the car, careful not to bang the door shut in the normal way. It was as though any real-life sound would break the spell, wake me up and send me speeding home. If I were truly awake I would know I had no business here. Clea was my business, none of the rest of it. And she was safe. Dev didn't think it was Chris who'd shot her, but Chris *had* tried to mess with her head, and for that I did not forgive him. I recalled Dev's icy observation that "forgive" was my kind of verb, not his. *Right Dev, it is. I'm as rock-ribbed a judge as any Tucker who ever breathed.*

I mounted the front steps, my sneakers silent against the gray deck, and paused before turning the polished brass bell handle. I knew that with the sound, I was committed; I could not turn tail. The handle was cold to my touch. I turned it and pulled myself over the edge. Now I was fully inside the dream, and there was no way out. I bashed the door furiously. Rang again and bashed some more, as though every extra second he took to answer were crucial—and unforgivable.

Suddenly, a light went on, and there he was: faded denim cutoffs, bare chest, bare feet, but eyes as sharp as bits of broken green glass. As the smile spread across his face, I had the odd feeling that he knew, better than I did, why I'd come—that he'd expected me.

"Come on in," he said. "I've been to your house, you want to take a look at mine?"

I started to step over the threshold, but my foot pulled itself back. My heart pounded me the message that I did not want to be inside Chris Held's house.

"I want to talk to you, Chris. And I want to do it out here."

"Chicken?" The eyes caught the porch light and glinted at me. "We're past that, Emily."

It took a beat for me to get what he meant; that's how past it we were. "Thanks for the memory," I said coldly. "But I'd prefer the fresh air anyway." I stepped down off the porch. "Come on, Chris. Chicken?"

"You're a funny lady, you know that?" he said, sauntering down the steps, graceful as Astaire, to join me. "One part rich bitch, one part nutcase, one part pretty hot."

"Those the same fractions you found in Ariane?"

His eyes shut for a moment, and his face turned serious, as close to sad as I'd seen it. "No. Ariane was something else; a whole nother thing. That what you came to find out?"

I couldn't seem to stand still. I paced as I talked, the way I did when I was trying to memorize lines. "Not mainly." I turned and looked him full in the face. "You didn't kill Zach, Chris."

He took his time: not rattled, just thinking. "Maybe I did," he said in a voice edged with teasing superiority.

"Nah. Ariane killed him, while he was sleeping or making love—or trying to. You were just the good maintenance man; you took his body away. That's what you do, isn't it? Clean up rich people's messes?" I wanted to goad. I also wanted to hurt, and saw that I had.

He closed the space between us in a few long strides to

stand closer than I wanted and half a head taller, looking down at me. "You don't know chickenshit about anything. You never had to work for money in your worthless life."

He was quite right. Sure I'd waitressed when I first landed in Hollywood; sure I'd played those little clubs. Fun, kind of like camping out. Fun, because if at any moment I'd dialed my grandmother's number, her check would have been in the mail. I hadn't chosen to, but the choice was there.

I felt like moving out of his range, and forced myself to stay put. "So you're a self-made man. Good for you. Exactly what kind of license do you imagine that gives you? I'm up to my eyeballs with your movie: how Chris the Magnificent overcame his bad beginnings, toughed it out, started a business, supported his mother—"

"Let's skip my mother," he snapped, like a kid in a street fight.

"You know what pisses me off?" Before I even started on the answer to my rhetorical question, he cut in.

"Sure I know," he said. "Clea." Cool again—Chris was back to being Chris.

"That you'd try to pin it on her, play head games so she'd pin it on herself. Well, let me tell you," I barreled along, my chest swelling with pride in her, "she didn't buy what you were selling for a second. She was playing too, putting herself on the line because she was afraid Heaney would go after her father."

"Her father?" He shook his head slowly. "The Major's too smart for that, and even old Weemsy isn't dumb enough to really believe *Bart* could make it with Ariane. Or have the balls to deal with a dead body." His smile returned. Its message was contempt.

"Is Weems also too dumb to know that you made it with Mrs. Weems?"

"Private business." The smile widened into a grin. "Just like Emily Silver."

"You were a great fuck, Chris," I said evenly, making the word its ugliest. "I'll write you a reference, okay? Let's get back to Bart. You were saying?"

"I was saying that my uncle wasn't even enough for a wackout like Wendy."

"So you took her on, like a bit of charity work to help him out? Nice of you."

"Nice for Clea baby," he agreed, relishing what was coming next. "If I hadn't been getting it on with Wendy, I wouldn't've been there the night your buddy tried to take herself out." He was standing close enough to see my face change, as he'd expected it would. Shrewd Chris: he guessed Clea hadn't told me that detail. "Surprised you? Her daddy was out of town overnight. She knew I'd be coming."

"Was it an extra little thrill for the two of you, rubbing a sixteen-year-old's face in your little affair?" Clea had learned her games early, at her mother's knee. Wendy Held was beyond my hatred; I could only be glad she was dead. But my loathing for Chris now was drenching and dirty. "You are such an asshole," I said, biting out the words one at a time.

"Clea would be dead but for me."

"She might not have tried to kill herself but for you. Ever think of that?"

I could have been speaking Chinese. "Hey, grow up, Emily. Life happens; shit happens; parents do what they do. You oughta know that," he added with a zinger in it. I came close to giving him back his "Let's skip my mother," but didn't allow myself the indulgence.

"After you parked Zach's car at Kennedy, what were you supposed to do with his body?" I asked instead. "Dump it in the Hudson?" He looked at me blandly and didn't answer. "Come on, Chris, it's just you and me." I ran my hands down my body, clothed as it had been since the disastrous morning walk with Clea, in tee-shirt and shorts—no room in either even for a wallet. "See? Noplace I could stow a recorder. You can always deny it later," I wheedled. "So, in the Hudson?"

"Something like that."

"But you dumped him down my coal chute instead, and stuffed him in the freezer. Why the change in plans?"

"Work it out." Suddenly he'd turned angry. No—on second thought, less angry than embarrassed. Chris, embarrassed? I studied his face, which looked sad, and suddenly almost innocent.

"You wanted to marry her," I said softly.

"She would've married me," he countered, not quite convincing himself.

"But you couldn't wait, right? What is it, five years till someone missing's declared dead?"

"Seven."

"What was it you couldn't wait for, Chris? Her or the money?"

"I didn't have to wait for her." He laughed a laugh cold as a frozen corpse. "The money, Emily. The money. Can you imagine what a kick it would've been? What a high?" Another laugh—this time, pure bliss. "Christopher Maddock Held the Third, of Millbrook: a millionaire ten times over anything his fucking granddad ever dreamed of having. I would have ditched that stupid castle in about ten minutes, and we'd have bought—"

"She'd never have married you," I said.

"You snob cunt. I was the best she ever had." We were on his turf. "And she was the best anyone ever had," he added, tasting it: a three-star meal recollected—a religious epiphany.

My skin puckered in a sudden wrenching shiver of need to get free of the sight of him. I headed for my car on the run, the instantly desperate flight of a nightmare, and heard his own long steps pound quickly behind me. I felt the warmth of his breath on the back of my neck.

Then I heard the shot, so close it seemed to explode in my ear.

I pivoted and hit the ground in time to watch him fall, slow motion and without a sound, beside me. I inched my palm out to just under his nose, and felt nothing. His sea-green eyes were vacant of sex or anything else.

The voice was, as always, quiet. "Straight through the heart. A clean kill. Good." She seemed to appear out of nowhere, ghostlike in a pale beige shift. *Jane comes on little cat feet.* The rifle rested easily against her shoulder, as she bent just slightly over his body.

I looked up at her. "Are you going to kill me?" No emotion but curiosity made its way into my question, because there was nothing else inside me. It was still, in some way, a dream.

"Of course not," she said, with flat northwestern good sense. "Why would I want to kill you?"

"You tried to yesterday."

"No, I tried to wing you yesterday, and winged Clea instead. I was sorry about that, but not very; it was her own fault."

"What was?"

"Jumping out that way, changing my shot. But if I wanted to kill you, Emily, you'd be dead. I just wanted to slow you down." The voice remained quiet, but took on a harsh edge of dislike. "People have a right to their secrets, and ones like you never respect it." Our eyes stayed locked on each other. After a moment, she held out her hand to me—the hand that wasn't cradling the rifle. "Here, let me help you up."

I grabbed onto it; my bad ankle had given itself a wrong turn as it hit the ground. "Why, Jane?"

"Because he was perfect." Her eyes gleamed the way I'd seen them gleam when she talked of a painting or a rug or a table. "And they'd have caged him up like something in a zoo, gawped at him, ruined him. You understand, there was no way in the world I would let that happen."

I'd seen her passion on display for weeks, without beginning to perceive its shape or dimension. Now I did understand—too late to matter. But a glimmer of something began to shine through to me: perhaps there was something *she* didn't understand. "Jane, do you think that Chris killed Zach Terman?"

"He did. Or she did. That's really not my concern. I knew he was mixed up in it. That Sunday, I was there at the train dropping my dealer off. I saw Chris coming out of the station, and before I could honk, he ran to a car. And he kissed her, the woman with the beat-up face; the one I'd just met at your house in the morning. I had no idea who she was. He kissed her and got into her car."

He was her ma-an, and he was doin' her wrong. "I see," I said, playing shrink to a love-crazed killer. "The sight of him kissing her. You must have felt so . . . betrayed."

She looked at me like a teacher at an especially foolish child. "No, no. Betrayed by Chris? He was a perfect lover. I wouldn't expect to own him any more than I would a Rembrandt or a Leonardo. He made love when and where he wanted to. Me, her, you. But he lied to me that day. He told me that there was a plumbing emergency in Amenia. And then when you found her husband's body and it turned out that his car was parked at the airport, I began to wonder about why Chris would be at the station, when he said he was in Amenia. He never took trains. Of course, if he drove that car to Kennedy, he'd have to get home some way, wouldn't he?"

"Seeing him kiss her at the train station? That was enough to make you shoot him?"

"No, that made me wonder. *You* made me shoot him," she said with a pitying half smile. "It was your fault. You couldn't leave it alone."

My hand flew to my mouth. The fear that had been so strangely absent flooded into me now, and I didn't believe I would leave here alive.

"You were all over the place, snooping. Well, I've been doing some snooping of my own these few days, very unlike me. I even went into that stifling city to see where Terman's studio was, and to see whether you'd show up there. You did."

I stared like a charmed snake. Wanting—not wanting—to know what would come next.

"These last few nights," she went on, "I've camped out in Chris's woods, in case somebody came for him and I had to end it. And I was right: you did come. Next, it would have been the police, so it didn't pay to wait. I heard everything you said."

I had killed Chris. And now, with awful symmetry, he would reach back and kill me.

Tires grated furiously against the gravel. A car door slammed. Seconds later, Dev stood there, his breath loud and ragged with running. The gun in his two-handed grip was trained on Jane.

"You won't need that," Jane said calmly. "I was going

to put a call in to Troop K as soon as Emily and I were finished talking.''

Dev did not shift his position. ''You sure he's dead?''

''He's dead,'' I said. *Straight through the heart. A clean kill.*

''Put the rifle down, Jane,'' Dev said. His face seemed cast in stone. Even his mouth barely moved as he spoke. She didn't give the rifle up, but wrapped her other arm around it instead, holding it close, as though it were a living thing.

''Give it here, Janie.'' Liam's voice, reassuring, pan-flat Boston, the brogue gone. He appeared out of the shadows, behind Dev to the right of him, and held out both his hands.

It was full standoff for long seconds. Then she walked slowly to him and handed it over. ''It's good to see a friend's face, Liam. I'm glad you came.'' Reasonable, so reasonable. Good that the kill was clean; good to have a friend along when you went to the police. Good.

The dream mist was entirely dissipated. The beginning creep of dawn was coming in unexpectedly chilly for July. A long shiver ran through my body, suddenly weakening my knees. Chris had died: the death penalty for being a stud; the death penalty for ambition; the death penalty for crossing Snooping Silver's path.

''Your car, Dev?'' Jane asked politely.

''My car, Jane,'' he answered. ''Go on, why don't you get in. I'll be there in a second.'' He jerked his head at his father. ''Keep her company, Liam. But let me have that rifle first, before you shoot yourself in the foot with it.''

Liam handed it to him. Then he looked at me. The blood-shot blue eyes were like an old soldier's, just off his final battlefield. ''Did she shoot Clea?''

''Yes. She meant it to be me.''

He shook his head. ''Let it go, Emily,'' he said as he turned to follow her. ''It's over now.''

Dev wrapped his arms tight around me. The gun in his pocket dug painfully hard into my side—the lethal steel of the grim present. It wasn't over. Too many things waited to be done. My own arms reached round Dev's shoulders, double-locking us together, but only for a moment.

''Go do what you have to,'' he said. His throat sounded

clogged. "I'll tell Heaney you'll be at Troop K in an hour. I don't think he'll give you longer before he comes looking."

"Probably not. An hour should be enough. More than enough."

"I don't approve, but you know that, don't you? Watch yourself. Please. I think I'd find the world flat without you."

37

Though it was just past six, Jamie Warburton was up and dressed, running the grounds with his Dobermans, who charged my car like a pair of black knights on crusade, teeth bared in impressive snarls.

"Pal, Friend, down. Sit!" Jamie's voice rang out sure and confident. He did not need to repeat the command. The dogs dropped their rumps to the ground and sat tea party perfect, gazing at their master, who doled out a single approving head pat each. "You're here very early, Emily." He looked at his large digital watch. "Six oh nine."

"It is early, yes. You're wonderful with your dogs, Jamie. I admire that."

"We always had dogs in Chicago. When I was three years old, I got a Lab pup to be just mine. Father got him for me. His name was Ahab, but I wanted him to be Pal. That was in 1975."

"Who named him Ahab?"

"Father named him Ahab, but I called him Pal anyway. Father hit me. But then he stopped hitting, and my dog was Pal, like he was supposed to be." His eyes were cherub-blue, lighter than Ariane's, and clear as a child's. Just now, they seemed to cloud with remembered resentment. "Father was the boss of everything. He didn't like my sister Ariane."

"Why not?" My heart felt overgrown and sickish in my chest. I hated what I was doing.

He shrugged. "I don't know. I liked her. She'd play ball with me and take me for walks. We would have fun. But Father said no, and I had to listen or he'd lock me up. I couldn't cry either; Father said only babies cry. I'll go get her for you now."

He didn't need to. As I turned to look, Ariane stood in the doorway, a long cotton robe of deep blue wrapped and tied around her. Her hair was braided in a single plait which fell just below her shoulders. The sleep glaze in her eyes appeared real, but I wondered now whether anything I thought I knew about Ariane was real—ever had been.

"Emily, what's happened?"

"I think I'll come inside, Ariane."

When the door had closed behind us, she switched briefly into gracious-hostess mode. "Would you like some—?"

"No, Ariane. Please. No. This isn't a social call. Let's go into some room with two chairs—I don't give a flying fuck which room—and talk. There is not much time."

"I see," she said, stiffening to take a blow she knew was coming. "We'll go up to my bedroom. I find I can't stand being among the things down here. So many of them red and velvet, like fresh-spilled blood." Her tone was cool, though, against the overheated words.

I'd been in her bedroom only once, and as I entered it now, I had a painful memory of rifling through her bureau drawer, holding in my hand her lace underpants—flesh-colored, Chris-smelling.

"Did Chris go to the police, or did Dev bring them to him?" she asked. Her face was as serene as a cameo, but her lips were not quite closing after the question, as though readying themselves to moan. They were beautifully shaped, sensual: the top one a wide, curving bow, the bottom a shallow arc of melon slice. But I'd never noticed them before. Suggestible Emily—good quality for an actor, all that suggestibility. Presents problems offstage, though.

"Chris is dead," I said, making myself look at her. "It was my fault. I went there, to his house to make him tell me."

It absorbed very slowly into her. I imagined I saw it hit her skin, and seep through, turning acid as it made its way deeper inside.

"Jane shot him with a rifle."

"Jane," she repeated, uncomprehending, as though the syllable were simply unfamiliar. "Jane. The decorator, you mean?" Her expression blurred in confusion.

"You didn't know about Jane?" I asked it gently, feeling, against all sense, for the first time in my life, protective of Ariane.

The hollow above her collarbone deepened with a long intake of breath. After she'd held it for a moment, like a drag on a cigarette, she let it go. "No, I didn't." Her hand went absently to her forehead to brush back a nonexistent strand of stray hair. "It wouldn't have mattered. Nothing mattered for Chris and me, but each other. Jamie, of course, but even Jamie didn't exist for me sometimes. I had my neat world, under control. That was important to me, more important than I think you can imagine. And then, one day, I saw Chris. He was putting a new roof on Jamie's group home. He . . . He was all there was." She bent her head slightly to one side and studied my face. "I don't believe you can understand that, Emily. You're such an innocent. In some ways I envy you."

"An innocent?" A little snort of a laugh escaped me, a sort of shock of recognition. "And I concentrated on being such a bad girl."

"A rifle? You said she shot him with a rifle?" She looked suddenly troubled in a different way. "Are you sure she was the one?"

"Entirely sure. I watched it."

"Ah," she murmured in relief. "I'm so glad it wasn't Bart who killed him."

"I don't believe that Bart could kill anyone."

"Don't say that." Her tone sharpened. "People do things they never dreamed they could do. Terrible things. Did that woman shoot Clea, too?"

"Not on purpose. She meant to wing me, put me out of action. She thought I was getting too close to finding out about Chris and Zach's body."

"Chris told her?" The suggestion of that betrayal was visibly crushing.

"No, he didn't tell her. She saw him get off the train on the way back from parking Zach's car. She watched him get into your car, kiss you. She'd met you only a few hours before at my house." As I flashed back to that day, I felt my own pangs of betrayal. "Ariane, just tell me straight. When you came that Sunday with your black eye and swollen jaw, had you already killed him?"

Her eyes shut off. "Yes, I had already killed him," she said tonelessly.

"So your little visit to innocent, gullible Emily, that talk about how Zach was going to leave you for another woman, all of it was part of your alibi." I grabbed hold of sarcasm like Sweeney Todd's razor, meaning to cut her to ribbons with it. "The beaten, abandoned wife. Who did it to you really? Chris? He made it look really good."

"Oh Emily." She sounded genuinely surprised. "No. No, that's not the way it happened at all. Everything about Zach and me—the troubles he had with sex, the way violence would sometimes help him . . . And how much I loved him for his little-boy ways, that, too—all of it was true.

"When he came home that Saturday evening, he was in a foul mood. It was late; he hadn't shown up for dinner. I didn't know at the time, of course, but he'd been first with you, then with Clea. I put some cold salmon out for him, some wine. I wanted to talk with him, you see, about Jamie coming to live with us. But he was so wound up. I knew what was coming, and I . . . God help me . . . for once, I couldn't bear it, maybe because I'd been with Chris early that morning. I hope that wasn't the reason, but I'll never be sure.

"Usually, I'd go along, say the things I knew Zach wanted to hear: saucy words of defiance, so he could react as the dominating man, and give me a few slaps." The disgust was plain on my face; I wasn't even trying to hide it. "It was pathetic, I know, but it gave him such pleasure, and . . . I wanted to give him pleasure. But that night, I somehow couldn't stop myself. I wasn't saucy, I was cruel; I said terrible things, terrible sexual things about him. He hit hard, very hard. Then he took me, and had me. And then he fell asleep. But right before he did, he looked up at me with a nasty kind of smile, and he said, 'Never. Brother lamebrain's never living under my roof.'

"I stared down at him, his face, his neck; the Adam's apple popping out: that little round bony lump. I never even thought about it, Emily. My hand raised up, and it came down. Then it was over, as fast as serving a ball. No, not that fast," she said, her voice flat. "He choked for a minute—maybe less—but his eyes opened . . ." Her hand came up now as far as her mouth, and covered it, pressing hard against it. To hold back words? To keep from being sick?

What rotten luck for her—for all of us—that she'd called Chris. Sexy, shrewd, ambitious Chris, too voracious to wait for the money. If only she had called Bart instead, Zach's body would be long lost in the Hudson by now, and Bart would never have betrayed her, never have pushed her, never have told—not with bamboo under his fingernails.

She stood. "I think it will be better if I go to the police than wait for them, don't you?" she asked, calm having washed over her face like a sea wave while I wasn't looking, wiping it clean. "I'll need to contact a lawyer first, of course. Bart said he'd find the right person."

"And when did he say that?" I was stunned.

"Last night. He saw, as you all did; he understood. He is such a dear man."

"And strictly a friend."

"Always. A pity: I have never been able to choose sex. It chooses me. It arrives; it astounds. It's different for you." She smiled like a waxwork. "You should be grateful for that. And now I really must call Bart." Her eyes came back from the dead, livened with energy of purpose. "I have Jamie to think of."

I rose and walked after her. "Ariane, I spoke with Bailey Hutchison Saturday."

Her lips made a soundless "oh." "I was a child. I didn't realize how different I was from other people in that single way. Barth, Bailey, Tom, poor Matthew: they trusted me, and I . . . destroyed them. I live with it, and pay for it. I promised myself nothing like that would happen again. But of course it has. How is Bailey?"

"She seems very well. She's head at Fletcher now. She and Tom are back together. Look, I didn't mean to dredge up all of that for you. But what about Jamie?"

She walked quickly to me, and grabbed my arm in an iron tennis-champ grip. "Emily, if you've ever valued anything about me, listen to me now. My father was a cold and vindictive man, obsessed with my mother and with notions of dirty sex about her. And with me as a demon replica of her.

Do you know he would never let me hold my baby brother on my lap? Never let me brush Jamie's hair or push him in his stroller? Jamie has complete recall. Two things about autists: meticulous memory and truth-telling. Jamie doesn't know how to lie. I have never touched my brother besides as a loving sister. I swear on my life and on his.

"Ask him, if you feel you need to. And believe him. *Believe me!*"

EPILOGUE
· · · · · · · · · · · · · · · · · · · ·

Though August has only just crossed the line into September, the air has a definite snap to it. Not yet, but soon, Orchards will enter its namesake-starring season. Six acres of spreading, carefully pruned trees will hang heavy with ripe Hudson Valley apples: McIntosh and Macoun, Baldwin and Winesap.

These weeks, I've confined myself, moving from kitchen to library to my old bedroom: three spaces that are unchanged from my childhood. Jane's artistry is too apparent in the other rooms, and painful for me to see.

Dev and I talk little. It's as though a splint of silence braces the shattered thing between us, part of both our flesh and bone. All we can do is hold close together while it heals. Night after night, we've slept—tangled arms and legs—in my old white bed, which isn't really big enough for two people. Sometimes, we've escaped into making love. But only sometimes.

Each time I play it all back, my memory rearranges—lays it out another way. Maybe that's the truth of memories, that every time the movie reruns itself, it actually alters in ways mostly too subtle to notice.

Jane's trial is on its way to being over. It's gone very quickly; she was not much interested in its outcome. The only fire she showed was in her refusal to utter any words of blame about Chris, and few words of any kind about him. The papers say that Jane will be found guilty of your standard crime of passion, while in a state of temporary insanity.

The truth is more complicated. Unless, of course, it isn't. Jane appears placid, satisfied—quietly matter-of-fact as ever. I offered to pay the cost of a high-powered lawyer, but she refused, preferring an understated local who works by the numbers. She will serve time in a prison or hospital of some kind, and the prospect does not seem to distress her. Odd for someone who lives for beauty and cannot breathe in New York City.

Ariane's trial is expected to begin in several weeks—a different story entirely. She has marshaled herself in her own defense with all the intelligence and vigor she brings to a tennis court. With the formidable help of a famed criminal lawyer, and Bart Held at her side, she is determined to get herself acquitted: a battered woman reacting in fatal split-second violence to defend herself, covering up the death only at the urging of her late lover, Chris.

Is that true? True enough that I will be a witness for the defense. As she reminded me, before she turned herself over to Heaney and Weems, she does have Jamie to take care of. I find I believe in her purely sisterly devotion to him, and believe too that his life would blow apart if she was forcibly removed from it.

Believe, disbelieve: so much does come down only to that.

A note of comic relief: Claudine Augier, Canadian film-maker *extraordinaire*, phoned last week. After an initial geyser of enthusiasm for the superb qualities I would bring to *Arden!* the bare-bones truth, which eventually wended its way through the wires, seemed to be that the cash I might bring was even more appealing. Her research into my family, which she'd flashed at our meeting, had evidently been more comprehensive than I knew. Now, plans for points and producer's credits tripped off her tongue at me. Apparently, if a possibility had ever existed for Miramax backing, it existed no longer. And Marty and Bobby were "off into other things."

So was I, I told her pleasantly.

And I was. Yesterday Bernie Clegg called with an "I told you so" about *Arden!* and asked if I'd be coming home after the trial. When I said I didn't know, he grudgingly allowed that Lincoln Center would begin rehearsal for a revival of *Heartbreak House* in November, and might be interested in me.

It seems to me that *Heartbreak House* is, all things considered, too suitable to pass up.

Liam stayed around for Jane's trial, and even more, I

think, to make sure Clea was going to be steady on her pins. She seems to be. The sling is finally off her arm, and she and Bart have come to an open-ended truce. No, better than that: a compact of compassion. I know she worries about him, perhaps with reason. She is counting on Ariane's acquittal, counting on the warmth of that friendship to sustain her father.

Her term at Vassar begins in a few days, and already she is making plans to transfer somewhere west—Stanford, maybe—next year. I doubt Bart will give her any flak, and her big sister Emily will give her as much encouragement as she'll take. I must be careful not to go over the top, though. It remains hard for me to see and honor boundaries, but I'm trying to learn. The specter of Celia Silver is always close at hand when I require a negative example.

The morning Liam left, we had a last cup of tea, both of us aware that he would be returning to an apartment two blocks away from the bar that was no longer his. An empty apartment; no Ethne there.

"You can change your mind and stay," I said.

"Are you kiddin'?" He trotted out the abandoned brogue for an exit appearance, to paper over the awkwardness. "I'm sicka the sighta the botha yez. A man needs his privacy."

I hadn't planned it, but it needed no planning. I unstrapped the too big watch from my wrist and handed it across the table to him. "I want you to have this. It would make me happy."

At first, his hands stayed where they were, cradling his teacup. "I shouldn't. What happened, happened, and I can't wash it away. Florio would spin in his grave."

"I'm not sure about much these days, Liam, but Mike would understand that I don't need it anymore, and I think he'd understand why you should have it."

I hoped he would. Liam is still Liam. From time to time, he and Dev will certainly go at each other like mad dogs ready to slip their leashes, and all three of us will occasionally see in our heads a large-handed drunk knocking a slender ten-year-old boy to the ground.

Our eyes met and he let go of the cup, took the watch

and clasped it on his wrist. It fit—not perfectly, but well enough.

Dev reaches for my hand now, across the same kitchen table.

"Is there someplace in this joint to plug in a word processor?"

A smile that feels entirely unfamiliar comes on fast enough to split my face. "Do you have some use for one?"

"You never know."

"In eighteen rooms we ought to be able to work something out." I give a pull at his hand. "I can show you the master bedroom right now, if I remember the way."